# “I didn’t realize you were famous…”

“Do you think I’m in danger? That this person would hurt me?”

It was a question Donovan wasn’t sure he could answer. He didn’t want to scare Kelly, but he didn’t want to lie to her either. “Any time someone is delusional, believes things that aren’t real, it’s hard to predict what they’ll do. We don’t know how unstable this guy is, so it’s probably best to assume he is capable of anything just to be safe.”

Kelly took a deep breath and let it out slowly. “Thank you,” she said.

“For what?”

“For helping to keep me safe. And for giving it to me straight instead of trying to scare me into doing what my uncle wants me to do.”

One day.

Donovan had known Kelly for all of one day, and yet he knew in his bones that nothing would stop him from keeping her safe.

Dear Reader,

When I was brainstorming ideas for another Grace Note Records story, I wanted to focus on a character connected to the music but not directly related to the making of it. I remembered how much I loved the disc jockey from *Love Songs and Lullabies* and how she had figured out Sawyer and Piper were meant for each other before they did. I decided to make Kelly the heroine, but who would be her hero?

Donovan is logical, rational. Feelings aren't his thing. When he lets his feelings be in charge, he does things like get himself put on desk duty. He's also the guardian for his niece and nephew, a job he doesn't feel prepared to have. I love writing troubled teens and adorable littles, and Donovan got one of each.

Family plays a big part in this romance because our family is where we first learn about love and trust. Donovan and Kelly both carry some baggage from their pasts that shape how they view love and family. I hope you enjoy their roller-coaster ride to that HEA.

Visit me on Facebook and Twitter or on my website: amyvastine.com.

xoxo,

*Amy Vastine*

HEARTWARMING

# *Falling for Her Bodyguard*

---

*Amy Vastine*

Recycling programs
for this product may
not exist in your area.

ISBN-13: 978-1-335-51077-8

Falling for Her Bodyguard



This edition published by arrangement with Harlequin Books S.A.

For questions and comments about the quality of this book, please contact us at CustomerService@Harlequin.com.

**Printed in U.S.A.**

**Amy Vastine** has been plotting stories in her head for as long as she can remember. An eternal optimist, she studied social work, hoping to teach others how to find their silver lining. Now she enjoys creating happily-ever-afters for all to read. Amy lives outside Chicago with her high school sweetheart husband, three teenagers who keep her on her toes and their two sweet but mischievous pups. Visit her at amyvastine.com.

**Books by Amy Vastine**

**Harlequin Heartwarming**

***Grace Note Records***

*The Girl He Used to Love*
*Catch a Fallen Star*
*Love Songs and Lullabies*

***Chicago Sisters***

*The Better Man*
*The Best Laid Plans*
*The Hardest Fight*

*The Weather Girl*

"Snow Day Baby" in *A Heartwarming Thanksgiving*

Visit the Author Profile page
at Harlequin.com for more titles.

To all those who open their hearts and homes
to kids without parents who can care for them.
You're truly a blessing!

# *CHAPTER ONE*

"OH, NO. NOT AGAIN."

"They were here when I got in. I was going to warn you, but I didn't want to ruin your morning."

Kelly Bonner snatched the bright pink envelope that stuck out of the humongous bouquet of multicolored roses that overwhelmed the small office space at K104 Radio with their scent. She pulled out the card, knowing it wouldn't shed much light on the sender. The flowers weren't the first gift from an anonymous admirer to arrive at the radio station.

*Pink symbolizes the happiness I feel when I think of you.*
*Lavender represents my love at first sight.*
*White reminds me of your purity.*
*Orange is for the deep desire I feel.*
*Red symbolizes the love we'll share FOREVER.*

A chill ran down her spine. Romantic words if they had been written by someone Kelly was in love with or even knew. These weren't from a boyfriend. Kelly didn't have one.

Another gift. Another note about them being in love. First, it had been the singing candy gram. She thought it was a joke, a prank courtesy of someone at the station. Then came the chocolate-covered strawberries, the earrings and the bottle of perfume. Something about these gifts and notes made her blood run cold.

She tossed the card down on the desk.

"No name again?" Nancy Oliver was the station's production assistant and Kelly's best friend. They had bonded when Nancy started as an intern around the same time Kelly landed her job as the afternoon on-air personality for the biggest country station in Nashville.

"Of course not. This guy wants to remain as creepy as he can." Kelly tried to shake off the eerie feeling that overcame her every time one of these anonymous gifts showed up.

"I thought it was sort of romantic in the beginning. Now, I think it's time to call your uncle. Maybe he can trace where the gifts are coming from, get you a name at least."

"My uncle Hal has bigger fish to fry than some fan with a crush."

Nancy adjusted her glasses. "Isn't the advantage of having a cop for an uncle that he can scare away the stalkers?"

"He's not a stalker. And knowing my uncle, I'd have a twenty-four-hour armed guard following me around for the rest of my life if he heard what was going on." Kelly's uncle was a captain for the Metropolitan Nashville Police Department. He was also extremely overprotective, always had been, but his sense of obligation to watch over her increased tenfold when Kelly's dad died three years ago.

"When I was little, I wanted to be so famous that I'd have to have a bodyguard who would clear a path for me through the throngs of wild fans who would always be trying to get to me," Nancy said.

"I only want fans who let me come to them through the radio. No bodyguard needed." What Kelly needed was this guy to reveal himself so she could let him down easy and be done with the gifts. "I have a show to do. Feel free to take those home with you or throw them away. I don't care which," Kelly said, gathering her notes for today's show.

"Kelly, Kelly, Kelly. How are we this fine afternoon?" Stan Benson was the station's promotion director. His thinning blond hair was parted to best maximize coverage of his growing bald spot. "We have the first round of charity concert tickets to give away today. And good news… They agreed to let *you* onstage to kick things off."

"Me? Not Travis and Holly?" Travis and Holly were the morning team, who were usually assigned the fun promotional gigs.

"When I talked to Dean Presley over at Grace Note, he said they were hoping you would do it. You always treat their artists well when they come in here for some press. He likes you. And why wouldn't he? You're our rising star."

She liked the sound of that. With her contract ending soon, she'd been working tirelessly to gain listeners, asking for more opportunity to promote the station and get her name and face out there so she'd have some bargaining power when they discussed her renewal. Stan's willingness to give her a chance was huge.

"Well, I appreciate the chance to support the station. I've been looking forward to that concert. To get to be a part of it is awesome."

Stan grinned and was back on the move. "The more you're in front of the public, the better," he said over his shoulder before turning the corner.

Kelly was determined to do whatever it took. If they wanted her to make public appearances every day, she would. Working in radio was a dream come true and she planned to do this for the rest of her life if they'd let her. Maybe they would if things kept going the way they were. She entered the studio with an extra bounce in her step.

"Someone looks extra happy today," Lyle Conrad, the show's producer, said once she put on her headphones. He sat in the control room, separated from Kelly's studio by a glass wall. Off-air, he could talk to her through the headset and on-air, he typed her messages through the computer. "Anything to do with those flowers out front? I didn't know you were dating someone."

"I'm not." The thought of the flowers had the opposite effect on her mood. "I think I might have a misguided fan. One who thinks we're destined to be together."

"Ah. We've had a couple of those over the years around here. Don't worry. Eventually, they get the hint and move on with their life."

"Let's hope so." Kelly didn't need the distraction. She didn't even have time for a real boyfriend, so Mr. Anonymous was out of luck.

"Caller number ten wins two tickets to the sold-out Grace Note Records Concert for the Kids on Saturday, June twenty-ninth," Kelly announced about halfway through the show. "We're talking Sawyer Stratton and Piper Starling, the Good Ol' Boys, Finch and Wells, and the one and only Boone Williams. This is not a show you'll want to miss, Nashville."

She clicked the button to play the commercial she had cued up before answering the calls as they came in. Clicking through the lines, she let the non-winners down easy. "Hi, you're caller eight. Thank you. Bye. Hi, you're caller nine. So close! Have a good one."

She switched on the VoxPro recorder before clicking on the winner. These calls were prerecorded just in case someone got a bit too excited and said something not exactly FCC-approved. Lyle gave her the thumbs-up and she pressed the last blinking red light.

"Hello, you are caller ten and our winner!" Usually, callers hollered or screeched when they heard they won, but this one was quiet. Another reason to record these calls—it allowed Kelly the chance to edit it and remove the dead air. "Hello, can I get your name?"

"That depends," the deep voice on the other end of the line replied. "Is this Kelly?"

Something about the way he said her name caused a shiver to run down her spine. "It is. Who is this?"

"Someone who's been wondering if you've been receiving my gifts. It's been very disappointing not to hear from you."

Her secret admirer. Now was her chance to finally find out who he was. "I've gotten several gifts lately. I've been waiting for a name so I could thank you properly."

"Which gift was your favorite?"

"That's hard to say. I'd really like to know who you are."

"Are you wearing the earrings I gave you?"

Kelly exchanged looks with Lyle. This guy wasn't going to give up his name even for concert tickets. Her commercial break was almost over. There wasn't time for all this creepy chitchat. Lyle typed her a message to put the call on hold so he could take over.

She did as Lyle suggested and turned the call over to him. Cutting their conversation short was the best option. Maybe being short with him would end this infatuation. Lyle messaged a few minutes later that the guy had hung up and the new winner was a very nice lady named Rhonda from Brentwood.

The rest of the show went off without a hitch. Kelly threw it to the next deejay and set her headset on the desk. She met Lyle in the hallway outside. He was tall and lanky with arms so long it was almost like he wouldn't have to bend over to pick things up off the floor.

"Great show, Kel."

"Thanks. Too bad we didn't get the name of my secret admirer. I just want the gifts to stop."

"You don't have to worry about that guy anymore. Not only was he not happy when I took over the call, but he was downright annoyed when I told him you already had a boyfriend and weren't interested in his gifts."

"You what?"

"I solved your problem. Now, he thinks you have a boyfriend and maybe he'll back off and start stalking someone else," Lyle said with a shrug.

Kelly felt a calming sense of relief. "Let's hope so. I mean, the part about him backing off, not the part about stalking some other woman."

"I'm here to help whenever you need."

"What about me, Lyle?" Nancy joined them in the hall. "Are you here to help me, too?"

Lyle's cheeks flushed red. "Of course, Nancy. Do you have a stalker I can scare off?"

"You scared off Kelly's stalker? Well,

you're our hero." She touched his arm and his face got redder.

Kelly, Lyle and Nancy went to her office to plan for the next day's show. When they finished, Kelly said goodbye to Nancy and she and Lyle headed out to the parking garage together.

"You and Nancy are close, right?" he asked as they entered the elevator.

"We are."

"Do you think she'd ever be interested in getting dinner with someone like me?"

"Someone *like* you or the actual you?"

Lyle rolled his big blue eyes. "The actual me. I'm bad with rejection. If you could give me a heads-up on my chances, I would be forever in your debt."

Kelly had suspected there was some interest on his side of things for a couple of months. He laughed at all of Nancy's jokes. Especially the ones that weren't even a little bit funny. He had memorized her coffee order even though it was some ridiculously long demand that would drive any barista to quit. And today, the man was completely flustered by a simple touch.

"Honestly, I don't know, but I could ask."

"Don't be super obvious about it, though. If

she's not interested, I don't want her to know I am."

His fear of being vulnerable was relatable. Kelly wasn't the biggest fan of being 100 percent up front about her feelings, either. Being open meant the possibility of being hurt. Being hurt was no fun. She would make sure Nancy knew nothing if there wasn't a chance. "I've got your back on this one, buddy," she assured him.

Instead of thanking her, Lyle stopped dead in his tracks.

"What's the matter?"

"That's your car, isn't it?" He pointed behind her.

Kelly spun around and gasped. Both headlights had been smashed and on the hood of her car someone had keyed the word *TEASE* into the paint.

"This is my fault," Lyle lamented.

Kelly's heart beat double time and it was hard to breathe. She scanned the parking lot, fearing that her secret admirer turned hater was still nearby. No one else was around. The garage was eerily quiet. It was definitely time to call Uncle Hal.

"WALSH! GET IN HERE, right now."

Hal Bonner was not the kind of boss you

wanted to cross. He was similar to all of the commanding officers Donovan had ever had in the Marines. Unfortunately, Donovan had been on the captain's bad side ever since he had lost his temper and broken the jaw of a known drug dealer. The guy completely deserved it but had better lawyers than Donovan had expected. While the case was under investigation with Internal Affairs, Donovan was stripped of his gun and badge and stuck on desk duty. It was worse than prison.

"Sir," he said, standing in the captain's doorway.

"Come in and shut the door."

Donovan did as he was told and waited for permission to sit, something the military had ingrained in him. Captain Bonner didn't look up from his computer because he was too busy typing. Two fingers pecked at the keys. Technology wasn't his strong suit.

Captain glanced up and noticed Donovan standing there. "For the love— Sit down!" he snapped. He shook his head as Donovan complied. "If only I had been there to say, 'Don't break his jaw,' you wouldn't be in this mess, apparently."

Donovan was very good at following commands but did have a tendency to let his emotions get the best of him in the field. That had been an issue in the Marines, as well.

Captain finished typing and rubbed his eyes. The man looked exhausted. "I'm putting you on a special assignment."

Donovan sat up a little straighter. Special assignment sounded so much better than desk duty. "I'll do anything you need me to do, sir."

"Glad to hear that." He jotted something on a scrap of paper and handed it to Donovan. "I need you to go to this address and pick up my niece, Kelly. You will then spend the rest of your shift watching her. I have squads sitting outside her place at night, but I need someone on her during the day. Wherever she goes, you go."

Babysitting? Desk duty wasn't sounding so bad all of a sudden. "Sir, I don't—"

"You don't what? You don't think you want to help me keep my niece safe from harm?"

"No, sir. That's not what I was going to say."

"Good, then it's settled. I've got some unidentified jerk running around Nashville obsessed with her. Yesterday, he vandalized her car. I want to make sure he doesn't get the chance to lay a hand on her. You start now."

Donovan tried to think of something to say

that could get him out of this, but there was nothing. Nothing that would change Captain Bonner's mind. Babysitting someone in relationship trouble was worse than desk duty.

"Goodness, Walsh! Stand up, walk to your car and go to the address I gave you," Captain said in a huff.

Donovan did as he was told.

He said a silent prayer that she wasn't in high school. If Donovan had to spend the whole day surrounded by teenagers, he might just quit. Living with one was bad enough.

"Where you headed, Walsh? Did they put you on administrative leave?" Detective Steven Dillon was Donovan's partner.

"Special assignment. I have to go babysit his niece—" he pulled out the piece of paper with her name and address on it "—Kelly. Know anything about her?"

Dillon's head fell back as he laughed. "Oh, man. My only words of advice are look but do *not* touch. Captain will crush anyone who even thinks about having inappropriate thoughts about that woman. Good luck with that."

Not a teenager at least. Donovan wasn't worried about having inappropriate thoughts about anyone. Once his niece and nephew were out of his house, he planned to live the rest of his life very much alone.

He drove to the apartment building and took note of his surroundings. It was a quiet street. Not a lot of cars. No traffic lights or businesses nearby with cameras, however. The complex was secure but there was no one manning the entrance. He punched in her apartment number in the intercom.

"Hello?" A voice came through the speaker.

"Miss Bonner, I'm Detective Walsh. Your uncle sent me. I'm supposed to—" he wasn't sure she'd take too kindly to him calling it babysitting "—keep you company today."

There was no answer and no opening of the door. Donovan buzzed the apartment again.

"Hang on." She sounded exasperated.

She was annoyed? He was the one who had to follow her around doing whatever mundane things she had on her agenda for the day. This could be a bigger nightmare than he imagined.

A woman on her phone pushed open the door. "I understand you're trying to protect me, but this is a little extreme don't you think?" she said as she jogged down the steps and onto the sidewalk. Ending her call, she turned around and glanced up at Donovan. Her dark hair was pulled back into a ponytail and her eyes were covered by aviator sunglasses. "Well, come on. He's going to send you to the station regardless of what I have to say about it."

This must be the niece. Dressed in jeans and a black T-shirt knotted at her hip, she didn't give him many clues as to what she might have to do today. Donovan could see why Dillon told him Captain was protective. She was attractive, albeit a tad rude. She stormed ahead before coming to an abrupt stop.

"I was about to call for a car, but I assume you have one?"

Donovan moseyed up beside her. "I do. Where are you headed in such a hurry?"

She took off her sunglasses, revealing the most stunning crystal-blue eyes. "The station," she said in a flustered tone. "I have a meeting before my show."

"Station?" The only station Donovan was aware of was the one he just left.

Kelly's head rolled back and she sighed. "He didn't tell you anything, did he?"

"I was directed to go where you go, miss. That's what he told me and that's what I'll have to do."

"I work at K104, the radio station. I need to get there in the next twenty minutes or my station manager is not going to be happy with me. This would be the same station manager who will hopefully be renewing my contract soon and I really don't need her to be unhappy. Maybe I can drive? Which car is yours?" She held out her hand as if he might actually consider relinquishing his keys to her. That was not happening. No one drove his truck except him.

"I'm right over here," he said, pointing to his black F150 and wishing he had asked for one of the station's cars. Being on desk duty meant he was only allowed to use his personal vehicle.

Kelly didn't follow him. "Since when does the Nashville PD drive around in pickup trucks?" she asked. "Can I see your badge?"

Donovan grimaced. That was a problem. No gun or badge. "Funny story," he said, slowly spinning around to face her and the can of pepper spray that was pointed at him.

## *CHAPTER TWO*

"STAY WHERE YOU ARE." Kelly fumbled for her phone. How could she have been so stupid as to not ask for identification? She redialed her uncle. "Tell me your name again," she demanded from the stranger.

"Walsh. Detective Walsh."

Kelly's heart was thumping so hard that it was becoming a distraction. Her hand shook so much that she feared she'd trigger the pepper spray before finding out who this guy was for sure. At the same time, she prayed he didn't attack her before her uncle picked up. "I don't know any detectives who forget their badge at home."

"I didn't forget it." He sighed as if she was irritating him. "I can show you the piece of paper your uncle wrote your name and address on."

"I'm not going to argue with you, Kelly," her uncle said when he answered the phone. "I won't pull him, so get used to it while I hunt your stalker down."

"The guy here says his name is Detective Walsh, but he doesn't have a badge or a cop car. He's about six-three, has short-cropped brown hair, no facial hair. Built like he could wrestle an alligator and win. He's wearing navy pants, a pale blue button-down and a green tie. No jacket."

With his hands on his hips, her possible stalker stared down at his feet. If he wasn't who he said he was, he didn't seem very nervous about a real detective showing up.

Uncle Hal gave a little chuckle. "That's my guy, Kell Bell. He is who he says he is. He's doing this as a favor to me, so he isn't carrying his badge."

Kelly lowered her pepper spray and took a deep breath in hopes her heart would slow down now. "I don't love this plan, Uncle Hal."

"I know, sweetheart. But it's the only one I've got right now. If anything happened to you..."

Kelly understood he was only doing what he thought best. She was the daughter of police officers. Her dad had been a homicide detective and her mom was a desk sergeant in Knoxville. Growing up, her curfew was earlier than all of her friends' because her parents couldn't bear it if anything bad ever happened to her because they knew *exactly* what kind of bad things could happen.

"Okay, he says you are who you say you are," she said as she hung up the phone.

Detective Walsh acted as if this was how he spent every Wednesday. He unlocked his truck, completely unfazed by what had happened. "Pepper spray is a terrible way to protect yourself, by the way."

"It stopped you cold," she replied, feeling defensive. She'd spent her life trying to prove she could take care of herself and now *another* cop was telling her that she couldn't do it.

"That's because I had no intent to do you harm. If I had, I could have easily turned your pepper spray against you."

Who did this guy think he was? "Oh, really? Well, I wouldn't have hesitated to spray you in the face, and this stuff will incapacitate anyone."

He shook his head and opened the passenger door for her. "First of all, the wind was blowing away from me and toward you. Secondly, pepper spray is not guaranteed to stop everyone. If your attacker is drunk or on drugs, he might just get angrier."

Kelly climbed in the truck and put her seat belt on, letting his comments sink in. She hadn't noticed the wind. It couldn't have been strong enough to blow it back at her, could it? Detective Walsh got in the driver's seat.

"And what if that little girl over there was asthmatic or that older lady and her dog walked through the cloud and inhaled it?" he asked. "You could have done serious damage to some innocent people."

Kelly hadn't considered how it could affect anyone other than the attacker. She suddenly had the urge to throw her pepper spray in the garbage. "So, what would you suggest I do to keep myself safe?"

"Have you ever taken a self-defense class before? Your body is really the best weapon."

Her mother had been trying to get her to take one for years, which was probably why she hadn't. She lived in a safe neighborhood, didn't run around at night alone and believed people—for the most part—were good. Until yesterday, she had never felt like she needed to protect herself that way. The pepper spray was an emotional impulse buy last night after she dropped her car off at the body shop.

"I'll have to look into it."

Their drive continued in silence once she gave him the address of the station to put into his phone's GPS. The quiet unnerved her. Detective Walsh only seemed to speak when he needed to. Kelly, on the other hand, talked for a living. Silence was dead air.

"I wish I had time to stop for coffee. Everything in my life feels off because of this." The meeting with Caroline was important and Kelly was so distracted. The impression she wanted to make today was not of some discombobulated airhead. Detective Walsh had nothing to add. He was not helping ease her anxiety in the slightest.

"So what did you do?" she asked as they came to a stop at a busy intersection. His eyebrows pinched together. She clarified, "To lose your badge and gain the responsibility of babysitting me?"

His jaw ticked. "Let's just say I am not a big fan of drug dealers and they aren't fans of me, either."

"Well, I have the opposite problem. I have a fan who thinks he's in love with me and that I cheated on him with a make-believe boyfriend."

The line between his brows reappeared. "He thinks you have a make-believe boyfriend?"

"No, he thinks I have a real boyfriend who is really a make-believe boyfriend. I don't have a boyfriend. I'm single. And not dating. Not because I can't find someone, I just don't have the time to put into a relationship. My job keeps me busy," she rambled. Detective Walsh clearly didn't care if she had a boyfriend or not. "Are you married?"

He glanced at her for a quick second. "How about we keep the personal business sharing to a minimum?"

"Right." Kelly fidgeted with her hands. He wasn't wearing a wedding ring, so chances were he wasn't married. His brown hair was cut short like they wore in the military. He sure looked a lot like those Navy SEAL guys on the covers of her mom's old romance novels.

His phone rang just as they neared the station. The caller ID showed it was a high school calling. Detective Walsh groaned and clicked the phone icon on his steering wheel.

"Hello?"

"Mr. Walsh? This is Dean Higgins again. I'm sorry to bother you," the voice said through the car speakers.

"What can I do for you, Mr. Higgins?"

"Well, I'm sorry to say I have Graham here in my office."

Detective Walsh pinched the bridge of his nose. "What did he do this time?"

No ring, but he had a kid. Maybe he was

divorced. Or didn't like wearing rings. Either was possible.

"He decided to skip math class again and we found him vandalizing the library."

"I wasn't vandalizing," a new voice shouted in the background. "It's called art. I was improving the overall aesthetics of this dump you call a school. You should be thanking me, not giving me detention."

"You've surpassed the limit for detentions, young man. Vandalism is a crime. I could have turned this over to the police."

"You called him, didn't you? You just turned it over to the police. Thanks a lot. Now I'm dead."

Oh, boy, could Kelly relate to this poor kid. She knew better than anyone the fear associated with a call home from school when your parents were cops.

"Tell him to stop with the dramatics," Detective Walsh said, cutting in. "He has no one to blame for this other than himself."

"We have a lot of concerns about the acting out Graham has been doing lately. We've tried to be understanding and compassionate. I know that things have been hard since his mom—"

Detective Walsh didn't let the man finish. "What's his punishment? In-school suspension? Saturday school? Does he have to pay to clean up the graffiti?"

"Well, sir, because he not only was truant from class but also vandalized school property, we're going to issue an out-of-school suspension for the rest of today. We need you to come pick him up."

Detective Walsh pulled the car over. "Hang on a second." He pressed the mute button on his phone. "You good getting out right here?" he asked Kelly.

She was still a block and a half from the radio station, but who was she to argue with him? It was obvious he needed to handle this situation with his son. "Um, sure."

"I'm guessing there are people at work who can watch you until I get back?"

Kelly felt a burning sensation in her chest. She wasn't a child. She didn't need to be watched. "I'll be fine," she replied, unlatching her seat belt and getting out of the truck. "You don't have to come back. I'm sure I'll survive."

"Your uncle gave me orders. I'll be back."

"Sounds like you already have your hands full."

Detective Walsh scowled. "I'll be back."

Kelly shut the door and watched him make a quick U-turn. Some bodyguard he turned out to be. Not that she needed one. Once she was inside the station, no one could get to her. She just needed to get inside the station.

A block and a half never seemed so far. Kelly was suddenly hyperaware of how many people walked along 16th Avenue. Since when did downtown Nashville feel like New York City? Someone rammed his shoulder into hers and didn't even bother to apologize. Someone else brushed past her in all kinds of a hurry. She clutched the bottle of pepper spray in her pocket. Of course, she'd never be able to use it. What if some innocent person had an asthma attack because she released a cloud of pepper in the middle of this busy sidewalk?

She entered the building that housed the station and paused in the entryway to catch her breath and slow down her racing heart. She made it. Without her bodyguard. Kelly could do this. She didn't need anyone to babysit her. As she got on the elevator, she made a mental note to look into some self-defense classes at the gym. Couldn't hurt to be a bit more prepared.

"Kelly!" Stan greeted her. "You made it. I heard about what happened yesterday. You okay?"

"I'm good. My car, on the other hand..."

"I don't understand what possesses people to do hateful things," he said, shaking his head. "We really should get some security cameras in the parking garage."

As much as Kelly appreciated Stan's sympathy, she had a meeting to get to. Caroline Yates, the station manager, would not accept any excuses for being late.

"I'm actually on my way to talk to Caroline. Maybe I'll bring that up with her."

"Oh, didn't she call you this morning? She decided last-minute to have you be on location at the opening of the new Great Barbecue over on 4th. They're a huge sponsor of the show and offered to let us do a remote broadcast. Lyle is already over there setting things up and Travis and Holly have been talking about it all morning."

Kelly had to push down the anger that was building at not being given ample warning about this. She couldn't let it get back to Caroline that she wasn't up for anything the woman threw at her. If Caroline asked her to jump out of an airplane while juggling flaming bowling pins, she would have to strap on that parachute and give it her best shot.

She plastered on a smile. "Good thing I skipped breakfast. Sounds like I might get to eat some brisket for lunch."

IF GRAHAM KNEW what was good for him, he would not say one word on their ride home.

"I can't believe they're dumb enough to send me home for ditching class. Obviously, I didn't want to be in class. They're actually giving me exactly what I wanted by suspending me."

Apparently, he did not.

Dressed in his usual jeans and '90s band T-shirt, the troubled teen flipped down the visor and checked his reflection in the small mirror. He had blond hair and a narrow nose like his mom but green eyes and a strong, wide jaw like his dad. Their oldest was truly a perfect blend of the two of them. Too bad he didn't act like either of them.

"I wonder what I have to do to get expelled."

Donovan gripped the steering wheel tighter. "You do not want to find out what will happen to you if you get expelled. Trust me on that."

"You gonna beat me up like you beat up the other bad guys in this town? Huh, Uncle Donovan?"

"You're really working hard to make your mother and father proud, aren't you?"

"Yeah, well, dead people can't be proud or disappointed, can they?"

Donovan couldn't really argue with the kid

about that. He understood Graham was angry at the world for taking both his parents way too early. The fifteen-year-old and his little sister, Avery, had been dealt the worst hand life could deal, but that didn't give Graham permission to make things worse.

"Point is, you should want to act in a way that would have made your parents proud," Donovan said. "I guess we can talk about why you aren't when we meet with your guidance counselor tomorrow morning. All this posturing and acting out isn't getting you anywhere."

"That's where you're wrong. It's getting me out of school, isn't it? I'd say it's getting me exactly where I want to be."

There was no talking to this kid. Why Donovan's sister would have named him the guardian of her kids after she died, he'd never know. He was not cut out for this parenting stuff. He didn't have the patience for obnoxious, know-it-all teenagers. The only reason Avery liked him was because she was seven and liked everyone. Kids were still sweet at seven, but give that little girl seven more years and some hormones... Donovan might not survive it.

"Give me your phone," he demanded when they pulled up to his house a few minutes later. "No phone when you're grounded. Which you are, by the way."

"What if there's a fire and I have to call 9-1-1 for help?"

"Run over to the neighbor's house and ask them to call for you."

"But what if I fall down the stairs and break my leg? I can't run to the neighbor's house then. I could bleed out because I couldn't call for help."

"I guess you better be extra careful walking up and down the stairs."

Graham let out an exaggerated sigh. "I hate you," he said before throwing his phone in the back instead of handing it to Donovan. He climbed out of the truck, slamming the door behind him.

This must be some kind of karmic payback for the things Donovan said to his parents in anger growing up. He rolled down the window. "No friends allowed in the house and bring me your video game controller!" If Graham was going to hate him, might as well give him enough reasons.

Graham stormed up the driveway. "Come get it yourself!"

*Inhale. Exhale.* Days like this made Donovan feel like he was completely in over his head. He had no idea how to get through to his nephew or if he was handling all of these discipline issues the right way or not. He knew he should talk to him, but talking about feelings wasn't exactly Donovan's thing.

After retrieving the game controller, Donovan headed back to the radio station. Hopefully, Miss Bonner wouldn't mention his disappearing act to Captain. Thanks to Graham, she had been unguarded for almost an hour. How much danger could she be in while at work? It wasn't like anyone could get to her while she was at the station.

He made it to the reception desk and waited patiently for the receptionist to get off the phone. Instead of Muzak, a live stream of the station played in the background. As soon as the receptionist hung up the phone, he stepped up to the desk.

"Hi, I'm Detective Walsh. I'm here for Miss Bonner," he said, realizing once again how much harder it was to introduce himself without a badge to flash.

"Is this about what happened to her car? It's terrible someone would do that to someone as sweet as Kelly."

"That's why I'm here."

"Well, I'm glad the Nashville PD is taking this seriously."

Donovan was glad she was glad, but he'd

be happier if she called Miss Bonner out here so he didn't have to worry about Captain finding out he had been MIA. "Can I speak with her?"

The woman grimaced. "Oh, she's not here."

That was impossible. He had dropped her off almost an hour ago. There was no way she got kidnapped just outside this place. He could feel the sweat begin to bead on his forehead. Donovan couldn't imagine what the captain would do to him if he had to call and say he lost the man's niece.

"Are you sure? I actually drove her to work this morning. Maybe she slipped past you?" A guy could hope.

"No one slips past Juliette Delgado. I see everyone who comes in. I saw Kelly arrive this morning, but I also saw her leave."

Why did this assignment feel more like dealing with a certain class-skipping teenager than a reasonable adult?

"Any chance you know where she went?"

Ms. Delgado's expression didn't give him much hope that she had the answer he was looking for. "I do not, but I can find you someone who might."

"Perfect."

While he waited for her to make a call, a voice came over the radio. "I have to admit,

I'm a bit jealous of Kelly today. She's going to be coming to you live from the brand-new Great Barbecue over on 4th Street. If you love barbecue as much as I do or just want to see Kelly Bonner in person, you should really head on over there for lunch today."

Donovan didn't have to wait for Ms. Delgado, but he did need to get over to Great Barbecue before Miss Bonner's stalker beat him to her.

## *CHAPTER THREE*

"IS THERE ANYTHING else you need?"

Kelly plugged in her laptop and checked to make sure she had a Wi-Fi connection. "I think I have everything," she said to Dominick, the manager of Great Barbecue. She looked to Lyle. "Are you good?"

Lyle was busy shoving some coleslaw in his mouth. He nodded and gave her a thumbs-up.

Kelly couldn't help but laugh. "We're good."

Dominick was decked out in jeans and a black Great Barbecue collared shirt. He had an easy smile and twinkling blue eyes. "You sure you don't want to sample something before your show starts?"

"I am definitely going to pig out, just not right now."

Barbecue was messy and Kelly didn't want to get their small work area dirty. They were given a table against the back wall in the dining area of the new Great Barbecue. It was a small restaurant in an older part of Nashville that was undergoing rapid gentrification. What it didn't have in terms of square feet, it made up for in charm. From the exposed brick walls to the picnic table–style seating, everything had a down-home feel. There were even paper towel rolls at every table for those messy fingers.

"You should try everything on the menu," Lyle said, giving the corners of his mouth a wipe. "This place is amazing."

"Maybe this is where you can bring Nancy on your first date."

Lyle's eyes went wide. "Did you talk to her? Did she say she's interested? Does she like barbecue?" Kelly smirked, making Lyle a bit paranoid. "What? Did you talk to her?"

She pulled her phone out of her back pocket. "Maybe I did, maybe I didn't." Pretending to scroll through her text messages, she could see Lyle's face turning red.

"Come on, Kelly. Don't mess with me." He came around to her side of the table and tried to get a look at her phone screen.

"I'm not messing with you," she said with a giggle, holding her phone against her chest so he couldn't see.

"That's exactly what you're doing. Come on! Did you ask her? What did you say? What did she say?" He gently tried to tug the phone away from her.

"Stop," she protested as he almost succeeded. She turned her back to him and he wrapped his arms around her. They playfully wrestled for the phone until Lyle flew backward. In the blink of an eye, he was facedown on the ground with Detective Walsh on top of him, growling at him not to move. As if poor Lyle would fight back.

All eyes were on them and everyone was frozen in their spot. It was as if they believed Detective Walsh's words were meant for them, as well. Kelly was the only one who had the ability to intervene.

"What are you doing?" she asked as she attempted to push the detective off her friend and producer. He was as strong as a bull and as stubborn as a mule. He wouldn't budge.

"What am *I* doing? I'm doing my job. This guy was all over you."

"*This guy* is my producer. Please let him up." Kelly scanned the room. People whispered to one another. Phones were out and texts were definitely being sent about what just happened. This would end up on someone's social media. Caroline would not be happy if the station got bad press because of her.

Detective Walsh helped Lyle back on his feet and apologized for the misunderstanding.

"Are you okay?" Kelly scanned Lyle for any injuries. He wasn't bleeding. She prayed there were no broken bones.

He did still appear a bit dazed. "I'm fine," he said, giving his neck a rub. "You could have told me you hired a guard dog."

"I didn't. My uncle sent him, and I thought I had gotten rid of him."

"Yeah, we need to talk about that," Detective Walsh said. "I left you at work. That was where you were supposed to stay until I got back."

He had some nerve. She motioned for him to follow her away from all the prying eyes and ears to the back hall by the restrooms.

Once they were alone, she laid into him. "Let me make something clear. I did not ask for you to be assigned as my bodyguard. I have a job to do—"

"So do I," he interrupted. "And when you aren't where you're supposed to be, it makes my job a little harder."

"It makes your job harder? You were the one who abandoned your duties. My boss sent me here. What was I supposed to do? Tell her I couldn't go on location because the cop my uncle sent to babysit me had to go deal with some personal issues?"

With his hands on his hips, his head fell forward. "I'm sorry about that," he mumbled at the ground.

"What was that? Did I hear an 'I'm sorry'?"

His head lifted and their eyes met. "I'm sorry I had to leave. I take my job seriously, and you know your uncle. I don't want him to think that I wasn't making your safety a priority."

Of course he was more worried about her uncle than her. Truthfully, she was more worried about Caroline than anyone else.

"Listen, I am under a microscope right now. I can't have you attacking innocent people while you're watching me. My contract at the station is on the line. I don't want to get you in trouble with my uncle, but I have to call him and get him to back off on this bodyguard idea."

Detective Walsh held his palms up. "Whatever you want to do is fine by me. I'm not going to stop you from calling your uncle, but I am asking you not to throw me under the bus when you do. Your job is on the line and so is mine."

She didn't want to get the guy in trouble, but she had to make a case for getting rid of him at the same time. "I'll do my best," she promised.

Kelly started back to her makeshift work area but Detective Walsh touched her arm. "This is a bad idea, by the way. Leaving yourself out in the open like this. Shouting it from the treetops exactly where you are and how long you'll be here. It makes you an easy target."

"How is it any different than being at the studio? He knows where I am every day I work."

"Yeah, but can he walk right into your studio? Can he sit a few feet away from you during your entire show? Whoever your little stalker is, he can get his hands on you here if he wants that."

Kelly wrapped her arms around herself. She sure hoped he didn't want that. There wasn't a chance this guy would really show his face. Was there?

"Well, you're here now. If he was spying on me and saw what you did to Lyle, I should be fine."

Detective Walsh tipped his chin. "For today. Until you call your uncle. In the future, you need to think about this kind of stuff."

She had been so gung ho about getting rid of her bodyguard a few seconds ago, but now, it seemed like one of Uncle Hal's better ideas. Her uncle would catch this stalker, obsessed fan, whatever he was. She wouldn't need someone to protect her forever.

DONOVAN HAD BEEN on a few stakeouts in his day. This wasn't exactly like those but close. Instead of sitting in a car all day, he got to hang out at one of his favorite barbecue places and eat the free food the manager kept bringing him. Standing behind the table where the radio station crew sat to do their show, he slathered the pulled pork in some of the tangy and sweet Kansas City–style sauce.

"How's it taste?" the manager asked, checking in for the third time. Donovan wasn't sure if he was simply being generous or was afraid of getting slammed to the floor like that Lyle guy.

"It's delicious, sir. This might be even better than the brisket, and that was heaven."

The man's whole face lit up. He took pride in what he did and it showed. "Glad you like it. Can I get you anything else? Did you get some cornbread?"

"I'm good, thank you. I've had two pieces of cornbread. You guys make the best."

"Appreciate that. Let me know if there's

anything else we can do for you while you're here."

Donovan gave him a will-do nod before the manager did a quick check on Kelly and her crew. She was off-air at the moment and chatting it up with a couple of female customers. Kelly laughed at something they said and thanked them for stopping by. She had a way with people. There was something very down-to-earth about her that people seemed to be attracted to.

"Kelly Bonner, I am your biggest fan." A man the size and height of a professional basketball player appeared at the table. Donovan could see Kelly's back straighten and her shoulders tense. He set his sandwich down on the counter behind him and quickly wiped his hands. He had let the food distract him from watching the room.

"Glad to hear it. Would you like to spin our wheel and win yourself a prize?" she offered. Kelly's producer had set up a prize wheel that listeners could spin for radio station paraphernalia or free food from the restaurant.

"Can I win a dinner date with you if I spin?" he asked, causing Donovan to inch closer.

"You can definitely win dinner," she replied, ignoring the come-on.

"This place is fine for lunch, but I want to take you somewhere real nice. I know this great Italian place on the north side of town." He placed his hands on the table and smiled down at her like a fox in the henhouse.

Donovan stepped in. "Sir, I'm going to need you to back away from Miss Bonner, please. Either spin the wheel for your chance to get your hands on a free can cozy or get in line for lunch."

The man stood up and reached into the inside pocket of his suit coat, pulling out a business card. "I don't need any can cozies, but if you want to have some of the best lasagna you've ever tasted, give me a call." He slid the card across the table.

Kelly's producer picked up the card. "I love lasagna. I'll drop your card in our drawing for tickets to the Grace Note concert."

The guy looked like he was about to say something when Kelly said, "Good luck and thanks for listening to K104."

Taking the hint, he made his way to the register to buy himself some lunch. Donovan hoped he himself had never made a woman feel that uncomfortable before and been so clueless about it. He prided himself in being able to read people better than that.

"Sorry we had to interrupt your lunch back

there," Kelly said, cracking a smile. "I think this is the first time since we've been on the air that I've seen you empty-handed."

Donovan tried not to roll his eyes.

"Do you think that was the guy?" her producer asked. "I listened to him talk, hoping I would recognize his voice."

"That wasn't him," Donovan said.

"How do you know? You didn't hear the guy when he called yesterday," Kelly challenged.

"I know because you told me your stalker is angry at you for saying you had a boyfriend. That guy strode up to you like there wasn't a chance you'd reject him. I'm less concerned about the men who approach you than the guys who hang back and watch you without saying a word."

Kelly scanned the room with wary eyes. She bit down on her bottom lip.

Her producer put a hand on her shoulder. "Don't worry, Kel. Between me and Detective Walsh, no creep is going to touch you."

"You're sweet, Lyle, but I'd like to be able to take care of myself."

Donovan admired the way she thought, and given the ease with which he took Lyle down earlier, her friend wasn't going to be much help if things got physical. It was best she learned to defend herself.

"Maybe you could get some pepper spray," Lyle suggested.

Kelly glanced back at Donovan and fought a smile. "I hear that's not the best idea, actually."

Maybe she wasn't as stubborn as he'd assumed.

Lyle's computer chimed. "Shoot, you're on in thirty seconds."

Kelly put on her headphones and Donovan slipped back behind her. It was his turn to scan the room for anyone out of the ordinary.

There was a group of women gathered around one of the tables. Their laughter came in bursts in between their raucous conversation. There was a dad and his two kids at another table. Both kids had to be under the age of five. The older child knocked over his cup and spilled red punch. His dad jumped up and grabbed the roll of paper towels off the holder at the other end of the table to wipe it up. The man's patience was admirable. He didn't yell or make the little boy feel bad for spilling; he simply had his son help clean it up.

Donovan wished he had that kind of patience with Graham and Avery. He was a military man who was used to always having things in order. Clutter wasn't something that existed on a military base. Kids created clutter without even trying. His niece and nephew were like two tiny tornadoes who could mess up a room in the blink of an eye.

A group of thirtysomething professionals walked in together. Behind them was someone wearing a dark blue hooded sweatshirt. He wasn't with them but stayed close enough to them that Donovan couldn't get a good look at him.

"We're going to be hanging out for another hour, so I hope you'll come on in and spin our wheel of prizes and enter for your chance to win two tickets to the Grace Note Records Concert for the Kids," Kelly said into her microphone. "Speaking of Grace Note, let's play the new song from Boone Williams. This is 'One Mountain at a Time.'" She clicked a button on her laptop and took off her headphones. "I cannot wait until the real promo for this show starts. You think I'll get an in-studio interview with Boone Williams? I have been in love with him since I was six years old."

Lyle laughed. "Careful, you don't want him getting a bodyguard because you're the obsessed fan."

Donovan's attention was split between

Kelly and the guy in the hoodie ordering his lunch. The group of work buddies came over to the table and took turns spinning the wheel and chatting it up with Kelly and Lyle. The lone wolf sat in the far corner with his back to the radio station's setup. It began to irk Donovan that he couldn't see the guy's face. He didn't even know what color his hair was.

Something inside his head told him to get a better look, so he waltzed over to the mystery man's table. "Want to spin the wheel for some prizes? They're giving away free pulled pork sandwiches on your next visit."

The guy didn't move. "No, thanks."

"Come on." Donovan tried to cajole him. "You can sign up to win tickets to some big concert, too. Boone Williams is going to be there."

The guy kind of chuckled. "Don't need any tickets. Especially to Boone Williams."

Donovan still couldn't see his face but could tell he had a baseball hat on under that hood and sunglasses on. "You got something against Boone Williams? Kelly over there loves him. You know, Kelly Bonner. From the local radio station."

"Everything all right over here?" The restaurant manager was back with a worried expression and a tray full of cornbread slices.

"Can I offer you gentlemen some cornbread while you wait for your food?"

Finally, the guy turned and looked over his shoulder. "I'm not going to say no to that."

The manager's eyes nearly popped out of his head. "Boone Williams?"

"He's not interested," Donovan said, getting a good look at this creeper. The man was in his forties. Dark hair under his hat and hood. Strong jaw. No visible scars on his face.

"Boone Williams!" a petite brunette from the table of women shrieked.

Before Donovan knew it, pretty much everyone in the place, save the dad and his two kids, was huddled around them asking for pictures and autographs. That was when it hit him.

"Ah, Boone Williams."

## *CHAPTER FOUR*

"I CAN'T BELIEVE that Boone Williams walked into my Great Barbecue for lunch." Kelly helped Lyle load up the station van with the last of the equipment.

"Oh, it's your Great Barbecue now, is it?" Lyle slammed the doors shut.

Kelly smirked. "You know what I mean. He must have heard me on the radio and couldn't stay away."

"I'm pretty sure the guy had no idea there was a radio station inside. He was definitely trying to avoid being recognized. My guess is he did not plan to show up where someone was playing his song and giving away tickets to see him in concert. Walking into your show was probably his biggest nightmare." Detective Walsh had an affinity for being no fun.

"Okay, so I know he's a private guy, but I don't think he'd call it his biggest nightmare to walk into a restaurant where I'm doing my show."

"Your Great Barbecue. Your show. Someone sure is all about what's hers," Lyle teased.

Kelly nudged him with her elbow. "Keep it up and I won't put in a good word for you with a certain someone we both know."

"Did I mention what a great show you had today?" Lyle asked, changing his tune. "Top-notch, Kel."

"I'll meet you back at the station," Detective Walsh said, backing away.

She was happy to be free of her shadow even if it was only for the short drive to the radio station. When she got back to her office, she would call her uncle and see if there was any other possible solution to this problem. Maybe she could convince him there wasn't really a problem. Yes, the guy messed up her car yesterday, but maybe that was it. He was mad, got his revenge and now he would move on.

She could hope.

"It's overkill to have a bodyguard, don't you think?" she asked Lyle. She wanted him to agree with her and put the lingering doubts she had to rest.

"Maybe," he answered quickly. He glanced her way. "I don't know. Maybe it's not. This guy had to know what car you drove to mess with it, which means he's watched you come and go. That's a bigger deal than someone sending you gifts in the mail. A bodyguard might be what you need until your uncle finds the guy."

It bothered her to think about being watched. How long had that been going on? Was he still watching without her being aware? The thought made her skin crawl.

At the station, Kelly contemplated asking the detective to stay in the parking garage instead of coming inside. She hadn't yet explained to Caroline that she had been given private security and wasn't sure how that would go over with the boss yet. He was there to open her door as soon as Lyle parked the van, however.

"If you can give me a quick tour of your office, I should be able to wait outside for you to finish up. It would be helpful for me to have a lay of the land in case anything was to happen while you were inside," he said.

The relief was immediate. Kelly's shoulders were no longer tight. "That sounds like a good idea. I'll show you around right now."

He offered to help Lyle carry the equipment into the building. With his arms full, he used his body to hold the elevator doors open for her. Kelly noticed the scar on the left side of his neck as they rode the tiny elevator up. She wondered how he got it but didn't ask.

"Do you have a first name?" she asked instead. "I'd like to be able to introduce you as a friend of mine if we run into my boss."

He stared at her with his hazel eyes. Outside they had looked greener, but inside they were a golden brown. "You can call me Donovan."

"Okay, cool. You can call me Kelly instead of Miss Bonner. That sounds so formal and I'm not really a formal person," she said. Donovan nodded and Lyle snickered. If he had been close enough, Kelly would have given Lyle's shins a little kick. She hated that the detective made her feel so awkward. Maybe now that they were on a first-name basis, he would lighten up and things would be a bit more relaxed. "Donovan. That's a good name."

"My mom thought so," he replied.

For some reason the elevator was taking forever and silence made Kelly nervous. "Anyone ever call you Don? Donnie? Dono?"

"No. And please don't try to be the first."

The elevator signaled they had arrived at their floor and the doors opened. No nicknames for the detective. At least he had a first name. Calling him Donovan made things feel less threatening. Hopefully, the only person she'd have to introduce him to was Nancy. Caroline liked to stay in her office anyway. It was unlikely they'd bump into her during the quick tour.

"Kelly, you're back already?" Caroline, in her red power suit and killer heels, stood next to the reception desk because of course she wasn't in her office like she usually always was. Kelly's luck lately kind of stank.

"We're baaaack." Kelly regretted saying it that way the moment it came out of her mouth.

Caroline's sense of humor was nonexistent. She appeared more annoyed than amused. "I need to talk to you. Who is this?" she asked, staring at Donovan, who had a box full of K104 promotional material in his hands.

Kelly hoped her broad smile didn't come across as fake as it was. "This is my friend Donovan. He was kind enough to help us carry things up from the van."

Juliette, the receptionist, frowned. Her eyebrows pinched together behind her glasses. "Aren't you the police officer investigating what happened in the parking garage?"

Donovan looked to Kelly for help. Of course, he must have introduced himself to

Juliette when he was here earlier, and Juliette never forgot a face.

"He is," Kelly answered. "He's a friend, who also happens to work for the police department. It's nice to have friends on the force, right?"

"Nice indeed. Well, I hope you figure out what happened," Caroline said to Donovan before turning to Kelly. "You remembered to lock your car, right?"

"My car wasn't broken into. It was vandalized."

"Oh, well, it's still important to lock up. When you don't, you invite trouble. That's all I was trying to say."

Kelly reminded herself not to take offense. Caroline didn't get where she was by thinking bad things just happened. She was a strong believer in being in control of one's destiny. In Caroline's mind, if Kelly wanted something, she simply had to work hard for it and she'd get it.

Kelly wanted a new contract.

"You wanted to talk to me?"

Caroline fiddled with her earring. "I did. Come on back to my office."

"Lyle, can you show Donovan around before he has to go?" Kelly asked, wanting to get the detective out of there as quickly as possible.

"Yeah, sure," Lyle replied even though it looked as if he'd rather do anything other than that.

*"Thank you,"* she mouthed as she followed Caroline back to her big, corner office.

Caroline's office was immaculate. Everything was in its place. The only thing on her desk was her mammoth computer monitor and keyboard. Her tidiness was as intimidating as she was.

"I know you're anxious about your contract coming to an end soon. I want to reassure you that there is a place for you here at K104."

Kelly nearly leaped out of her seat. "That's great. Thank you. I love it here and I definitely don't want to be anywhere else."

"That's good. But I do need to put some serious thought into where you fit in the lineup. There's been some discussion about moving you to the morning spot. I need to know you're willing to do what it takes to help this station maintain its top spot in the ratings."

The coveted morning spot? The most listened-to time of the day? Kelly wanted to do cartwheels across Caroline's spacious office. "I am willing to do whatever you want me to do. I have some great ideas that I wanted to run by you, as well."

Caroline held up a hand. "Hold on. I'm not looking to brainstorm with you. I want to *challenge* you."

Kelly swallowed hard. She was up for any challenge, but the way Caroline said it made it seem a bit scary.

"Whatever you want."

Caroline opened a file drawer to her left. She pulled out a folder and set it on the desk. She handed Kelly a flyer for the farmers market near Bicentennial Capitol Mall State Park.

"I've heard you've been asking to do some more promo for us. Stan keeps trying to convince me that you're the next big thing here and I should let him find more ways to use your popularity," Caroline said, making it clear she didn't agree with him yet. "I'd like to see what kind of draw you really are. I've agreed to let you make more public appearances. We'll start with sending you out to this farmers market every Friday after your show for the rest of the summer. There are also a few smaller concerts we're sponsoring that I'd like you to attend before we have you onstage at the Grace Note fund-raiser."

"I'm happy to do all of that." This was what

she had been begging Stan to let her do. Finally, Caroline was on board.

"Great. Once we see how things go, we can meet to discuss your new contract and a possible move to mornings."

"Thank you so much, Caroline. You won't be sorry you gave me this chance."

Kelly practically floated back to her office, where Lyle and Donovan were chatting with Nancy.

"Someone looks happy," Nancy said when Kelly walked in.

"Maybe that's because Stan has finally convinced Caroline to give me a chance to prove my worth around here."

Lyle and Nancy applauded. "That's awesome!" Lyle said. "Did she offer you a new contract?"

"Not yet." Kelly stepped over the pile of promo material on the floor and sat down on the corner of her desk that surprisingly didn't have anything on it. "But she's going to. She wants me to get out and do more promotion at some of the concerts we're sponsoring and at the farmers market every week."

"But you told her about your stalker and how it would be safer if you were here in the studio instead of out there in the public for the time being," Donovan chimed in. It felt like he took a pin and popped her balloon.

"No, I didn't tell her that because that would have made her very unhappy, and a very unhappy boss means bad things for my impending contract negotiations."

Donovan rubbed his forehead as if she had given him a headache. "The detectives working on your case aren't going to crack it in one day, Kelly. Having you out in the public is going to make it a lot harder to keep you safe."

"Maybe there's nothing to worry about. Maybe he's done with me. He messed up my car and thinks I have a boyfriend. It could all be over."

Donovan shook his head. "It's not over."

DONOVAN DIDN'T KNOW why he was so sure that Kelly's stalker wasn't through with her yet, but he had such a strong feeling about it, he couldn't ignore it. Hearing that her job was going to take her out of the studio and out in the spotlight again (and on the regular) made him uneasy.

His phone alerted him to a text. The officers investigating the vandalism had some luck getting some surveillance camera footage from outside the parking garage and were going to follow up on a couple leads. Perhaps they would wrap this up faster than he thought.

"What's your cell number?"

Kelly rattled off the number. Donovan put it in his phone and sent her a text message so she could contact him.

"That's me," he said when her phone chimed. "Let me know when you're ready to leave and I'll be waiting in the station's lobby for you." He wanted to do a little investigating on his own while he had some time.

"I just need to plan for tomorrow's show and I'll be ready to go."

Donovan left her and her friends to finish their work. He stopped to talk to Ms. Delgado before heading down to the parking garage.

"Can I ask you a question about the items that were delivered here for Miss Bonner?"

The observant receptionist tilted her head. "Sure, what do you want to know?"

"I'm wondering if you remember how the packages were delivered. Did they come through the regular mail? Or maybe delivered by someone from wherever the gift was purchased?"

Juliette shook her head. "Same guy every time. Except for the singing telegram. That was a different guy, obviously. But all the rest were delivered by a young guy with sandy blond hair."

"Can you remember anything else? Was he tall or short, fat or thin?"

"He was about your height. Sturdy-looking guy. I remember faces better than I remember other things about a person."

"Did he appear to work for a delivery service? Was he wearing a uniform?"

"No uniform. One time he was wearing a hat, but it wasn't from a delivery company." She paused for a moment. She pursed her lips and rubbed her chin. "It was a college hat. Alabama maybe. Their colors are red and white, right?"

That was an excellent observation. "You are a gem, Juliette. If you see this man again, would you please call me?" He snatched a pen out of the holder on her desk and wrote his cell number on a scrap of paper. "And if he comes when Kelly is here, could you contact me right away so I can ask him a few questions. If she's here, I'll be nearby."

"Absolutely. Whatever you need, Detective."

Donovan headed down to the parking garage to take a look around. The officers who were investigating had probably done their due diligence, but it never hurt to have an extra pair of eyes searching for any clues that the stalker may have left behind.

There were no cameras in the garage. No way to be sure who had vandalized Kelly's car. On the lower level, there was a valet. The officers had surely asked them if they had seen anyone suspicious. Donovan had one question for them the officers wouldn't have known to ask, however.

Two men with jackets that clearly identified them as the valets were finishing up with a customer, who tipped the one who had retrieved the car. Once the man had driven off, he counted the wad of dollar bills.

"Hey there, can I ask you guys a couple questions?" Donovan asked.

"Questions about what?" one of them asked. He had a young face and dark hair the same color as Kelly's.

"My name is Detective Walsh and I was wondering if you guys were working here yesterday afternoon."

"We already talked to some cops earlier today," the other one said. His hair was light brown and his complexion pale, like he didn't get out in the sun much. He was built like a marine. Strong and thick.

"Yeah, I know. I'm just following up."

"You got some ID?" the dark-haired one asked.

Why was it that when he didn't have his badge, everyone wanted to see it? "You two aren't in trouble. I just need to know if you were working yesterday and if you saw anyone suspicious hanging around."

"He asked you if you have any ID," the light-haired one said. "If you're a cop, you should have a badge or something."

Donovan inhaled sharply. "I don't have my badge on me, but I—"

The dark-haired one pulled his phone out. "Maybe we should call those cops from this morning and tell them someone real suspicious is nosing around and asking weird questions, pretending to be a cop."

"Go right ahead. They'll be able to vouch for me and then you two can finally answer some questions."

"I wasn't working yesterday," the dark-haired one said, putting his phone back in his pocket. "That's what I told the cops this morning, so it doesn't matter if you're a cop or not. I can't help you either way."

"What about you?" Donovan asked the other one.

"I was here, but I didn't see anything."

"Have you ever noticed someone coming

here to deliver things? Going in with flowers or packages and coming right back out?"

The dark-haired one shook his head. "We don't pay attention to people who aren't asking us to park their cars, man."

"I've seen a guy," the other one said.

"What did he look like?"

"Skinny guy. Maybe as tall as you."

"Do you remember what color hair he had or anything about what he was wearing?"

"I think he had red hair. Maybe. I don't know. I wasn't checking him out or anything. Yesterday he parked his car down here, got out with a bunch of flowers and was in and out in a matter of minutes."

"Was he ever wearing a hat? Maybe you saw a red hat not red hair?"

The valet shrugged his shoulders. "I don't know. All I can tell you is I saw him a couple times. He was definitely a skinny guy."

"If you guys think of anything else, please call the officers you talked to this morning. They would appreciate anything you can remember."

They both agreed to do so but didn't seem like they were going to lose any sleep over who was stalking Kelly Bonner. Donovan headed back to his truck to wait for Kelly's call. His phone rang, but it was Avery.

"Hey, kiddo. How was school?"

"Fine," Avery said. Based on the sounds in the background, she must have been rummaging around in the pantry, finding herself a snack.

"How was after-school club?" Donovan had Avery stay after school for a couple hours with one of the neighbor girls whose mom also worked. It cost more than he liked, but it was worth the peace of mind it brought him to have her supervised by someone other than her brother.

"Fun." She wasn't usually a one-word answer kind of kid. Graham was rubbing off on her regardless of Donovan's attempt at preventing it.

"You thanked Mrs. Finnegan for dropping you off at home?"

"Of course I did, Uncle Donovan."

"Good. I'll be home at my regular time. Is Graham hiding in his room?"

"No. He's watching Davey play some video game."

Donovan moved his phone to the other ear. He must have misunderstood her. "What do you mean he's watching Davey play a video game? He's not supposed to have anyone in the house and he doesn't have his controller."

"Davey's not in the house."

"How is Graham watching him play if he's not in the house?"

"He's outside."

"Davey's outside or Graham is outside?"

"Davey is outside and Graham is inside."

"And Davey is playing video games from outside."

"Yep."

Donovan pinched the bridge of his nose. The kid was creative. He'd have to give him that. "Don't say anything to Graham. I don't want him to know I know he's watching Davey play video games, okay?"

"Okay. Can I watch TV in your room for a little bit?"

"Sure. I'll be home soon." Very soon. He hung up with Avery and dialed Kelly. She was going to have to leave work a little early whether she liked it or not. Donovan could only stand to stink at one job today and apparently parenting was what he was the best at failing.

## *CHAPTER FIVE*

"YOU'RE REALLY NOT going to tell me why we have to go to your house right this second." Kelly felt she had displayed an abundance of patience with Donovan today. He seemed to have a lot going on. Between whatever it was that got him put on desk duty and whatever these issues were at home, the man was a mess.

"I need to handle a situation at home. It should take me no more than a couple minutes. I promise."

Speed limits did not seem to apply to the detective this afternoon and rolling stops were no big deal. Kelly held her breath as they ran a very late yellow light.

"If I drove the way you are, you would probably give me a ticket. Or ten."

He didn't slow down. "I'm not a traffic cop. I don't write tickets."

"I meant that I would get pulled over by a cop. You're a cop." Donovan was so literal it was painful. "You're also breaking all the traffic laws. Can you ease up just a bit?"

"I need to get home. I promise to get you there safely."

Kelly's idea of safe must have been different than his. They crossed the Cumberland River and turned onto a residential street a couple miles east of it.

"You can stay in the truck," he said, pulling into a driveway and jumping out.

Donovan's white Craftsman had a bright red door. There was a detached garage in the back and an American flag hanging from the flagpole out front. From the outside, it was kind of cute. It wasn't where Kelly expected someone like Donovan to live.

A teenage boy sprinted out of the backyard and down the street. Kelly wondered if that was Donovan's son. No one was chasing after him, so maybe not. The front door opened and a little girl came out.

Two kids.

The little girl waved at Kelly. She couldn't have been older than seven or eight. Kelly waved back. A smile spread across the girl's face and she ran up to the truck. Kelly opened her door.

"What's your name?" the girl asked.

"My name's Kelly. What's yours?"

"I'm Avery. Are you friends with my uncle?"

Uncle? That made more sense than Dad.

"I am. Your uncle didn't tell me he had such an adorable niece."

Close up, Kelly could see that Avery was missing one of her front teeth when she smiled. She had brown pigtails that were tied up with ribbons. It was a fancy do for someone living with her uncle. Donovan didn't strike her as the pigtail-making type. Maybe there was an aunt inside, as well.

"He didn't? He likes me better than Graham. Did he tell you about Graham?"

"I heard about Graham this morning. Was that who just…went for a run?" she asked, choosing her words carefully.

"No, that was his friend Davey," Avery replied. "Uncle Donovan said Graham couldn't have friends over, but he didn't listen. Uncle Donovan says Graham's ears must be broken because he never listens."

Kelly tried not to laugh. "You both live with your uncle?"

"Yeah, my mom and dad are in heaven, so he takes care of us."

That wiped the smile right off Kelly's face. "Oh, I'm so sorry, sweetheart."

Avery didn't seem bothered by her loss. The resiliency of youth was amazing. "Do you want to come inside? I bet Uncle Donovan is done yelling at Graham."

"I don't know. Maybe we should hang out here until your uncle comes outside. We wouldn't want to get in the middle of whatever is going on in there."

"Want to jump on my trampoline with me?" she asked with a tilt of her head.

Kelly decided there was no harm in getting out of the truck if she didn't go in the house. "I can watch you jump on your trampoline. Do you know any tricks?"

"I know lots of tricks! Come on, I'll show you." Avery took Kelly by the hand and led her bchind the house.

There was a paver patio off the back with a table and chairs for entertaining and outdoor dining. One of the chairs was pulled away from the table and sat right in front of the sliding glass door. The fenced-in yard was well maintained. There were flowering hydrangeas and manicured bushes around the house and in the corners of the lot.

"Watch me do a flip," Avery said, kicking off her shoes and climbing up on the trampoline that sat in the center of it all.

"Okay, just be careful." The last thing she needed was for the kid to break her neck on Kelly's watch.

Avery and her pigtails bounced and bounced.

Once she was high enough, she did a somersault in the air and landed on her bottom.

"That wasn't a good one," she said, getting to her feet.

"I thought it was pretty good."

The sliding glass door opened and Donovan stepped out on the patio. "Avery, come on inside." He didn't sound angry, but he didn't sound pleased, either.

"Everything okay in there?" Kelly asked.

"As okay as it's going to get. Sorry she bothered you. She should have gone to her *room* like I asked her."

"You guys were yelling too much. I hate when you yell," Avery complained as Kelly helped her off the trampoline.

"I wasn't yelling. Graham was yelling. I was talking in my normal voice."

"Nope, it was your mad voice. I heard it."

Kelly had known the man for less than twelve hours and even she knew what his mad voice sounded like. It could certainly make someone feel like they were being yelled at.

"Your mad voice is kind of scary," Kelly said as they joined him on the patio.

He frowned. "I don't have a mad voice. That's not even a thing."

"I'll point it out the next time you use it, so you can be more self-aware," Kelly offered.

"Wanna see my room?" Avery asked. Without waiting for an answer, she tugged Kelly toward the door.

Kelly resisted, not wanting to assume that Donovan was fine with her going into his house. "I would love to see your room…*if* it's okay with your uncle."

Avery had obviously been trained at the best adult manipulation school around. Her puppy-dog eyes were in full effect. She clasped her hands together and began to beg. "Pleeeeeeeease, Uncle Donovan. Pleeeeeeeease let me show her my room."

"I'm still working, Avery. I need to get Miss Bonner home." The man was ice.

"It will only take a minute. I want to show her the mural Graham painted me."

"Well, now I'm really curious," Kelly said, waiting to see if he would give in.

"Please," Avery continued to beg. "I never get to have friends over. I just want to show her for one minute."

She was breaking Kelly's heart. Both her parents were in heaven and she never got to have friends over. How could he say no? He couldn't. He thawed immediately and was a puddle at her feet.

"Fine. Go ahead and show her your room, but I do need to get her home."

"Yes! Come on, Kelly."

Kelly smiled at Donovan as she followed the little munchkin inside. It was nice to see that he had a soft spot underneath that tough-guy exterior.

The inside of the house was just as unexpected as the outside. It wasn't simply a house; it was a home. The open-concept layout made the first floor appear bigger than it was. The couches looked extremely comfortable and there were some of Avery's art projects hanging on the refrigerator.

A bag of potato chips sat open on the coffee table along with several soda cans. There was no angry teenager, though. Something told Kelly he was probably locked in his room.

"My room is upstairs," Avery said, leading the way. Her pigtails swished from side to side as she walked.

Avery's room was magical. Three of the walls were painted a soft blue while the wall her bed sat against had the most beautiful mural of a castle in the sky. The stone castle sat on a pile of clouds. Each one of the four turrets had purple flags flying from the top and there was a large rainbow arching over it. Above that, there were two heart-shaped clouds with halos.

Kelly's throat tightened and tears threatened to burst from her eyes. Little Avery had her mom and dad watching over her bed every night.

"I asked Graham to add a unicorn but he said he's not that good at painting animals yet."

"This is amazing, Avery. It's so beautiful. Your brother is very talented."

"Too bad he thinks he can draw on any wall he wants now." Donovan leaned against the doorjamb with his arms crossed over his chest.

Kelly remembered the call he had taken this morning. Graham had vandalized the library and been suspended. She could only imagine what a difficult time the kid was going through. She was a grown woman who had only lost one parent, and even that was unbearable sometimes.

"And this is my reading corner. Uncle Donovan built me this bookcase and got me this purple beanbag chair. Purple is my favorite color." Avery plopped down on the chair and pulled a book off the shelf.

"Well, your uncle is full of surprises."

"Want to read a book with me, Kelly?" Avery asked.

"We have to go, little one," Donovan said,

straightening up and dropping his arms to his sides. "I'll read one with you after dinner."

"But I want to read one with Kelly. Can't she stay for dinner? We're having spaghetti and meatballs. Uncle Donovan makes giant meatballs as big as my head. Do you like spaghetti and meatballs?" Avery asked Kelly.

"As big as your head?" The man was getting more interesting by the second.

"They are not as big as your head," Donovan corrected his niece. "Come on and get your shoes on. You and Graham have to come with us because I can't trust your brother here unsupervised."

"But she loves spaghetti!"

Kelly giggled at her persistence. Donovan certainly had his hands full with his niece and nephew.

"She never said she loves spaghetti. Please go get your shoes on."

It was clear that he did not want a dinner guest. No amount of adorable begging was going to get him to change his mind. Not that Kelly wanted to stay. Considering why they were here, dinner was likely to be a bit tense.

"I like spaghetti, but I really need to get home. Maybe we can have dinner another time, okay?"

Avery looked absolutely crestfallen. “Fine,” she grumbled as she brushed past him and out the door.

“Sorry about that. She lacks boundaries. I’m not sure how to teach her them without making her think she can’t talk to anyone. She’s at that age where everything is black or white. She never sees gray.”

Kelly shook her head. “She’s adorable. Don’t discourage her from being her sweet self.”

“Sweet until she doesn’t get her way. Lucky for her and unfortunately for me, I have a hard time telling her no. If you hadn’t turned her down, I fear I would have forced you to eat spaghetti with us.”

Had she not met Avery in person, it would have been harder to believe that she ruled this roost with her cuteness. Although that was clear, so much more was not. Kelly was naturally curious and she had about a million and one questions. How did Avery and Graham’s parents die? How did the kids end up with Donovan? Did he cook anything other than spaghetti and meatballs? Did he build other things besides bookcases?

“Well, I really do need to get home.” Kelly knew today was not the day to ask any of them. She walked past him and into the hall.

"But you owe me spaghetti and meatballs as big as my head some other day because *that* I have to see."

THE LAST THING Donovan imagined happening today was bringing a woman into his home and having to discourage Avery from inviting her over for dinner. One of Jessica's final requests was that he promise not to bring women in and out of the kids' lives. To be fair, his sister didn't specifically ask him to remain single. In fact, Jess had begged him to try harder to let people in, but in his line of work, vulnerability meant death. Donovan understood it was unlikely a woman would kill him if he let her get close, but he was who he was and so far everyone he had ever dated wanted more than he was willing to give. That meant it was better he drop out of the dating game until the kids were grown.

Donovan's biggest concern was that he'd be responsible for his niece and nephew having to suffer any more losses. A father and a mother were enough. He didn't want them to get attached to someone only to have them disappear.

He knocked on Graham's door. "We leave in two minutes. You better be in the back seat of my truck when I'm ready to pull out of the driveway or else."

Donovan had no idea what the "else" would be but hoped the threat of the mysterious else would be enough to encourage Graham to do as he was told. Why did parenting have to be so hard?

"If it makes you feel any better, I hear that once you get through the teenage years, it's smooth sailing," Kelly said as they headed downstairs.

"Considering he's only fifteen and she's barely seven, I'm not sure if that's good news or bad. The light at the end of the tunnel is so far away, it's a tiny pinprick."

"Well, maybe she'll be less trouble. She might learn from some of the trouble he gets in."

Kelly was quite the optimist. Donovan had lost the ability to see the bright side a long time ago. Since Oliver, Donovan's best friend and Jessica's husband, was killed in the line of duty and Jessica was diagnosed with incurable cancer, Donovan only expected the worst. Since his sister died, every day was similar to his time in the military. It was all about survival—his and the kids'. He didn't have the luxury to hope for more than getting through each day still breathing.

"Can Kelly sit in the back with me?" Avery asked as she came skipping through the house.

"I would love to sit in the back with you, Miss Avery." Kelly gave one of Avery's pigtails a gentle tug. "Did you do these pigtails yourself?"

Avery giggled and the sound squeezed Donovan's heart. His niece's resiliency was her most amazing quality. She had more experience with tragedy than most adults, yet she could still smile, skip and laugh.

"Uncle Donovan always does my hair in the morning. I wanted a French braid today, but he said there wasn't enough time."

Donovan wasn't surprised by the shocked look on Kelly's face. Six months ago, no one would have been able to convince him that he would know how to do a little girl's hair. "Someone was a sleepyhead this morning. If you want a French braid you have to get out of bed earlier."

"You know how to French braid hair?" Kelly asked.

"Mommy taught him everything before she went to heaven. They had to practice every day because he used to hurt my head when he combed out my knots."

Kelly pressed her lips together and had that look in her eye that always made him uncomfortable. Avery didn't understand how talking about her mom might make other people feel and their sympathy was sometimes too much. The sooner he got Kelly back home, the better.

"Let's get in the truck. It's late."

A door slammed upstairs and Graham came stomping down the steps. He had on a black sweatshirt with the hood pulled up. With his hands in the front pocket, he trudged past all of them and out the front door.

"Kelly might have to sit in the front seat, Avery. I don't think Graham is going to want to sit in front with me."

"No!" Avery chased after her brother. "Graham! I'm sitting in the back with Kelly. You have to sit in the front."

As much as Graham hated Donovan, he loved Avery more. He didn't even argue; he just got into the passenger's seat. He might be trouble, but that boy would take care of his sister until the day he died.

He apologized to Kelly again. "Today has been kind of a nightmare. I promise it won't always be like this."

"It's okay," she said, placing a hand on his arm. The contact made him suck in a breath. "Don't apologize for being a good uncle."

He didn't feel like a good uncle. He felt

like he was barely cutting it. Maybe she was just being nice, maybe she saw something he didn't. Either way, he appreciated the compliment.

They all got inside the truck and Donovan headed back to the city. Graham stared out the window and didn't say a word. Avery, on the other hand, talked nonstop. Kelly patiently listened to her go on and on in excruciating detail about her day at school. She even described everything she ate for lunch.

"At recess, we played tag and I was only it one time because I am super fast. I had my fast shoes on."

"You have fast shoes?" Kelly asked, making Donovan chuckle. Avery had a pair of sneakers that he told her would make her run faster. He had to be careful what he said around Avery because she did not doubt anything he told her.

"They're pink with silver sparkles. I wanted purple ones, but Uncle Donovan said they were fast shoes and I would run faster in them and he was right."

"I think I might need him to buy me some of those shoes," Kelly said, making eye contact with him in the rearview mirror. Those blue eyes were mesmerizing. "At the gym, I run on the treadmill and I can never go as fast as the guy who works out next to me. He always teases me."

"Uncle Donovan, do they make the fast shoes for grown-ups?"

"I don't know, Avery. I'm guessing not the same exact ones."

"Shoes don't make you fast, Avery," Graham said from under his hood. "You're fast because you're fast. You don't need stupid shoes."

"They are too fast shoes and they're not stupid!" Avery asserted. "Uncle Donovan said they are, so they are."

"Uncle Donovan lied."

"That's enough, Graham," Donovan warned. "Don't make your sister upset because you're mad at me."

Graham pushed back his hood and glared at his uncle. "Do the shoes really make her fast? Are they magic shoes or did you tell her that because you were tired of shopping and you couldn't find any purple shoes like she wanted?"

Donovan gave him a pointed look. "I said that's enough."

"You're such a hypocrite." The hood went back up. "You punish me for every little thing I do, but you lie to my sister every day."

Donovan had no rebuttal. He was wrong

and he was right. They drove in silence for a full minute.

"They are fast shoes, Graham. They are," Avery said in her tiny voice. No one said anything after that until they pulled up in front of Kelly's building.

"Do you want me to check your apartment?" he offered. Her building wasn't one of the most secure places to live. Someone could sneak their way in with a little patience.

"I'll be fine," she said, opening her door. "If I see anything suspicious, I'll text you."

She gave Avery a hug and promised to eat dinner with them next time she came over. That was a good answer. As long as they never ended up back at his house, they could avoid spending an awkward meal together.

"See ya tomorrow," Donovan said before she shut the door. He waited until she was safely inside before putting on his blinker so he could pull out into traffic.

"I think she's my new best friend," Avery said.

It made perfect sense why he had decided not to bring people into the kids' lives. Avery got attached so quickly. He had thought this would be easier since he had no intention of getting into a relationship with anyone. But Avery could bond with a complete stranger in five seconds flat, and Kelly wasn't a girlfriend. She wasn't even a friend. She was a job assignment.

"Who was that? Why did you offer to check her apartment? Why are you going to see her tomorrow?" Graham asked. Donovan was surprised he was curious enough to say something.

"That's my boss's niece. She works at a radio station and someone was…being mean to her. I have to help keep her safe until we can find that person."

"Why would someone be mean to Kelly?" Avery asked. "She's so nice."

"It's hard to explain, sweetie."

"Is someone trying to kill her?" Graham asked.

"Someone is going to kill her?" Avery screeched and then burst into tears.

"Are you serious right now?" he said to Graham. Donovan was ready to tape the kid's mouth shut. Did he not understand how saying something like that could scare his sister? He tried to console Avery. "No one is going to kill Kelly. She's totally safe."

His phone chimed with a text. Don't leave! was all it said.

Adrenaline flooded Donovan's body. He hoped he hadn't told Avery another lie.

## *CHAPTER SIX*

STANDING OUTSIDE HER door with the "apology" note in her hand, Kelly suddenly felt completely vulnerable. She dropped the sheet of paper on the floor and pulled out her phone as she made her way back to the elevators. She pressed the down button on the wall as her heart pounded.

How did he get in her building?

The elevator doors opened as she began to text Donovan not to leave. An unfamiliar man stood inside and the fear of the unknown made her turn and run for the stairs instead of joining him. She probably looked like she had lost her mind, but she didn't care. Whoever this stalker was, he could get in here. She flew down the stairs while trying to send off her text. When she got to the ground level, she pushed the door open and bumped right into another man.

"Are you okay?" he asked.

The panic that overwhelmed her made it impossible to answer. She was in the midst of a fight-or-flight response and her brain screamed, "RUN!" She pushed away from the stranger and sprinted out of the building, hoping Donovan wasn't very far away. His truck was still where she'd gotten out. He didn't hesitate to jump out of the truck.

"What's the matter?"

"He was in there."

"Right now?" Donovan pulled her behind him, putting himself between her and the building.

The scariest thing about that question was she had no idea if he was or not. "I don't know. He left a note on my door, so he was."

"You're fine," he said, putting his hands on her shoulders and looking her right in the eye. His voice was calm and unwavering. "Take some deep breaths. I'm going to have you get back in the truck, but I don't want you to scare Avery, okay?"

Kelly glanced back at his truck and could see Graham staring at her wide-eyed. She couldn't see through the tinted back windows but assumed Avery was doing the same. She didn't want to alarm the children, but she couldn't stop her heart from wanting to break through her rib cage.

"Look at me, Kelly," Donovan said sternly. She did as she was told. "You're safe. I'm right here. I won't let anyone hurt you. Take some deep breaths. Slow and steady."

She inhaled through her nose and exhaled out of her mouth, following his example. Her body began to relax and her heart rate went back to normal.

"Thank you," she said, meaning it more than ever.

"I'm going to call the detectives in charge of the vandalism while you wait in the truck with the kids, okay?"

Kelly nodded and got in the truck. Avery stared at her with fear in her eyes. Kelly put on her bravest face even though she felt anything but.

"Hey, sweetie. I decided I have to try your uncle's spaghetti and meatballs. I thought I could live without them, but I can't."

"No one is trying to kill you?" Avery squeaked out.

The question caused some more heart palpitations. "What? No. No one is trying to kill me." At least she hoped no one was.

"Why did you look like you were running for your life?" Graham asked from the front seat.

"I was afraid you had already left. I was just trying to catch you." She patted Avery on the leg, hoping she was convincing enough.

Graham scoffed. "You're just like my uncle," he said, turning around to face the front. She wasn't fooling him, but Avery seemed pleased with that answer.

Donovan got in the truck. "We need to park. I have some work friends stopping by and I need to talk to them for a minute."

"But we have to get home and make Kelly spaghetti and meatballs as big as my head," Avery protested.

Donovan made eye contact with Kelly through the rearview mirror. "Do we?"

"That's why I came running out," she explained. "I decided dinner sounded too good."

"Right. Well, we just need to wait a couple minutes. It shouldn't take long and then we'll make dinner."

Donovan started the truck and drove around, looking for an open spot. It didn't take as long as Kelly had feared for the detectives to show up. Donovan asked the kids to stay put while he and Kelly talked to his "work friends."

"I thought it was a note from the association or something. It was just taped to my door," Kelly explained to them. "I didn't even think about the fact that no one else had one on theirs."

"Did you notice anyone suspicious when

you came in or went out?" one of the detectives asked.

"No one on the way in. On the way out, everyone looked suspicious, but I think that was more my fear than them being dangerous."

They had a few more questions and took the letter as evidence. Kelly went into her apartment to grab an overnight bag. Donovan suggested she spend the night at her uncle's while they did some investigating. The detectives were busy canvassing the floor when she finished locking up. They knocked on a few of her neighbors' doors to ask them if they had seen anyone hanging around who didn't belong.

The letter had been some sort of apology for messing up her car. He also stated he was disappointed that she had gotten the police involved. Kelly had wondered how he knew that was true. He assured her he wouldn't hold a grudge if she was sorry for hurting his feelings. He understood she might be confused about her feelings because he hadn't revealed himself to her yet, but he would... soon.

She didn't want him to. Kelly wasn't confused. She wanted him to go away.

"Are you okay?" Donovan asked her as they made their way back to the truck.

"I'm disappointed more than anything. I had this hope that he was done with me because we had ruined his fantasy. I just wanted him to disappear."

"Well, it's concerning that he knows you talked to the police. That means he's closer than we thought. I'm also wondering if he knew where you lived all along or if he followed you home last night. Everything else came to the station before today. That has to mean something."

Kelly could feel the anxiety returning. "I'm sorry I told Avery I was coming over for dinner. I'm sure you want to get rid of me for the night."

"It's fine. It was a good excuse. Graham got her all upset by asking me if I was protecting you because someone was trying to kill you."

That didn't help keep the fear at bay. This stalker was obsessed, but he wasn't going to kill her. She was going to keep telling herself that until she believed it. "No one is trying to kill me."

Donovan gave her a gentle pat on the back. "No one is trying to kill you. Plus you have the entire Nashville PD looking out for you. No one is going to do anything to Captain Bonner's niece."

His words were reassuring. Uncle Hal

always had her back. For the first time in forever, she was grateful for his overprotectiveness.

They got in the truck and drove to Donovan's house. Avery was full of questions on the way back. Trying to downplay what was happening wasn't as easy to do when being interrogated by the most curious seven-year-old on the planet.

Graham was out of the truck before Donovan had it in Park. Kelly offered to help Donovan cook dinner. She wasn't much of a cook, but she could handle filling a pot with water so they could boil the noodles.

"We have to make the meatballs first. Right, Avery?"

"Meatballs first because they take the longest because they're so big." Avery pushed a step stool by the sink and began washing her hands. Donovan had her trained quite well.

Kelly noticed the chalkboard menu on the wall by the refrigerator. Every day of the week had a different dinner listed next to it. Today was spaghetti and meatballs. Tomorrow, chicken enchiladas were planned. It was fascinating how organized Donovan was. There was something very attractive about a man who could cook and braid hair but still exude manliness.

"The only thing my dad knew how to cook was hamburgers on the grill," Kelly shared, taking her turn at the sink to wash her hands. "Truthfully, he wasn't very good it. Sometimes the burgers were more like hockey pucks."

"You can't eat hockey pucks," Avery said.

Kelly's eyebrows lifted. "Exactly."

That earned her a chuckle from Donovan. "Hopefully, the meatballs will be to your liking."

"I love them," Avery said. She was clearly Uncle Donovan's biggest fan.

Donovan had all the ingredients out on the kitchen island. Kelly didn't even realize meatballs had eggs in them. Avery situated herself in between the two adults and Donovan gave them both a job.

"How are you at chopping onions?" he asked Kelly.

"I'm probably good."

"Have you chopped onions before?"

"Not really. I'm better at doing this..." She pulled out her phone and pretended to call someone. "Hello, I'd like to order some food for takeout." She put her phone down. "The delivery guy from Johnny's Grill and I are practically best friends."

Avery slapped her hand against her forehead and giggled. Donovan moved the cutting board back by him.

"I think I'll chop the onions while you help Avery measure out the other ingredients. You can pour things into measuring cups and spoons and then dump them into the bowl, can't you?"

Kelly picked up one of the measuring cups. "I can handle that."

"I'll help you," Avery whispered to her. Her big brown eyes were framed by the thickest lashes. She was the sweetest thing.

Avery added bread crumbs to a small bowl and Kelly poured a half cup of milk in there, as well. Avery stirred it a bit and then left it so the bread crumbs could soak up the milk. In the bigger bowl, Donovan had placed two kinds of ground meat. Avery and Kelly both added a pinch of salt and pepper. They put in some garlic and parsley, as well.

Donovan sniffled and pretended to wipe tears away. "I'm done with these onions. They always make me cry."

Avery's giggle was the perfect remedy for the anxiety Kelly had been feeling about her situation. "He always cries when he does the onions. I don't know why it's so sad!"

"Your uncle is a very sensitive guy."

Donovan smirked and pushed his sleeves up. "Who is going to crack the eggs for me?"

Avery raised her hand. "Me!"

"Probably a good idea. For some reason when I make scrambled eggs for breakfast, they're always a little crunchy from little bits of shell."

"Ew! You're not supposed to eat the shell."

"I know. I don't try to eat them. It just happens."

"It's a miracle you have survived this long on your own," Donovan said. "I also feel bad for your future children."

"My future children will be fine," she argued. "I plan to marry a man who can cook or one who loves eating out as much as I do. Maybe I'll even marry the delivery guy from Johnny's Grill."

"When's dinner going to be ready?" Graham called down from upstairs.

"About forty minutes!" Donovan yelled back. "Why don't you come down and help?"

"No, thanks!" he said before slamming his door shut.

Donovan scowled. "I'm going to take his door off if he does that again."

"I was a big door slammer when I was in high school," Kelly admitted. Her parents used to make her so mad when they would set so many annoying limits. It was like they didn't trust her judgment at all. "Sometimes it's the only way to let off some steam."

"I think he can find other ways that don't damage my house."

Kelly realized she had crossed a line. She shouldn't get in the middle of Donovan and his nephew. She had no idea what was going on between the two of them. "You're right. I didn't mean to mind your business."

DONOVAN WASN'T LOOKING for parenting advice from someone who didn't have any children herself. "Who's ready to get their hands dirty and make some meatballs?" he asked, changing the subject.

"Me!" Avery was ready for everything. The child's energy was limitless. "Don't forget to make them super big, Kelly. These are not baby meatballs."

"These are as big as your head," Kelly said with a wink.

"Not exactly that big," Donovan reminded them. He used his hands to mix everything together in one bowl. Grabbing a handful, he rolled it into a ball. "This is as big as we want them."

The three of them made eight giant meatballs, so they could each have two. Into the oven they went. The rest of the meal Donovan would finish on his own. He had Avery wash up and Kelly went outside to make a phone call to her uncle.

It was frustrating to be on the sidelines in this investigation. Being the bodyguard meant he didn't get to solve the crime. His only role was to stop anything else from happening to her. Donovan wasn't a fan of being reactive instead of proactive, but his hands were tied. It was better than desk duty. He had to remember that.

Graham came downstairs and opened the refrigerator. "There's no more soda?"

"I think the six cans you drank today were enough."

His loud sigh was like nails on a chalkboard.

Donovan stepped in front of Graham before he could walk out. "I need you to behave yourself during dinner. Kelly's uncle is my boss. It would be helpful if you could make a better impression or at least be civil."

"I'm pretty sure your boss isn't going to fire you because I don't kiss up to his niece like Avery does. I don't think they care about me that much. At all, really."

"I'm not worried about being fired. I'd like

Kelly and her uncle to know that I value respect and having pride in who you are."

Graham didn't flinch. "You don't respect me. Why should I show you or anyone associated with you respect?"

Donovan didn't know how to get through to him. "I'd give you respect if you respected yourself. You walk around here with this giant chip on your shoulder and take no pride in anything you do."

He got nothing back but an eye roll. No comeback meant maybe he knew Donovan was right.

The sliding glass door opened and Kelly came inside. At the same time, Avery came downstairs all clean.

"Hey, Avery, can you help your brother set the table?" Donovan asked, hoping Graham wouldn't leave Avery to do it by herself.

"I can help," Kelly offered. "Can you show me where the plates are, Graham?"

"Oh, can I? Can I?" Graham said mockingly. Even though it was clear he was displeased with the chore, he went to the cabinet with the plates and pulled out four.

"What am I going to do?" Avery complained. Only this little one would be disappointed that she didn't get a chore.

"You can watch the water in the pot and tell

me when it's boiling so we can cook the noodles." There wasn't really anything else she could do. The four of them worked together to get everything ready. It was disconcerting how normal it seemed. He'd known this woman less than a day and she was about to be a part of their family dinner.

*Family dinners.* That was the other big rule Jessica put into place. She wanted the kids to have dinner together as often as possible. That was the time for the three of them to reconnect, to hear about each other's day and to show the children that the family unit was important.

Most of their family dinners had consisted of Avery monopolizing the conversation with the tales of her day. Graham didn't seem to mind having to share less because his sister shared more. Donovan was trying his best to do everything the way his sister asked him to, but it was proving more difficult than he ever imagined.

Protecting the kids from unnecessary attachments seemed to be just as hard. There was Kelly engaging both kids in conversation about her job. Somehow this woman had insinuated herself into his family in a matter of a few hours.

"Do you listen to Finch and Wells?" she asked Graham.

"Sometimes," Graham answered. He handed her forks to place by the plates on her side of the table. "They aren't my favorite, though. I'm more into Boone Williams. He was my mom and dad's favorite. They were always playing his stuff in the car and at our house."

"For real? You're not going to believe this, but your uncle met Boone Williams today."

"No way." Graham's head whipped around with a skeptical look on his face. "You met Boone Williams?"

"Kelly's station was doing her show from the new Great Barbecue that opened up in the city. He showed up and was trying real hard to go unnoticed."

"Your uncle thought he looked suspicious and was harassing him until the restaurant manager came over and recognized him," she said, ratting him out.

Graham smirked. "You had no idea who he was, did you?"

"He was trying very hard not to be noticed. I wanted to make sure he wasn't the guy who was…being mean to Kelly." He had to be careful about saying the wrong thing around Avery.

"There's no hiding when your uncle is

around. Boone was very gracious, though. He took pictures and signed some autographs for the people who were there. I've interviewed him once in the studio when his new album came out. He's really a nice guy. You would like him."

"That's cool," Graham said.

"Did you ever interview Piper Starling? She's my favorite singer," Avery asked without tearing her eyes away from the pot of water on the stove. The child was dedicated.

"I have interviewed her a couple times. She's probably the nicest person I have ever met."

That got Avery's attention. She completely abandoned her duty and joined them at the table.

"You met her? Can I meet her? Do you have her phone number? Are you friends?"

There was something so charming about the sound of Kelly's laughter. "I wouldn't say we're friends. I wish. She's going to be a part of the Grace Note concert at the end of June. If your uncle is up for it, I might be able to get you tickets and backstage to meet Piper *and* Boone."

With that one little promise, she managed to create a massive ruckus. Both of them were in his face, begging Donovan to let them go to the concert.

"Whoa, whoa, whoa. I'll look into it."

That wasn't a good enough answer. They continued with their pleading. Donovan glared in Kelly's direction. Rookie mistake to mention it to the kids before asking him if they could go.

"Guys, let me give your uncle all the information before you attack him," Kelly said, trying to rescue him. "I think we'll have better luck convincing him if we back off."

"That sounds like a great idea," Donovan said. "The water is boiling, Avery. Do you want to help me put in the pasta?"

"I just want to say one more thing," Avery said, holding up one finger. "Piper Starling is the nicest person in the world. Don't you want me to meet the nicest person in the world?"

She was good; he would give her that much. Too bad elementary school didn't have a debate team. Avery would be the captain if they did.

"I will take that into consideration when I make my decision."

"That means he's going to say no," Graham said. He tossed the napkins down on the table. "Of course he's going to say no because it would be awesome and he never lets us do anything awesome."

Donovan was offended by that comment. He tried to give them positive experiences all the time. "I do lots of awesome things with you."

"Not as awesome as meeting Piper Starling. That would be the most awesome," Avery said with a hand on her hip and a tilt of her head.

"I probably should have learned my lesson to mind my own business, but I would be remiss not to mention that a portion of the profits from the show are going to benefit Nashville's Children's Hospital. If you buy something at the show, it helps a really good cause."

He should have stopped her when she mentioned minding her own business. There was no going back now. The kids were back to pleading with their hands clasped and Graham even on his knees.

"You wouldn't be doing it for us. You'd be doing it for the sick kids. Come on, Uncle Donovan, we'll do anything," Graham begged.

Suddenly, inspiration struck. "I'll make you a deal. I'll take you to the concert if you can manage to stay out of trouble for the rest of the school year. No more calls from your dean and the ticket is yours."

Graham's arms fell to his sides. All the excitement seemed to leave his body. Was it really such an impossible task? He never got in trouble when his mother was alive. Donovan believed he could do it if he would simply try.

Avery, on the other hand, jumped up and down with her arms raised victoriously. "I'll stay out of trouble! I can do it! I want to meet Piper Starling!"

"What about you, Graham? Do we have a deal? There's less than a month left of school. Three weeks. I think you can do it."

Graham stood up and shoved his hands in his pockets as he stared down at his feet. It couldn't possibly be more important to him to be a troublemaker than to do something that was apparently "so awesome."

"Fine," Graham mumbled at the ground.

"Fine? Did you say fine?"

Graham lifted his head and rolled his eyes. "I said fine."

Donovan felt like he had actually won a small victory with that concession. Maybe Kelly had helped him instead of making things worse. Maybe Donovan would be okay with this tiny intrusion if it led to something positive for Graham.

# *CHAPTER SEVEN*

SPAGHETTI WITH MEATBALLS as big as your head was now Kelly's favorite meal of all time. It was so delicious she could hardly believe she had helped make it. Her skills in the kitchen were not something to write home about.

To show her gratitude for letting her encroach on his family time, she offered to help with the dishes. Donovan was reluctant but didn't stop her. Avery was allowed to watch some TV while Graham, who was still grounded, went back to his room.

"I'm sorry I put you on the spot about the concert. I know I put being the cool lady at dinner above your rights as their guardian."

"You were definitely the cool lady at dinner. I'm not sure any other dinner guest will ever be able to compete."

Kelly had seized the opportunity to do something that could bring some joy into these kids' lives. She hadn't thought of it when Graham mentioned liking Boone Williams, but when Avery shared her love for

Piper Starling, the lightbulb came on. She was relieved Donovan found a way to make it a win-win for both him and Graham.

"It's sweet that Graham is such a big Boone fan like his parents were. I used to listen to Johnny Cash over and over because he was my dad's favorite." Music had this wonderful way of connecting people. It was one of the reasons she loved her job so much.

"My sister was definitely a country music lover," Donovan said as he handed her another plate to dry. "Before she got sick, she had big Tennessee hair. It was platinum blond and covered in so much hair spray it probably could have doubled as a helmet. Every year for Halloween, she'd dress up like Dolly Parton. Dolly was her first love before this Boone character came along."

Kelly smiled at his memory. Stories like that warmed her heart. "I think I would have liked your sister."

"Everybody loved Jessica." Donovan's jaw tightened and his eyes closed for a second.

Kelly could feel his loss in the center of her chest. "How long has she been gone?"

"Three months," he said barely over a whisper. He cleared his throat. "She and the kids moved in with me about six months ago so she could oversee the transition. She taught me how to do Avery's hair and transformed my bachelor pad into something out of one of those shows on HGTV. The kids started at their new schools. She made sure they had everything they needed. Well, almost everything."

Kids needed a mom. Kelly's eyes began to tear up. She swallowed down the lump in her throat and tried to think of the right thing to say.

The doorbell rang, removing the need to say anything. Donovan dried off his hands and went to answer it.

"Captain Bonner."

From one "uncle to the rescue" to the other. Kelly gave Avery a big hug goodbye before grabbing her purse and overnight bag by the door. Kelly's uncle was a towering mass of a man. He reminded her so much of her dad, his brother. They had the same dark hair and build. They both had these long legs and arms. They could easily get their arms around more than one person at a time for a bear hug.

"Thanks for coming to get me, Uncle Hal."

"Anything for you, Kell Bell. You know that. Detective, thank you for going above and beyond today. We can discuss a few things tomorrow morning at the station. Why don't you come in around eight thirty? I'll have

Kelly come with me to the office so you can take her to work from there."

It felt a bit too much like being a child passed between parents. As much as the note on her door had given her a fright, she still wanted to be able to take care of herself.

"I think someone should teach me some self-defense so I won't need a babysitter at all. Unless, of course, you catch this guy. Then I'd really sleep easy."

Uncle Hal dipped his chin. "He's not your babysitter. You are not a baby. I want you to be able to go about your business without looking over your shoulder. That's what he's for. He does the looking, you do the living."

"I get it, but if you don't find this guy, I can't have someone following me around the rest of my life. I will eventually need to learn how to fend for myself."

"This man is a former marine, a trained police officer." Uncle Hal put his hand on Donovan's shoulder. "No amount of self-defense training is going to compare to having him watching over you. And I will make sure they catch this guy. Don't you worry about it."

Another way he was just like her dad had been—Uncle Hal believed he could do anything. Justice would always be served under them. He also thought he always knew better than Kelly.

There was no point in arguing with him tonight. “Thank you for your help today,” she said to Donovan. “And thank you for dinner and the hospitality.”

“I’ll see you tomorrow, Miss Bonner.”

Kelly attempted to hold back a grin. Donovan was so formal in front of Uncle Hal. “Good night, Detective Walsh.”

Uncle Hal took her bag for her as they walked out to his car. “You should call your mother, by the way.”

“Please tell me you didn’t tell her what’s going on.” Kelly had purposely not called her because she knew her mother’s reaction would be over-the-top.

“Ha! You think I’m going to withhold this kind of information from Monica Bonner? I’ve known that woman longer than you’ve been alive. She’d be furious with me if I hadn’t informed her I was taking care of this.”

Kelly wasn’t surprised she didn’t have ten messages to call her mother immediately. It made sense that her mother was sitting at home in Knoxville, waiting for Kelly to call her. She was waiting and seething for sure. As soon as Kelly did call, her mother would unleash all her pent-up frustration.

"Thanks a lot," she grumbled, getting in his car.

"What? I figured you told her what's been happening. I thought I was only calling to assure her I was handling it."

There was no putting off the call. The longer she waited, the worse it would be. She clicked on her mother's contact information.

"Kelly Renee," her mom answered. "What a surprise to hear from you in the middle of the week. I thought you could only make time for me on the weekends."

Passive aggressive. Kelly's favorite. "Hi, Mom. I know Uncle Hal talked to you already."

"Oh, you mean when he called me to tell me that you've had some obsessive fan stalking you for almost a month and he finally crossed the line and damaged your car? Wouldn't it have been nice if my daughter had thought maybe she should tell her mother what was happening right from the start so we could have prevented things from escalating?"

Typical Monica Bonner. She believed she could prevent all the bad things from happening to Kelly as long as she was in control of her daughter's life.

"What were you going to do from Knoxville to stop this guy from sending me flowers? People send me gifts to the station all the time. I didn't think he was going to cross the line the way he did."

"This is what worries me about you. You are so naive, sweetheart. You think everyone has good intentions, that nothing bad is ever going to happen. You don't realize there are sick people out there, especially in a place like Nashville."

There it was. Her mom had always resented the fact that Kelly had chosen to move to Nashville. She'd assumed Kelly did it to get away from her parents. That had been one of the reasons, but there were others. True, it had been a relief to get some breathing room when she moved away. Being under her parents' watchful eye was hard enough when she was young. As a grown woman, it was unbearable. The main reason for leaving, though, was to get on Nashville radio. The opportunity at K104 was huge. This was the country music capital of the world and where she wanted to have a career.

"I'm sorry I didn't call you earlier, Mom." Arguing never got Kelly anywhere, so she accepted defeat. "It would have been great if you could have stopped my car from getting vandalized."

"I'm worried about you. Maybe you should come back to Knoxville. I'm sure with your experience in Nashville, you could get a job here at any station."

Kelly didn't want to work at "any station" in Knoxville. She wanted to renew her contract with K104. "I'm not going to let this person run me out of town."

"You won't even consider it? Even if it meant you'd be safe?"

"Mom." Kelly closed her eyes and rubbed her forehead, hoping to stop the headache her mother was giving her.

"It would be nice if you would at least *consider* it."

Not happening. Kelly had no intention of leaving Nashville. Not because of a stalker. Not because of her mother. Not for anything. But if she wanted to survive this phone call, she would have to lie.

"I'll think about it, but don't get your hopes up."

"Thank you for being somewhat reasonable. I believe that if you really weigh your options, you'll see that things could be a lot less complicated if you came back to Knoxville."

Kelly wrapped things up with her mom and once she hung up, she glared at Uncle Hal.

"What?" he asked, playing so innocent. "She loves you."

Her words came out heated. "This obsessed fan, stalker, whatever you want to call him is not going to ruin my life. I am not moving back to Knoxville. I will not let him keep me from doing my job. I will not be dependent on a bodyguard the rest of my life."

"You're more like your mother than you want to admit," Uncle Hal said with a laugh.

"How so?"

"She thinks all her problems can be solved by her and her alone."

"Exactly, she wants to control me and I just want to control myself. That's not the same thing."

"I understand wanting to be independent, but be accepting of help when it's given. I know Walsh can be a little standoffish, but he's a good cop. I trust him to keep you safe. Don't fight me on this."

Her issue wasn't with Donovan. It was the idea that no one trusted her to look after herself in the long run. "I'm fine with the help while you're investigating. I don't want to be guarded my whole life. That's all I'm saying."

"Then take a self-defense course. Be empowered, Kell Bell. But understand your mom and I simply don't want anything to happen to you. We aren't trying to ruin your life."

Kelly couldn't argue with that. She knew their actions and words came from a place of love and concern. *Be empowered.* Maybe that was the part that had been missing. She would have to change that.

DONOVAN NEEDED TO be at the police station by eight thirty, which meant that he needed the meeting with Graham's school counselor this morning to go quickly. Donovan wasn't a fan of counselors any more than Graham was, but he needed to step up so Graham would, too.

"I don't understand why we need to talk to Mrs. Mitchell. This is a waste of our time," Graham complained.

"We're here so you can assure Mrs. Mitchell that you plan to be a perfect angel for the rest of the school year. That is what we agreed to last night, wasn't it?"

Graham huffed instead of answering. Donovan would take that as a yes. If Graham wanted to go to that concert, there would be no more ditching class and no more graffiti.

A woman entered the main office. "Mr. Walsh?"

Donovan stood and shook her hand as she introduced herself.

"Thank you for meeting with us," he said.

If Mrs. Mitchell had on jeans and a T-shirt, Donovan was pretty sure she could be easily mistaken for a student. She couldn't have been very far into her twenties. She led them back to her office and took a seat behind her desk.

"I really appreciate you coming in, Mr. Walsh. I know we haven't really spoken since Graham's mom..."

"Died," Graham finished for her when she paused. "My mom died. My dad died, too. That was a couple years ago, though, so maybe that's not as important."

Donovan put his hand on Graham's knee and gave it a squeeze. "Come on. Don't."

"You've been through a lot in the last couple years and it can't be easy," Mrs. Mitchell said. "I want you to know that we all understand how hard it's been for you and we want to help."

"Can you make people come back from the dead?"

This was not how Donovan wanted this to go. "She's saying the school would like to help you deal with it. They don't want you to deal with it by ditching class and drawing on the walls. Two things that aren't going to happen anymore, right?"

"I will not get into any more trouble, Mrs. Mitchell. I promise." Graham could not have sounded less sincere.

"I'm glad to hear that, Graham, but I want you to know that if there's anything you want to talk about or if there is anything I can do to help make things less stressful for you, I want to be able to help."

"Can you get me out of math?"

Donovan was exasperated. "You have less than a month left. You're not dropping a class now."

"Is there something going on in math that I could help you resolve?" Mrs. Mitchell asked.

Graham sank in his seat. "Doubt it."

"Maybe I could try," she said.

Graham said nothing. Donovan couldn't stand the silence. "Graham has agreed to behave himself the rest of the school year. I think the summer will be good for him. I'm going to have him work part-time for a friend of mine. I think he'll come back next year a new man."

Mrs. Mitchell smiled sympathetically as if she felt bad for him for believing that was a possibility. "That's good, but I want Graham to remember that we're here if he needs us. I'm an excellent listener and if he needs to talk about anything, I'm here."

"He's got it. Right, Graham?"

"Sure. Can I go to class now? I don't want to be late to first period."

That was music to Donovan's ears. He wanted to be on time. He was going to behave himself. Everything would be fine.

Mrs. Mitchell wrote him a pass and sent him off. Donovan got up to leave, but before he could thank her for her time, she asked him to give her another minute.

"I am really worried about him, Mr. Walsh. I'm wondering if he's opened up to you at all."

"He doesn't tell me a lot. I do think that with some time, he'll be fine. Right now, we're all just trying to figure things out and find our new normal."

Mrs. Mitchell nodded. "I'm sure you are. Have you thought about having him talk to someone else? Maybe a grief counselor? I have some great references for some local counselors." She pulled out a piece of paper with a bunch of names and phone numbers on it.

"I don't think Graham is going to talk to a counselor."

"I'm going to give this to you in case you change your mind," she said, sliding the paper in his direction.

It was clear she wasn't taking no for an answer and Donovan needed to get out of there before she tried convincing him to get some counseling, as well. He took the referral list and thanked her for her time.

From one problem to the next. He headed for the station and prayed today wouldn't be as chaotic as yesterday. He hoped Kelly could have a normal day with no distractions or threats. He'd only known her *one* day and he already felt protective.

Donovan had driven this way to work since he started on the force. Today was the first day he noticed the billboard for K104 with Kelly's face smiling back at him. Her crystal-blue eyes were mesmerizing. Distractingly so. He slammed on the brakes, almost hitting the car that had come to a stop in front of him.

His heart felt like it stopped and then pounded like he had run the fifty-yard dash. One day. Not even twenty-four hours yet. He needed to get his head on straight. This was a short-term assignment while his case was under review with IA. Maybe he'd be done even sooner, if they found Kelly's stalker. He needed to maintain boundaries. No more dinner with the family. No answering personal questions. No more being Avery's new best friend.

"Walsh! Get in here," Captain said as soon

as Donovan set foot in the office. He was five minutes early. No reason to be in trouble already.

"Sir."

There was Kelly live and in person. She sat across from her uncle with her legs crossed and her foot bouncing up and down like an overactive kid who needed to get up and run around.

"Kelly and I were talking last night. She wants to learn some self-defense. I was thinking you could show her a couple things to make her feel more comfortable when she's on her own. She's only on the radio a couple hours. After that, he could give you some lessons. Right, Kel?"

"This may come as a surprise, but I do have responsibilities when I'm not on the air. I have to plan for the next day's show. I have station meetings to attend. I'm part of the station's road crew and go on location around town."

"No road crew while we're hunting down your stalker," Captain Bonner said, echoing Donovan's sentiments from yesterday.

"I can't *not* go, Uncle Hal. It's part of my job. I have to be at the farmers market every Friday and there are some concerts I have to make an appearance at over the next couple weeks."

"It's more difficult to keep you safe when you're out in public. Plus, I can't ask Walsh to work all day. He has a family to get home to."

"Then I'll take care of myself."

"I'll do it," Donovan said at the same time.

"You could work evenings? What about Graham and Avery?" Captain had been very understanding when Jessica's condition worsened and Donovan had to take off time to be there for her. His compassion extended to the children, especially after she died.

"It's not forever and it's only a couple of nights. I can work something out."

"You don't have to do that. I'll have people from the station with me. Lyle will be there or sometimes Trish goes out on those things."

"Lyle? The guy with you yesterday?" Donovan didn't trust that guy to protect himself. "I can come to a couple concerts."

Captain Bonner agreed. "I'm more comfortable with Walsh sticking with you if he can make it work."

Kelly got to her feet. "Once again, I don't really have a say, do I?"

"All I'm asking you to do is to accept some help," Captain said to her. "We talked about this."

"Fine. I'm accepting help. Don't expect me to be happy about it." She started for the door. "Come on, Detective. If I can get to work early, you won't have to stay so late."

She said nothing else even when they got inside his truck.

"Remember how scared you were yesterday when you found that note?" he asked, starting the engine. "Imagine how scared you'll be when this guy shows his face. Fear can be paralyzing."

Her long dark hair was down today and made the perfect curtain for her face as she stared out the window. So much for those boundaries he was going to set with her. Instead of keeping her at arm's length, he had attached her to his hip. And she was more upset about it than he was.

"I saw your billboard on the way to the station this morning," he said, hoping she'd look his way. "I never noticed it before, but now that I know who you are, I saw it right away. I didn't realize you were famous."

She adjusted the air-conditioning vent on her side. Why was he suddenly unable to stand the quiet?

"Avery woke up extra early this morning so she could get a French braid."

That got her attention. "I bet she looks extra adorable today."

"It's difficult to make that child *not* adorable."

That earned him a tiny laugh and put a smile on her face. "You're going to be in big trouble when she gets to be Graham's age."

"Don't remind me."

"I'm sorry for being in my head. I'm trying to figure out if my family is being unreasonable or if I'm being stubborn. Do you think I'm in danger? That this person would hurt me?"

It was a question he wasn't sure he could answer. He didn't want to scare her, but he didn't want to lie to her, either. "Any time someone is delusional, believes things that aren't real, it's hard to predict what they'll do. Do unstable people do dangerous things? Sometimes. Other times, they're harmless. We don't know how unstable this guy is, so it's probably best to assume he is capable of anything just to be safe."

Kelly took a deep breath and let it out slowly. "Thank you," she said.

"For what?"

"For helping to keep me safe. And for giving it to me straight instead of trying to scare me into doing what my uncle wants me to do."

One day. Donovan had known Kelly for all of one day, and yet he knew in his bones that nothing would stop him from keeping her safe.

## *CHAPTER EIGHT*

"If you were to plan the perfect date, where would you go and what would you do?" Kelly asked her best friend.

"That would be a fun question for tomorrow's show," Nancy said, jotting it down on her notepad. The two of them were working in Kelly's office after she got off-air.

"I'm not brainstorming, I'm legit asking you," Kelly said. "Where would you go and what would you do? Like for real, don't say a cafe in Paris and kiss at the top of the Eiffel Tower."

Nancy twisted her lips. "I have no idea. Where would you go?"

"It doesn't matter where I would go. It matters where you want to go. There has to be somewhere you love in the city—a restaurant or a romantic spot you've always wanted to go with someone special."

Nancy set down her notebook. "Why are you asking me? Are you planning something for my birthday? Because if you are, I do not want it to be a surprise. I hate surprises."

"I am not planning a surprise party." Getting some intel for Lyle was proving to be more difficult that she thought it would be. "I am asking you where you'd go on a date. Why would I ask you that if I was planning a party? I'd ask you where you'd like to party."

"Well, it would be a pretty terrible way to plan a surprise party if you straight up asked me where I would want to have a party. Duh. Then I would know for sure that you were throwing me a party."

Time for a different tactic. "Remember when you told me you really liked Lyle's new haircut?"

Nancy narrowed her eyes in suspicion. "Yeah."

"Were you telling me you liked it because you were pointing out a coworker got a haircut or because you thought the haircut made Lyle look nice?"

Nancy snorted. "What are you talking about?"

"Okay, I'm really bad at this." She was abandoning this plan to get secret information. "I don't know how to get information without being straightforward."

"What information?"

"Lyle has a massive crush on you and wants to know if he has any chance in the world or if he should learn to repress his feelings and move on."

Nancy was stunned silent.

"I know you've been working hard to get over Harrison. You guys broke up a good two months ago. I, for one, am hoping you are truly over him and his crooked eyebrow."

"He did not have a crooked eyebrow!" she said, snapping out of it.

Her ex-boyfriend absolutely had a crooked eyebrow. It was so crooked, it was extremely distracting every time Kelly had to talk to him. She so badly wanted to reach up and smooth that thing out or take some tweezers and shape it up.

"Do you or do you not think you could give Lyle a chance to sweep you off your feet?"

Nancy took a moment to think about it. "We work together. That could be a major disaster for both of us if we were to start a relationship and not see it all the way through. I don't think I could work here if Harrison worked here."

"I get that. But this is Lyle. He not only has a cute haircut but his eyebrows are perfectly symmetrical."

"Harrison did not have a crooked eyebrow. Stop saying that!"

Kelly leaned back in her chair and giggled. It was too easy to rile her up. "Okay, seriously. Think about it and let me know. I am not going to tell Lyle to go for it unless I know you're going to say yes."

"You sound more worried about Lyle getting his feelings hurt than you are about me having to quit my job if I go out with Lyle and we break up."

"Well, let's be honest. If one of you is going to break the heart of the other, my money is on you doing the breaking."

Nancy folded her arms across her chest. "Maybe you should go out with him if you're so concerned about his feelings."

Kelly did not have those kind of feelings about Lyle. She liked Lyle as a friend, not as anything more. "Maybe because he only has eyes for you and I am looking for someone a bit more..."

"Like that gorgeous hunk you're calling a bodyguard? Remember when I told you my bodyguard fantasy? I forgot to mention I wanted them all to look like that guy."

They were not going to talk about Donovan. "Leave my bodyguard out of this."

Nancy grinned. "Oh, look who's all defensive now. Don't tell me you didn't notice that he was good-looking."

She wasn't blind. Kelly was fully aware of how good-looking Donovan was. Looks were not the only thing that made a person attractive, however. Other things like kindness, compassion and a sense of humor were equally important.

"Are you telling me you'd rather date my bodyguard than Lyle?" she asked, turning the tables.

"I didn't say that!" Nancy wagged a finger at her. "I see what you're trying to do. If you don't want to talk about your hot bodyguard, we don't have to."

Kelly did not want to talk about Donovan. Or how cute it was that he braided Avery's hair this morning. Or how impressive it was that he could cook. Or how flattering it was that he noticed her billboard. He was a cop. A detective. She had grown up the daughter of police officers and had no intention of being the wife of one, which made dating one pointless.

"What am I telling Lyle?" Kelly asked, trying to steer this conversation back on course.

Nancy wasn't quick to answer. She chewed on her thumbnail for a few seconds. "He's one of the sweetest people I've ever met. I could see myself falling for someone like him."

"I can't lie. I have a good feeling about you two. And you know I'm never wrong."

Nancy let out a sharp laugh. "Never wrong?"

"What? I have a perfect record of matching people with their perfect mate." She had called the relationship between Piper Starling and Sawyer Stratton before they made their relationship public. She had guessed Rob from accounting was interested in Julie from marketing. She'd set up their social media expert with her fiancé. It was a gift.

"Says the woman with the worst dating history known to man. How am I supposed to trust you to pick the perfect person for me when you've failed so miserably finding the right person for yourself?"

"Hurtful."

"Don't deny it. Ben? Liam? Sammy? And don't make me mention Ian."

Kelly covered her ears with her hands. "Stop. I get it. I am terrible at choosing a man for myself. I am aware."

Kelly wasn't sure why she was so much better at matchmaking for others but only seemed to attract the wrong men over and over.

"I'm sorry. I don't mean to throw those guys in your face. You're right, Lyle seems like a good match for me. I'm just not sure I want to put our professional relationship in jeopardy."

Lyle would be so disappointed, but Kelly could respect Nancy's feelings and her boundaries. It was a shame, though.

When Kelly finished for the day, she went out to the lobby, where Donovan had stationed himself. Hopefully, he hadn't been too much of a distraction for Juliette. He had wanted to be where people came in if they were delivering gifts or if they were there to…kidnap her or something.

"How long do you bake it for?" Juliette asked.

Donovan was leaning against the reception desk. "You only need to put it in the oven for ten minutes or until the cheese is melted."

Juliette wrote that down on the notepad in front of her. "I am making this tonight. My husband loves Mexican food."

"There are never leftovers at my house when I make those chicken enchiladas," Donovan said.

Kelly had no doubt that was true. If he cooked Mexican like he did Italian, it would probably rock her world. She wondered what it would take to get invited for dinner two nights in a row.

"Are we doing a recipe swap out here?" Kelly asked.

"Detective Walsh was telling me about the enchiladas he was making for dinner tonight and I had to steal the recipe," Juliette said with a smile. "He's been full of great ideas this afternoon."

Someone had made a friend. "I'm glad he wasn't in your way out here."

"In my way?" Juliette placed a hand on her chest. "Not at all! He kept me company on somewhat of a slow day."

"I appreciate your hospitality. Have a good night, Juliette," Donovan said. His gaze fell on Kelly. "You ready to go?"

"Ready when you are." She motioned for him to lead the way to the elevator. When they made it to the parking garage, they passed by the valet. "Have a good one, gentlemen," Kelly said to the two attendants.

"Good night, Kelly," Miller said. Carl just waved.

"You know those guys?" Donovan asked.

"I use the valet here and there when I'm running late and don't want to search the lot for a spot. They're nice guys. Always pretend fighting about who's going to get my car for me. They're funny."

Donovan nodded and looked back over his

shoulder at them. “Barrel of laughs, those two.”

“So when does my self-defense training begin?”

“I don’t know. What were you thinking? I’m not sure where we should go. Do you belong to a gym?”

“I go to the gym in my building, but that consists of a couple cardio machines and a few free weights. It’s not very big.”

“You don’t have any gym mats at your apartment, do you?”

Kelly chuckled. “No, I do not have gym mats in my apartment. Why do we need mats? Am I going to get to body slam you or something?”

Donovan’s turn to laugh. “No, there will not be any body slamming, but I do want to show you a few escape moves and for safety’s sake, it would be good to have some mats. I’ve got some at home. We could go there.”

“Of course you have gym mats.”

“To be fair, Avery has taken them over. She likes to do her ‘gymnastics’ on them,” he said, using air quotes.

Kelly could picture little Avery doing somersaults and cartwheels, believing she was the next gold medal winner. “Oh, Avery. She makes me fall more in love with her every time you bring her up."

Donovan's expression turned grim as he checked his watch. "Maybe we can get everything done before Avery gets home from school." He unlocked the truck. "Let's get you home so you can change clothes."

As much as Kelly wanted to prove to her uncle and her mom that she would be able to take care of herself, she felt the nerves creep in at the thought of going back to her apartment. "Do you think it's safe for me to be home tonight?"

Donovan shrugged. "As long as I do a sweep of the place before I leave, I think you'll be fine. Your uncle has someone patrolling your neighborhood all night long."

Knowing that would allow her to rest easier. Accepting help was her new thing.

DONOVAN KNEW HE needed to be more cautious about letting Kelly too close, but he still couldn't stop his mouth from inviting her over. Graham was home when they got there, but in his room. That was for the best. He figured he had about an hour before Avery would be dropped off.

"This is quite the workout area. I see how

you stay so fit." Kelly picked up one of his hand weights and did a couple of bicep curls.

His home gym was in the basement, complete with free weights, a punching bag, treadmill and power cage for bench pressing, squatting and deadlifting. Donovan used to work out every day when he was in the military. When he'd returned to civilian life, he needed to keep himself active.

"We're only going to do a couple things today. First, I want you to remember that the last thing you want to do is get into a physical altercation with someone. If you can get away, always do that instead. Be smart when you're out in public and do what you can to keep yourself out of harm's way."

"So the best self-defense is not having to use self-defense?"

"Correct."

"What are you guys doing down here?" Graham appeared at the bottom of the stairs.

"Hey, Graham. How's it going?" Kelly asked.

"I've been better. I've been worse. What are you two doing? Working out?"

Donovan was about to tell him it was none of his business, but Kelly answered. "Your uncle is teaching me some self-defense moves so he doesn't have to be my bodyguard forever."

"Self-defense? You're going to teach her how to fight?"

"Hopefully she learns how not to have to fight."

"But you have to show her some moves, right?"

It was unclear where this sudden interest was coming from. Usually, Graham couldn't care less what Donovan was doing. "I plan to show her a few escape moves. A way to use her body to get an attacker off balance so she can get away."

"Can I watch?"

"Sure," Kelly said at the same time Donovan said no.

"I mean, I don't mind if he's down here. Unless you don't want him to stay. He's your nephew. You decide," she said.

Now he wasn't sure what to say. "Don't you have teenager stuff to take care of?"

"Nope." Graham sat down on the workout bench.

Donovan hadn't been expecting to do this with an audience, but it didn't seem like he'd be able to persuade Graham to leave. "Like I was saying, the first thing to remember is prevention is the best self-defense."

"Yeah, but if someone is after her, trying to kill her, she really can't do that," Graham interjected.

"No one is trying to kill her," Donovan said sternly.

"Sorry we were vague yesterday," Kelly said. "We didn't want to talk about it in front of your sister, but I have an obsessed fan who thinks he's in love with me and wants me to be in love with him. I'm more afraid of him trying to kidnap me than kill me."

Graham sat forward with his elbows rested on his knees. "So he thinks he's in love with you because he heard you on the radio?"

Kelly shrugged. "I guess. I don't know who he is. Maybe I've met him, maybe he's only heard me on the radio. It's pretty strange."

"Well, I apologize on behalf of the men in the world. A real man doesn't make a woman feel unsafe," Graham said much to Donovan's surprise. Those were mature sentiments he wasn't used to hearing from the troubled teen.

"That's very sweet, buddy." Kelly seemed genuinely touched. "Thanks."

"Let's get started. Shall we?" Donovan asked, wanting to be done before Avery got home and came running down here. No doubt she'd invite Kelly for dinner again and Donovan would be left in that uncomfortable spot once more.

Kelly clapped her hands together. “Let’s go.”

“Prevention means being aware of your surroundings, staying in well-lit areas. If you are confronted, you should try to de-escalate the situation. Try to talk the guy down. In your situation, you want to remind this guy that he doesn’t want to hurt you.”

“I am a good talker. I’ll definitely try to talk him down.”

“If you have to really defend yourself, then you need to know the most sensitive parts of the body. The eyes, nose, ears, neck, groin, knee and legs are the most vulnerable spots on anybody. But don’t forget what I told you yesterday about an attacker being fueled by a lot of adrenaline and maybe drugs or alcohol. He might not feel pain the way an average person would. Hitting him might just make him mad.”

Kelly frowned with her hands on her hips. “You’re not making me feel very confident about fighting someone off.”

“Don’t think about it like fighting someone off. The key is getting away. Escape. You just need to give yourself a chance to put space between you and him.”

"What if there's more than one person?" Graham asked.

Both Donovan and Kelly turned their heads in his direction. "That's a good question," Donovan said. "I guess I'm assuming we're only dealing with one person in this case."

"Let's hope so," Kelly said, looking a little uneasy at the thought of anything else.

"I'm going to focus on one attacker for right now, okay?"

Kelly nodded. "Can we walk through what a confrontation might look like? You can tell me to strike him where it hurts, but how to do I know what to do when?"

"Hitting is the last option. Don't forget that." He needed to let her practice a few escapes. He grabbed her by the wrist, startling her. "I imagine he's going to do something like this."

"Hit him in the nose," Graham suggested.

"What part of 'hitting is the last option' did you miss?" Donovan looked at Graham before he tightened his grip on Kelly. "Escape is always your goal. If he grabs you like this, first, I need you to be loud. Back off! Let go of me! Be as loud as you can. You want to get other people's attention."

"I can be loud. But how am I supposed to get away when you're so much stronger than me?" She tried unsuccessfully to pull her arm away.

He tugged her close to him and she lost her balance, falling into him. She placed a hand on his chest to steady herself. Those crystal-blue eyes stared up at him and he lost his train of thought for a moment. It was a good thing he wasn't driving. He was even more under their spell when she was real versus a photo on a billboard.

He gathered his wits about him and took a step back. "Even though I'm stronger than you, there are weak spots you need to be aware of." He showed her his grip. "You want to focus on where my thumb is. Instead of pulling back, lean forward and rotate your wrist toward my thumb. See how my grip loosens? Jerk your wrist out right here."

Kelly did as he directed and was able break free. Her stunned expression was priceless. "I can't believe that worked!"

Graham was on his feet. "Can I try? Grab my wrist." He held out his arm. Donovan hadn't been planning on this being a group lesson, but he didn't think there was any harm is letting Graham try.

Donovan grabbed Graham's wrist and talked him through the escape. Even though he usually acted as if following directions would cause him to break out into hives, he did as he was told and was able to get loose.

"I don't get how that works," Graham said, staring down as his arm. "You are so much stronger than us."

Donovan did his best to explain how it worked and showed them two other hold escapes before he heard the sound of the front door slamming. He checked his watch. Somehow he had completely lost track of time.

"Graham? Uncle Donovan?"

"We're down here, Avery!" Graham shouted.

Seconds later, she was skipping down the stairs. "Kelly! You're back!"

Donovan could almost hear his sister laughing at him up in heaven. He had done exactly what he'd sworn he wouldn't do. He felt this enormous pressure to keep the kids happy but protect them from being hurt at the same time. If Graham and Avery didn't like Kelly so much, things would be easier, but that was clearly never going to be the case.

## *CHAPTER NINE*

"LAST NIGHT, I had the best chicken enchiladas I have ever tasted in my life," Kelly said into the microphone. "One reason they were so good was I had nothing to do with cooking them. The second reason they were so delicious was they were made with organic ingredients. And do you know where you can get some of the best organic food in Nashville? The Nashville Farmers Market. The Nashville Farmers Market is the perfect place to pick up fresh produce to make dinner tonight. If you aren't in the mood to cook or maybe aren't very good at it, like me, there are plenty of restaurants and ready-to-eat goodies. Not hungry? There's still plenty to do. You can shop or watch a demo or stop by and see yours truly. I'll be there tonight from four until six, giving away tons of stuff including tickets to the Grace Note Records Concert for the Kids. You know who's going to be at that show? This lovely lady—" Kelly cued the music "—is Piper Starling."

Kelly pressed the button to play Piper's new song and slipped her headphones off, letting them hang around her neck. She wondered if Donovan was listening to her show in the lobby. She knew they piped the music in there, but that didn't mean he was paying attention.

Hopefully, he wasn't annoyed if he was listening. She had only told him how good his food was about a hundred times last night because it had seemed like Donovan wasn't thrilled about her staying even though he had said it was fine. After dinner, he took her back to her apartment, made sure no one was hiding in there and left with nothing more than a *Good night, see you tomorrow.*

She couldn't help but be a bit paranoid about what she had done to make Donovan so standoffish, as her uncle would say. After the ups and downs of their first day together, she thought they had bonded yesterday. It was the perfect example of why she was terrible at finding the right man. She was terrible at reading the signs when it came to her own relationships.

Nancy came into the studio. "Are you going to have enough time to grab lunch with me or are you going to head straight over to the farmers market when you get off-air?"

"I was thinking about getting food at the farmers market. Do you want to come with me?" she offered, part of her hoping Nancy would say no so things wouldn't be more awkward with Donovan there.

"I have to meet with Stan after lunch to go over a few things. We'll go out on Monday. Deal?"

"Deal."

Nancy left with a smile and a wave. Relieved, Kelly put her headphones back on. Lyle, from the control room, spoke to her through them. "I don't mean to be a pest, but have you spoken to her yet? I'm starting to lose my nerve. Should I lose my nerve?"

The last thing she wanted to do was break Lyle's heart. On the other hand, if she didn't tell him the truth, Nancy would break his heart a lot worse.

She made eye contact with him and gave him a sad smile. "I'm not sure she's over her ex. I can try to talk to her again, but I got the impression she thinks it's too soon for her to date."

"I never liked that Harrison guy," Lyle said. The disappointment was all over his face. "Did you ever notice how one of his eyebrows was crooked? That bugged me so much."

"Yes! Thank you! It's totally crooked." It

felt good to have someone agree with her for once but bad to be right about how Nancy's disinterest would hurt Lyle. "I'm sorry the timing isn't right, buddy."

Lyle shrugged it off. "Thanks for feeling her out. Saves me a face-to-face rejection."

He pulled at her heartstrings. Nancy was missing out by not giving Lyle a chance. There was nothing worse than having unrequited feelings for someone.

Trish, the station's intern, was the only one joining Kelly at the farmers market today. Since they weren't broadcasting from there, Lyle wasn't needed. It was awkward explaining who Donovan was and why he was hovering by their booth.

"I'm going to grab something to eat before we set up. Do you want to come with me?" Kelly asked Trish.

"I ate at the station. I can start putting things together for you while you go eat." Trish was young and very motivated. She had boundless energy, reminding Kelly of a puppy with two modes—asleep and full-speed. Kelly couldn't have stopped her from doing everything on her own if she tried.

Nashville Farmers Market had two open-air sheds, a greenhouse, an enormous garden center and at least two dozen restaurants and shops. The market attracted local ranchers, dairy farmers and crafters. People sold their cheeses, baked goods and other farm-direct goodies like honey and jams. The fruit and vegetable stands were overflowing with produce. There was also an excellent deli in the Market House, along with a creperie that made chocolate hazelnut crepes that were pure heaven. Kelly had her heart set on one thing, though, a grilled cheese masterpiece from the Grilled Cheese People food truck.

"Did you hear me mention your enchiladas on the radio today?" she asked Donovan, who wasn't any more talkative this afternoon than he was this morning.

He nodded as they walked around, looking for something to eat.

"Those really were the best chicken enchiladas I have ever had. You're an awesome cook and you're a really good self-defense teacher. I'm beginning to wonder if you're good at everything you do. It's made me determined to find something you aren't amazing at."

"That won't be as hard as you think."

"We'll see about that." Kelly got in line at the Grilled Cheese People. "I'm buying you a very late lunch, by the way, so you better be looking at the menu."

Donovan ran a hand over the top of his head. "You don't have to do that."

"Actually, I do. You have made me dinner two nights in a row. I owe you and I won't take no for an answer. If you don't order something, I'll order for you and force you not to waste food."

Hands on hips, he relented. "Fine, but you don't have to do that."

"We'll just have to disagree. You know what you'll agree with me on? This will be the best grilled cheese you've ever had. Unless you make some kind of magical grilled cheese." That was possible. Her forehead scrunched. "You probably do, don't you?"

"Grilled cheese isn't that hard. I feel like even a self-proclaimed bad cook like yourself could manage it."

"Ha!" Kelly had tried to recreate her favorite Grilled Cheese People sandwich a few times and failed miserably. "I have a tendency to either get distracted while cooking it and burn one side or I watch it like a hawk and get the bread nice and brown but the cheese is not melted at all. I don't know what I'm doing wrong, but I can never get the cheese perfectly melty like they do."

"Sounds like you have the heat on too high."

"Wouldn't that make it more melted?"

Donovan grinned and Kelly felt a flutter in her stomach that she tried to rationalize as hunger. "I feel like even if I explain it to you, you will still be confused."

"You are not wrong. This is why I don't cook. It's so much easier to buy things that are made the way I like and ready to eat."

They got to the front of the line and Kelly ordered her favorite—buttermilk cheddar on sourdough with bacon and avocado. Just thinking about it made her mouth water. Donovan ordered a pizza melt with loads of mozzarella and pepperoni on a panini. They got their sandwiches and found a picnic table to sit down and eat.

"So where did you learn to cook? The military?" Kelly asked.

"No, not the military. I'm not sure I would be as good if I had learned to cook for a bunch of hungry marines. My mom taught me. She loved cooking so much, she was the kind of person who woke up in the morning and while she made breakfast, she'd start planning what she was going to make for dinner."

"I don't even think about what I'm making for dinner when I'm making dinner."

Donovan coughed a laugh into his fist.

"You have to be exaggerating how terrible you are in the kitchen."

"I don't believe you aren't good at everything and you don't believe I'm as bad as I claim. That's funny." Kelly's cheeks were hurting from smiling so much. "Maybe you can show me how to make something I can't mess up. If I manage to make something edible on my own, it will prove I'm right about you and you're right about me. We would both have to admit that you are good at everything and I am not as bad as I think I am. If I bomb, then you are right about you and I am right about me."

The space between his brows wrinkled. "The way your mind works both fascinates and scares me at the same time."

"I think that's the perfect way to find out who's right about who."

Donovan leaned forward, his elbows on the table. "You could purposely ruin the dinner just to be right about yourself."

"True," Kelly admitted. "But then I would be wrong about you being amazing at everything. If you can't teach me to cook, I have found your weakness. The beauty of this is either way, we'll both be right and both be wrong. We'll just find out about what."

"Okay..." He took a sip of his soda and

tipped the cup in her direction. "I accept this challenge."

"What are you going to teach me to cook?" She was excited by the possibilities.

"You have to give me some time to think about it. I have to carefully consider my options so I don't fail…or you don't fail. Wait, who do I want to fail?"

It was nice to see him loosened up. She didn't like it when he was all business. "Let's hope no one fails, I guess."

"I'm not sure I totally understand what we're doing," he said with a chuckle.

Kelly couldn't stop staring at him. He had very masculine features. He had a broad nose and a heavy brow. His prominent chin was square and his jaw strong. In contradiction to all that manliness, his eyes were soft. In the sunshine, they were more green than brown. Hazel was such an interesting eye color. It was like he was a chameleon, able to change color based on his surroundings.

Donovan dropped his gaze. "Why are you looking at me like that?"

"Your eyes. They're so interesting."

"My eyes are interesting? Have you looked in a mirror? Ever?"

Kelly rolled hers. "I know, I know. Mine are unusual."

"They're gorgeous."

His word choice made her cheeks flush. "Thank you. Some people think it makes me look cold. I always hear people say they look like ice. Yours are so warm. I'm jealous."

"I don't think they make you seem cold. Anyone who would judge you based on your eye color is missing out because you are quite the opposite. I've listened to you on the radio the last couple days, seen the way you interact with people. You don't need to be jealous of my eyes. You are a warm person."

Kelly took the last bite of her sandwich. This was why she was terrible at finding the right person. She found herself attracted to men who were wrong for her. Donovan was a perfect example. She was having these "feelings," but he was a cop for goodness' sake! Kelly would never end up with a cop. Never.

THE FARMERS MARKET was crowded on a late Friday afternoon. Donovan felt pressured to pay attention to everyone walking by the booth whether they stopped to talk to Kelly or not. If her stalker was there, he might not approach her but rather admire her from afar.

Anyone wearing a red Alabama hat got an extra once-over. Guys with red hair did, too. It was frustrating to have such limited information. He wasn't sure those two leads were even useful. In reality, Kelly's stalker could be anyone.

"Is that who I think it is?" Kelly asked as a man in a T-shirt and khaki shorts strolled past.

The blond turned and smiled. "Kelly Bonner, what are you doing here?"

"Promo for the station. Did you get a Friday night off from Johnny's? Who's going to bring me my food if I order from there tonight?"

"You would have been disappointed if it wasn't me?"

Donovan stepped a bit closer. Behind his sunglasses, his eyes were glued to this guy. Medium build. No distinguishing features.

"Of course I would!" Kelly replied. "You always remember to bring me extra ketchup."

"Glad to know I'm making a difference in the world," he said with a flirtatious grin.

All of Donovan's internal alarms went off. This was the delivery guy Kelly had talked about. He obviously was a bit infatuated with her. He claimed not to know she was there, but he could have easily lied to make it look like their meeting was coincidental.

"Want to spin the wheel and win a prize?" Kelly offered.

"Nah, that's okay, but can I get a selfie?" He held up his phone. "I need something interesting to post on Instagram and you're kind of a local celebrity."

Kelly didn't hesitate. "I don't know about being a celebrity but absolutely, we can take a picture." She came around the table and slipped her arm around his waist.

"Let me get one for the station, too," Donovan said, thinking on his feet. He could take the photo back to the station and see if Juliette recognized the man.

"Oh, good idea!" Kelly's intern chimed in. "We can put it up on social media."

Donovan took a couple and made sure he had a clear shot of the man's face.

"It was good to see you, Hunter. I'm sure I'll be ordering from Johnny's soon and hopefully you'll show up at my door with extra ketchup."

Hunter seemed thrilled by that idea. "For sure."

"I can take everything back to the station, if you want to head home," Trish said to her. Donovan gave Kelly the please-take-her-up-on-that look because it meant he could get home sooner than later, as well.

Thankfully, she accepted her offer and suggested they take turns each Friday returning their stuff to the station. He respected that Kelly had no ego about her. She saw herself as equal to the station's intern even though it was likely others would have taken advantage of the young woman's willingness to please without a second thought.

"What are we going to do once I get my car back?" Kelly asked as they made their way to the parking lot.

"I can follow you or you can keep riding with me. Whatever you want to do."

"You're giving me a choice?"

"Why wouldn't I?" he questioned.

"When both your parents are police officers and your uncle is a police captain, you get used to always following other people's rules."

No wonder she was always trying to assert her independence. "I'm not here to give you rules. As long as I can do my job, you can do things however you want."

Donovan's phone chimed with a text. It was Graham wondering when he was coming home and if he was still making dinner or if he would pick up dinner so they could eat right away. Someone was hungry.

"Everything okay?"

"Graham's starving and needs food. Now."

It was amazing how someone half Donovan's size could eat as much as he did.

"Growing boy. How tall was his dad?"

"Ollie was a beast. Six foot three and built like a truck." Donovan and Ollie had served together in Afghanistan and became friends. It was their friendship that led to Jessica and Ollie meeting and falling in love.

"There you go. He must be growing. Before you know it, he'll be bigger than you."

"I'm not ready for that." Donovan shook his head. "I'm not ready for a lot of things. It's hilarious that you think I'm this guy who has everything figured out, when I really have no idea what I'm doing half the time. My sister trusted me with the two most important things in her world and I pray every day that I don't mess them up."

Kelly stopped and so did he. She placed a hand on his arm. "Graham and Avery are two great kids. You would have to work hard to mess them up."

"I hope you're right." He kept telling himself he only had a couple of years left with Graham to do any major damage and Avery was the most well-adjusted child on the planet.

"Have you thought about what you're going

to teach me how to cook?" she asked once they got in the truck.

"I'm going to show you how to make my mom's specialty—goulash."

"Gou-what?"

"Goulash. It's a Hungarian stew made with macaroni."

"Aha! I know what macaroni is. You may be surprised, but I have successfully made mac and cheese once."

The only surprising thing about that was she'd only succeeded once. "How many times did you try to make it and fail?"

"I lost count. Did you know that if you overcook noodles they basically melt together like a disgusting paste? And if you don't cook them long enough, they crunch when you bite into them. Also disgusting, by the way."

Donovan couldn't keep a straight face. "You are a complete wonder."

"Maybe under your guidance, I'll become the best goulash maker in the world."

"Let's not get carried away. I thought it only had to be edible."

Kelly's laughter filled the cab of the truck. He liked the way her eyes crinkled at the edges when she laughed. "You do not get to be the judge, by the way. I need impartial judges. The kids are going to have to eat what I make and give me their honest opinion."

"My kids?" The warning bells in his head went off again. "You think Avery is an impartial judge? You could rob a bank and Avery would still think you were the nicest person she knows."

"Kids have a hard time pretending to like something that tastes terrible. You know it's true."

He couldn't deny it. Even when they were trying to be nice, their faces gave their true feelings away. "You're right. They would be the only ones to give it to you straight."

When they got to her building, Donovan went in with her to check her apartment. She didn't have a very big place. It was a two-bedroom, but Kelly used the second room as a cluttered office. The cleanest room in the house was the kitchen, probably because it never got used the way it was supposed to.

"All clear," he said, joining her in the hall where he had her wait.

"Well, you enjoy your weekend off duty. I'll be hiding in my apartment all weekend since I can't be wandering around town with my superfan looking for me."

Just like the last time the bells went off and the time before that, he ignored them. He couldn't leave her trapped in her apartment all weekend. "Maybe you could come over and learn how to make goulash tomorrow night."

"Are you sure?"

"I think I need to look into your little delivery guy friend before I leave you here with no other way to feed yourself."

"Hunter? He couldn't be. He's a nice guy. He's not stalker material."

"Why? Because he just 'happened' to run into you tonight? He had no idea you were there even though you've been talking about it on the radio for a couple days?"

Kelly's face fell. He didn't mean to make her feel bad for being a bit naive, but he needed to point out to her how easily it could be anyone she knew.

"It was sort of weird that he wanted a picture. What if I encouraged him without meaning to?"

"Let me look into him. Come over tomorrow and cook. We can even throw in some self-defense training if you want."

"That sounds...perfect," Kelly said. "Thanks for everything this week. I appreciate all that you've done to keep me safe."

Donovan gave her a single nod. He held the door open for her and wished her a good evening. He waited until he heard the click of the lock, letting him know she was safely inside for the night.

It wasn't often that he didn't cook dinner. Tonight seemed as good a night as any to splurge on some fast food instead. A couple burgers, some chicken nuggets and three french fries weren't going to break the bank. Jessica would approve as long as they ate it around the dinner table.

"So how was your day?" he asked Avery once they were all settled.

"I had a spelling test and I got them all right. Some of the words had four letters in them."

"Nice job." Donovan held up a hand for a high-five. Avery slapped it hard.

"You'll be spelling words like *constitution* and *bibliography* before we know it," Graham said before shoving half his burger in his mouth.

"What's a biblinographney?" Avery asked with a mouth full of french fries.

Donovan looked to Graham. "I have no idea. It's part of a book or something?"

"It's like the works cited when you write a report. A list of all the books you used for reference."

"That's right," Donovan said, trying to play it off. "I knew that."

"Sure you did," Graham said with an obvious air of sarcasm.

"Did you keep Kelly safe today from the mean guy?" Avery asked.

He'd been home ten minutes and she was already asking about Kelly. "I did."

"How come she didn't come over for dinner tonight?" Avery's questions persisted. "Doesn't she like french fries?"

Donovan assumed Kelly would have loved some french fries given that she had no issue scarfing down a basket of tater tots with her grilled cheese sandwich this afternoon. "She had to go home after work today, but she's coming over for dinner tomorrow."

"Yay!" Avery cheered.

"Again?" Graham questioned.

Donovan couldn't tell if he was asking because he was surprised or upset. He knew he shouldn't be bringing her over again, but he kept doing it anyway. If either of the kids had an issue with it, he'd have to cancel.

"Is that a problem?"

"No, I'm glad. I wanted to ask her something, so it's cool."

Cool? That wasn't a word Graham used very often to describe anything that Donovan had to do with.

"What did you want to ask her?"

"If I wanted you to know, I would have asked you," Graham said. "I want to ask Kelly, not you. It's private."

"Well, I'm your guardian and if you need to talk to another adult about something, I should probably know what it is."

"It's about girls. Do you know about girls? Are you a girl?" he sassed.

"I'm a girl!" Avery said, raising her hand like she was at school. "Tell me."

"You don't know this kind of girl stuff, Avery," Graham said, trying to let her down easy.

"Maybe I do," she asserted.

"You don't. You have to be older to know this stuff."

Donovan wasn't sure how to proceed. Graham needed the support of a mother-like figure. Donovan was afraid to let that person be Kelly. Not because she wouldn't be good at it. Maybe because he knew she would be.

# *CHAPTER TEN*

KELLY TOOK OUT her hair tie and marched back into the bathroom to get her comb so she could braid her hair instead. Why was she so worried about how she looked when all she was doing was going to Donovan's to cook dinner and practice some self-defense? Donovan was her bodyguard. He worked for her uncle. He was a police officer.

This wasn't a date. She didn't need to impress anyone, so why was she so worried about how she looked?

As much as she wanted to deny it, she was attracted to the man. Anyone with eyes would be. His looks weren't the only thing causing her to question her feelings. She was also impressed by him. He had so many layers.

When she first met him, she only saw him one-dimensionally. He was a cop and that was all she had to know about him. Then, she met his family and he became something more. He was a parent. He was a caregiver to two children, two *orphaned* children. Everything about Graham and Avery melted Kelly's heart. Lastly, he was a teacher, a coach, a mentor. He took on a leadership role when needed and did so with compassion and patience.

Her doorbell buzzed and her stomach was in knots. His patience would be greatly appreciated today. She would be testing it a bunch tonight. Besides asking him to wait for her to finish getting ready, it was likely she would ruin dinner. She didn't even know what goulash was until yesterday.

She hit the button to let him in the building and ran back to the bedroom to finish getting ready. The buzzer went off again.

Why was he buzzing twice? She hit the intercom. "Hello?"

"Did you seriously buzz me in without even checking to make sure it was me? You could have let your stalker in and not even known it."

Kelly couldn't believe she just did that. She hadn't been thinking. Well, she had been thinking. She'd been thinking about Donovan so much that she never imagined it could be anyone other than him.

She buzzed him up again and quickly changed out of her workout shorts and into some leggings. Checking her reflection in the mirror, she once again chastised herself for worrying about what she looked like. This was not a date.

Donovan knocked on the door and she sprinted out of her room to answer it. She yanked it open. "Sorry."

"You didn't even look through your peep-hole to see if it was me before you opened your door, did you?"

Kelly closed her eyes, so she didn't have to see the disappointment on his face.

"Kelly, you can't be so careless. You're letting people in the building without confirming who they are. You're flinging your door open, welcoming whoever is standing on the other side right on in."

She dared to look at him and he was definitely angry, but she didn't need to see him to know it.

"Did you hear that?" she asked.

"Hear what?"

"Your mad voice. Avery is so right about your mad voice."

Donovan shook his head and furrowed his brow. His patience had run out quick. "I am not using a mad voice. I am speaking in my normal voice."

Kelly disagreed. "That was not your normal voice. You weren't yelling at me, but you might as well have been."

He cocked his head. "Kelly, someone is out there trying to get to you and you just made it really easy to do so. I'm not yelling at you, I'm simply pointing out things you can't do if you want to stay safe."

"I don't know what I was thinking. Or why I wasn't thinking. I won't make that mistake again. I'm sorry."

"You don't have to apologize to me. I'm not the one who is going to be hurt if you are careless with your security, you are."

He was right about that. The only person who would suffer because of her thoughtlessness was her. She'd spent the whole day frustrated that she couldn't go wherever she wanted without constantly looking over her shoulder. Then when she should have been a tad bit paranoid, she completely let her guard down. This situation was the absolute worst.

Suddenly, something else hit her. "Why did you come up instead of texting me to come out?"

"Exactly!" He threw his hands up. "Something told me I should see how you manage a visitor. I hadn't expected to have this much to talk to you about."

She was embarrassed to have failed his test so miserably. "Can we get out of here? I'd like to get this cooking lesson over with because

I fear this dinner is going to go about as well as this little test did."

He held the door open for her. "I'm hoping for a major comeback. I thought we'd go back to the farmers market and get some of the ingredients. Fresh is best."

"So we won't be taking something out of a box and putting it in the oven? I am occasionally successful at that kind of cooking."

Somehow, she'd managed to make him smile. "You're occasionally good at heating something up in the oven?"

"I can burn water, Donovan. Okay? That's how bad I am at cooking."

"You can't—" He stopped himself from responding to her nonsense. "Let's go. I'm going to show you it's not as hard as you think it is."

The farmers market was bustling on a late Saturday afternoon. The fragrant smell of fresh flowers coming from the garden center caught Kelly's attention when they walked by. She checked the price on one of the hanging baskets full of purple petunias.

"I can't wait to buy a house someday. I want a big front porch with humongous hanging baskets and overflowing planters everywhere. I've dreamed of having a place with super cute window boxes bursting with colorful annuals under every window. My only fear is that I don't have a green thumb. My mom sent me a houseplant as a gift when I moved in and I managed to kill it in less than a week."

Donovan picked up two of the hanging baskets she had been looking at and asked, "Did you forget to water it?"

"I think I overwatered it. It drowned. I didn't even know that was possible. I thought plants needed water."

He chuckled once again at her ineptness. "I think Avery would like these. They're purple," he said as if he had to explain. "I'm going to get them for my front porch."

Kelly's heart skipped a beat. He was so sweet and thoughtful, she had to force herself not to sigh like a lovestruck teenager. She reminded herself that this was the same guy who came to her door to test her ability to take care of herself. That was something her mother and father would have done to her when she was younger.

In the market area, he had a very short list of things for them to buy. They needed one onion, a garlic bulb, a pound of ground beef, a bunch of parsley and three fresh tomatoes. Everything else he claimed to have at home for her to use.

"Did you go grocery shopping with your mom when you were a kid?" she asked as they walked through the aisles of produce.

"I don't remember going when I was little, but she did take me when I was in high school. She had a whole list of things she wanted me to learn to do before I graduated. It was sort of a how-to-be-a-successful-adult to-do list. She made me navigate grocery stores and Target. I still avoid that store on the weekends because of the horrors I witnessed there with my mom."

Kelly laughed, trying to picture Donovan afraid of a bunch of weekend shoppers. "I wish my parents would have done that with me. They were so busy making sure there were no boogeymen under my bed that they didn't even think about how to prepare me for the real world."

"I feel pressure to start doing it with Graham, but he has no interest. I tried to show him how to do laundry the other day and he acted like I was speaking a different language."

Trying hard not to visibly swoon at the thought of him teaching his teenaged nephew how to wash clothes, she focused her attention on the cart full of watermelons up ahead. "Should we get some fruit for dinner? These watermelons look good. Not that I know what a bad watermelon would look like. Do you know how to tell?"

Donovan picked up one of the melons and inspected it. He seemed to be weighing it in his hands. Flipping it over, he showed her the belly. "You want to make sure it has a decent yellow patch where it was laying on the ground. That means it's ripe." He hit the melon with the heel of his hand.

"What was that for? Did you pick up a naughty one?"

He cocked his head to the side and cast her a look that told her he was unimpressed with her humor. "You always want to tap the underbelly. A ripe watermelon will have a nice hollow sound. Underripe or overripe melons will sound more muted."

"You should have your own show on the Food Network. *Dining with a Detective.* Oh, I like that. I would watch that."

A smile tilted his mouth as he shook his head at her. "Let's get home and get dinner on the table."

When they got to his truck, his phone chimed with a text from Graham, who was wondering when Donovan was going to be home because Avery was annoying him by asking for a snack every five seconds. Another text came through that questioned how long it took to pick someone up.

"He loves to complain but can't stand it when anyone else complains. He has no problem asking other people to do things for him but is clearly being abused when someone asks him to do something. I don't know what to do with him anymore."

Kelly didn't know Graham very well, but she could remember being an emotional teenager. Graham had the added bonus of grief to muddle through. It had to be impossibly hard.

"I think you need to continue being patient with him."

"That's getting more and more difficult," Donovan confessed.

"Not only is he going through this typically self-centered phase of life, he's at a really vulnerable age to have lost both parents. There's probably a constant fight going on in his brain. Sometimes he wants to be independent and other times he's probably sad his parents aren't here to take care of him."

Dark brows rose in astonishment. "That's a really good point. I think if someone needs a TV show, it's you. I can't think of anything clever to call it, but I'm sure you could."

The way he smiled and nervously glanced at her left her boneless in the seat next to him.

He had this habit of making her feel things she was desperately trying to convince herself she would never feel for any police officer. But these feels were very dangerously real.

DONOVAN LET KELLY help him hang the flowers he bought for Avery when they got back to the house. He thanked her and did his best to reject the chemistry between them. She was the captain's niece. Captain was clearly not going to be okay with Kelly dating someone in his unit. Not that Donovan was thinking about dating her. That was not part of any plan he had. Taking care of his sister's kids brought enough drama into his life. He didn't need a girlfriend on top of it.

"Are you ready for your cooking lesson? This isn't going to be like making the meatball a couple days ago. You are going to do it all—I'm just going to guide you."

Kelly clapped her hands together. "As long as you're fine with having to pay for a couple of pizzas later when everyone is starved because the goulash was a disaster, I'm ready."

"Pretty flowers!" Avery said, coming outside.

"I was hoping you'd like them," Donovan said. "I thought of you the second I saw them."

"Did you buy Kelly some, too? Boys are supposed to buy flowers for the girls they like."

He kept his gaze fixed on Avery, refusing to look at Kelly's reaction to the little girl's question. "I bought Kelly some stuff to make for dinner. Why don't we go inside?" His voice was a hoarse croak.

Playing it cool was difficult when his heart was thumping in his chest and embarrassment surely colored his cheeks. He needed to set Avery straight, but explaining the intricacies of adult relationships to a seven-year-old was about as easy as teaching her quantum physics. Avery believed that everyone should be friends. She didn't discriminate and she didn't understand that grown-ups were sometimes more than friends.

"Thank goodness you're home," Graham said. "Avery was driving me nuts."

"I was not," Avery argued. "You're the one who was being annoying."

"I wasn't talking to you, Avery. Can you mind your business for one second?"

"Hey, be nice to your sister," Donovan warned.

Graham followed them into the kitchen. "What's for dinner?"

"Hello, to you, too, Graham," Kelly said.

"Hi, Kelly. What's for dinner?"

Kelly shot him a crooked smile. "I am making you guys goulash."

"Cool," Graham said with little affect.

Avery, on the other hand, celebrated by jumping up and down. "I love goulash!"

"Oh, great." Kelly's wariness was evident in her expression. "I have to make something you love." She glanced briefly at Donovan. "Wonderful."

"If you know they like it in general, you'll know they'll be honest about whether they like yours."

"They like it when *you* make it." She was legitimately worried. He could tell she didn't want to disappoint but feared she would.

"And I am sharing my recipe with you, so they will like it when you make it."

Kelly took a deep breath and walked to the sink to wash her hands. "Let's do this."

Donovan sent the kids away. Kelly couldn't handle the distractions. He handed her the recipe card and watched her carefully as she got started. He didn't do anything but talk her through it. He gave her little tips, like chew gum when chopping onions to prevent getting teary-eyed and how to shake garlic from its skin by using two metal bowls.

"Make sure to set the timer," he reminded her after she mixed the noodles in the sauce. "No one likes crunchy or pasty noodles."

"Okay, I have fifteen minutes. What do I do while I wait?"

"You could cut up the watermelon," he suggested.

She wiped her hands on a dish towel. "I think I can handle that."

"How much longer? I'm starving?" Graham called from the other room.

"About fifteen minutes," Kelly answered. "Want to help me with cutting up the watermelon?"

Donovan would have put money on there being no chance at all that Graham would lend a hand when he was hungry. Being hungry made him irritable and being crabby made him uncooperative.

"Sure," he replied much to Donovan's surprise. "Did anyone famous show up at the farmers market when you were working at it yesterday?"

"Nope. Nobody famous. How was school on Friday?"

"Same as every other day. Boring."

Kelly sliced the watermelon in half and

the two of them began removing the rind. "There has to be one class that isn't a complete snore-fest."

"The only class I like is art," Graham replied. "I'm taking this drawing and painting class and we're working on our final projects."

"Cool. What are you doing for it?"

He hesitated. "I'm drawing a portrait of my mom."

"That's awesome, Graham," Kelly said, briefly making eye contact with Donovan, whose heart clenched. He had no idea. Graham had never mentioned anything about art class until today.

Graham tried to downplay it. "It probably won't get me an A, but I don't really care."

"The grade doesn't matter. What's important is that you got to create a piece of art that means something to you. I think that it's great that you decided to paint something so special."

Donovan cleared his throat and struggled to keep his voice even. "I can't wait to see it."

Graham looked at him with eyes full of all the emotion he kept trapped inside.

Wishing he could tear down his nephew's walls, Donovan moved next to him and put an arm around him. Graham quickly shrugged it off.

"I'm fine. Don't worry about me," he said.

Donovan backed off. He had thought this was a chance to show Graham that he could be there for him. Once again, Graham showed he wasn't ready to let him in.

"You can't tell the people who love you not to worry," Kelly said from the other side of the kitchen island. "When you love someone, you worry about them all the time. It's just the way it is."

"Sometimes I just need everyone to worry less," Graham said.

Kelly let out a sharp laugh. "Man, do I get that more than you will ever know. Both of my parents are...well, *were* police officers. My mom still works for the Knoxville Police. No one knows about wanting people to worry a little bit less than me."

"Both of your parents are cops and your uncle is my uncle's captain?"

She nodded. "I always felt like they worried about me too much. But when my dad died, all I wanted was for him to worry about me—to call me up and ask me if I remembered to lock my door. Lucky for me, I have my uncle in town. I called him when my car got vandalized, and he dropped everything to help me."

Graham didn't miss a beat. "And now my uncle is worrying about you. If you really wanted them all to worry less, you blew it with that one phone call."

Kelly laughed. "You're probably right about that, but I would rather have more people who love and worry about me in my life than have no one who cared."

She stole another glance in Donovan's direction. He was appreciative of her sharing her story with Graham since they were so similar. Donovan gave her a friendly smile and she returned it immediately.

The timer went off and Kelly jumped. "Oh, my gosh, it's done. See how I get totally distracted and lose track of time. Good call on the timer."

He turned off the timer for her while she drained the noodles and mixed them with the other ingredients. "I think it's done."

"Hopefully, it's done," Donovan said. "You have to check and make sure. The chef should taste test before serving to the guests. Grab a spoon from the drawer to the right of the sink."

He'd supervised everything she did and there was no way this wasn't going to taste exactly like his goulash. He couldn't wait to see her expression when she realized she'd actually made a decent dinner.

"Here goes nothing," she said, dipping her spoon in. She puckered her lips and blew on the hot bite. Finally, she tasted it.

"Please tell me you didn't ruin it because I'm starving," Graham said.

The widest smile broke across her face. "I have no idea what it's supposed to taste like, but this is delicious!"

Donovan felt an enormous sense of pride. She had done it and he had helped her. Maybe he was a good teacher. He might not get through to Graham, who wasn't ready to accept his help. But when he was dealing with someone willing and able to take his advice, he was capable of making a difference.

"If the kids like it, you can't call yourself a bad cook anymore," he said, helping Graham get the cut-up watermelon into a bowl and on the table. Kelly placed the pan of goulash on the trivet in the center of the table.

"Thanks to you," she said before throwing her arms around him.

Donovan froze for a second, shocked by the physical contact. He softened and gave her a squeeze back. When she broke contact, he wanted to pull her back close. That desire startled him more than the hug.

"Avery, come and eat!" Graham shouted up the stairs.

She was downstairs in a flash. They all sat down at the table and Donovan opened up a napkin and placed it on his lap. The kids were busy spooning food on their plates while Kelly watched with a pleased expression on her face. She had made them dinner when she believed she was incapable of making anything edible.

"Can you pass the watermelon?" Donovan asked Graham, who was more than ready to feed his face. He pushed the bowl in his uncle's direction before digging in.

"Well?" Kelly waited impatiently for some feedback.

Avery took a bite of the goulash, too. Both kids took their time chewing and swallowing. Donovan could see Kelly's anxiety rising.

"Mmm! This tastes just like Uncle Donovan's," Avery concluded.

Graham didn't say anything, opting to shovel some more into his mouth instead and give her a thumbs-up.

"Kids don't lie," Donovan reminded her.

Kelly was beaming from across the table. She served herself a hefty portion and asked

Avery to tell her about her day. Donovan ate and watched his family interact with Kelly like she was one of them. As much as he doubted he was doing the right thing, in this moment, it felt a lot more like things were absolutely perfect.

## *CHAPTER ELEVEN*

AFTER SUCCESSFULLY COOKING DINNER, Kelly was given a free pass from having to clean up. She got to sit with her feet up in the family room while Donovan and the kids cleared the table, loaded the dishwasher and put things away.

"I could get used to this," she said with her hands behind her head. "Can you come over every night and clean up my kitchen, Avery?"

"No! You have to come here," Avery said with a giggle.

Kelly noticed the way Donovan stilled at the kitchen sink where he was hand washing some pots and pans. He was the king of mixed messages. One minute, he'd seem happy to have her there and the next, it was like he couldn't get her out fast enough.

"I really don't need to sit here like a princess," Kelly said. "I can cook *and* clean."

"You can switch with me," Graham said, holding out the dish towel he was using to dry what Donovan washed. "I'll be a princess."

"Graham!" Avery was exasperated. "You can't be a princess! You're a boy."

"Fine, I'll be a prince then. I'll be whatever gets to sit on the couch and not do chores."

Donovan flicked some suds at him. "You'll finish drying the dishes and accept your fate as faithful servant instead."

"See, I knew you thought of us as slaves. That's probably the only reason you agreed to take us in. Free child labor."

"Really, dude?" Donovan sounded displeased. "Don't go there with me. Especially in front of your sister."

"What's child labor?" Avery asked. Her little face scrunched up.

Kelly felt bad she had unintentionally started this whole conversation. She popped up and took the dish towel from Graham. "Child labor means kid jobs, like chores. Something lots of kids have to do," she said, looking pointedly at Graham. "It is far from a crime to ask kids to help with chores. My mom called it being a 'contributing member of the family,' so Graham is going to help you and I am going to help Uncle Donovan."

"I like that you're part of our family," Avery said, skipping over to the table to grab the drinking glasses.

Kelly opened her mouth and closed it again,

unsettled by how it made her feel to be included that way. She liked it, even though it clearly made Donovan uncomfortable. His jaw was clenched so tight, it had to be painful.

"She's not part of our family, Avery. Uncle Donovan works for her. He's her bodyguard."

Avery scowled at her older brother. "She can be part of our family if she wants to."

"That's so sweet, Avery. I am very fortunate to be a friend of your family." She hoped that would put the conversation to rest.

"The only way grown-ups become part of someone else's family is if they get married," Donovan said, snapping out of his stupor. "Kelly and I are not getting married. You have to be in love with someone to marry them. We are not in love. Does that make sense?"

"You could be," Avery said so plainly as if it was that simple.

"No, we can't," Donovan said crisply. "I don't feel in love with her. I like her. She's a nice person. She can be our friend, but I don't love her. I never will. Okay? Is that clear?"

Kelly's stomach was in knots and her face was burning hot. He was crystal clear. He was never going to be in love with her. There was no chance. Not the slightest bit of doubt in his voice. No mixed messages here. Kelly knew exactly where she stood and, if she really thought about it, was glad for it. She wasn't in love with Donovan. Sure, he ticked off a lot of the perfect-guy boxes but not all of them.

"I love you," Avery said, wrapping her arms around Kelly's waist and giving her a big hug.

A giant lump of emotion was lodged in her throat. She swallowed it down. "Thank you, sweetheart."

"Okay, you two are off duty. Kelly and I will finish up and then we need to do some work in the basement. Graham, you are in charge of watching your sister."

"Are you doing more self-defense? Can I come down and learn some more moves, too?" Graham asked. He was almost as excited about that as he had been about eating dinner.

"No, I need you to watch your sister."

"She can come down, too. She can learn self-defense, too. She's a girl. She needs it."

Donovan was having none of it. "You and your sister will stay up here. This is not up for discussion."

"Why? You let me come down there last time. This isn't fair," Graham complained.

Donovan ignored him as he plunged his

hands back in the soapy water and began washing the last of the dishes. Kelly gave Graham a sympathetic smile.

"You don't even get why I want to learn some things because you don't even care."

Donovan rinsed the last pot. He had said the discussion was over and he obviously meant it.

Kelly couldn't let that go, however. "What is happening that makes you feel like you need to learn how to defend yourself? Is something going on at school?"

"He doesn't care, so it doesn't matter."

Donovan gripped the edges of the sink and bowed his head. "I ask you every day how things are at school and you never want to talk about it. Don't act like I don't care when it's you who chooses to leave me in the dark."

Graham rolled his eyes and took off for his bedroom. Kelly felt sick. There was something going on at school, a reason Graham felt like he needed to learn self-defense. It wasn't her place to interfere, but she also understood that there was a breakdown in communication between uncle and nephew.

She hung up the dish towel and followed Graham upstairs. "Wait," she said when she got the top. "What's going on at school?"

"Do you know how hard it is to start at a

new school as a sophomore? Everyone at the school has known each other since they were five. No one cares about the new kid. I'm nothing but a punchline, someone for them to throw insults at because I don't matter."

"That's not okay, Graham. You need to tell someone at school."

"Oh, so I can be the new kid who also rats on everyone? That will make me *super* popular."

Kelly understood how hard it was for kids Graham's age to stand up for themselves, to get help from the adults. Her heart hurt thinking about how much this boy had been through only to have no friends at school to support him.

"I'm so sorry you have to deal with jerks. That's the last thing you should have to worry about. Please tell me there are some nice kids at your school. They can't all be heartless."

Graham pressed his back against the wall and slid down until he was sitting on the floor. "That's kind of what I wanted to talk to you about."

"You wanted to talk to me?" There was no way she could hide her surprise. She sat down next to him in the hall.

"I wanted your opinion because you're…a

girl. Well, you're not a girl, you're a grown-up, but you were a girl when you were younger."

"I get it. I'm a female. You're looking for a female perspective on something?"

He sighed and nodded his head. "If a girl always waits for a boy after a certain class so they can walk together, is it possible that means she likes him more than a friend or is he just overthinking things?"

Kelly's faith in Graham's generation was renewed. There was a girl. "Well, does she wait for him because they have the same class next period?"

"No, but the rooms are near each other."

"Does she talk to him any other time?"

"She comes to his locker sometimes and tells him funny things that happened to her. They also have chemistry together."

Kelly tried not to smile too big at the double entendre. "I would say she definitely likes him."

"But they also have the same lunch period and she sits with the guys from his math class who hate the boy and love to make his life as terrible as possible. At lunch, she pretends she doesn't even know him. She says nothing when the jerks she sits with say or do mean things."

All the faith that had been renewed a few

seconds ago was suddenly lost again. Peer pressure stank. "She could still like you, Graham. She just hasn't found the courage to stand up to those guys yet. Bullies get away with so much because people are afraid to stand up to them."

"That's why I want to learn some self-defense. I want to be able to stand up to them when they get in my face. I want to be able to get away from them when they think they can push me around because I'm not as big as they are. I hate being so short and weak. My dad was huge and so strong. My uncle is a beast. Why am I such a wimp?"

"You aren't a wimp. You're fifteen. You're still growing. You'll probably still be growing when you're in college."

"A lot of good that will do me over the next two years of high school."

Kelly playfully ruffled his hair. "Don't be so dramatic. You could grow a bunch of inches over the summer. You never know. Fortunately, you come from good stock. You're bound to be just as big and strong as your dad and uncle."

"What do I do about the girl?"

"You have to decide what you want. Are you happy with the way things are or do you want more? If you're content being her friend when it's convenient for her, then leave it alone. If you want to be treated better than that, maybe it's time you call her out. Does she want to be your friend or not? Don't let her pick and choose when she acts like it and when she doesn't."

"She could choose to not be my friend at all."

"That's unfortunately true." Kelly said a silent prayer that this mystery girl would not let Graham down. "That's why you need to think about it carefully. I'm sure it's nice to have someone be nice to you some of the time. Maybe that's better than having no one be nice all of the time."

"I'm going to think about it. Thanks for listening," Graham said, his voice thick. "I miss my mom so much sometimes. She was the only one who got me."

Tears welled in Kelly's eyes. She wiped them away before they could fall down her cheeks. Donovan might not ever love her, but Kelly was quickly falling in love with his family.

DONOVAN STOOD IN the stairwell with a pain in his chest he hadn't felt since the day his sister died. Listening to Graham spill his heart out to Kelly was almost too much.

He had planned to ask Kelly to mind her business and leave Graham alone to have his temper tantrum. He had no idea what the boy was going through at school. How isolated he felt. It explained a lot about why he was avoiding certain classes and why he hated school in general. Donovan had not made things better by ignoring his outbursts. There was a reason Graham was so passionate about things.

Donovan couldn't deny he also felt a bit jealous. Envious that Graham would open up to a practical stranger instead of him. Kelly had been to the house three times and she somehow managed to get Graham to tell her what had been going on the last six months at school.

Doubt once again clouded his thoughts. Why had Jessica asked him to take care of these kids? He wasn't good at it. He'd been struggling to gain Graham's trust and to curb Avery's insta-attachment to anyone who showed her some attention. Today was a perfect example of how miserably he was failing.

Pushing all that negativity down, he climbed to the top of the stairs. Kelly's head turned and her gaze met his. She nudged Graham and nodded in Donovan's direction.

"Why don't we all go to the basement to

practice a couple new moves," Donovan said, hoping for a positive response.

"I think that's a good idea," Kelly said. "Will you come down with us?"

"You were eavesdropping?" Graham accused.

Donovan exhaled a heavy sigh. "I don't want to fight. Can we not fight?"

"Aren't you tired of fighting with him?" Kelly asked Graham. "He wants to help. Let him."

Graham pulled his knees up to his chest and hid his face. Kelly stood up and held out a hand.

"Come on. Come with us," she said.

Graham took her hand and let her pull him to his feet. "I probably should come and make sure you're paying attention. I don't want that stalker to ever hurt you."

Kelly looked like she was about to burst into tears. She pulled him in for a hug. Jealousy crept back up and Donovan had to work hard to squash it. He needed to appreciate that Graham was connecting to someone, someone kind and with honorable intentions. He was a good kid with a big heart. In the midst of all his pain, he was able to show compassion for someone else.

In the basement, Donovan reviewed the

moves he'd taught them the other day. Kelly remembered them perfectly. She smiled proudly when he complimented her.

"Let's practice a couple attack moves. But I want to remind both of you, the smartest—"

"The smartest thing to do is to get away," Kelly and Graham said at the same time.

Donovan was glad they were both paying attention. "These are things I only want you to use as a last resort. Only if there is nothing else you can do to get away."

"We got it," Graham said.

"Watch this, guys," Avery said from the other side of the room. Everyone turned their attention to the seven-year-old with the jump rope. She skipped rope four times before getting tangled up.

They all clapped for her and Donovan encouraged her to keep practicing. His focus returned to the teaching.

"I don't want to get a call from the school next week, saying you're in trouble for breaking some kid's nose," he said to Graham.

The teen responded with bravado. "Only if he takes the first swing."

"Showing you this stuff is not me condoning fighting," Donovan clarified. "This is for her more than it's for you. She needs to know this stuff. You have other options even if they aren't cool."

"I'm not a rat."

"No one said you have to be a rat, but there are people at school who can help you if you're being bullied. People like Mrs. Mitchell."

"I'm not telling the guidance counselor," Graham said gruffly.

"Maybe we should save this conversation for later," Kelly interrupted. "I think Graham gets that you are not okay with him fighting. Right?"

Her cool head was frustratingly admirable. She had this knack for saying the right thing at the right time. Especially when Donovan's emotions were getting the best of him. Maybe there were some things he could learn from her.

"Do you remember the vulnerable spots on a body?" Donovan asked.

Kelly didn't flinch. "Eyes, nose, knees, legs, ears, throat and groin." When she noticed his surprise, she added, "Being stuck in my apartment for hours on end leads to lots of study time."

Donovan explained those were the places she wanted to strike if she needed to in order to get away. "Come over here by the punching bag and show me how you would hit it."

Kelly ran a hand along her braid. She may have been confident about where to hit, but she wasn't as sure of the how. She made a fist and cracked her knuckles with the other hand. Turning her body at an angle, she jabbed at the bag like she was trying to fluff a pillow.

Donovan suppressed a smile. "Okay, if you punch someone like that the only thing that's going to happen is you are going to hurt yourself."

She frowned. "I always got good feedback in my cardio kickboxing class from the instructor."

Cardio kickboxing was not the same as self-defense. At least Donovan knew now that he had some reteaching to do. Kelly would have to unlearn a bunch of bad habits she got from her fitness class.

He had Kelly show him her punching fist. He held on to her wrist and flipped her fist over. "Number one, never tuck your thumb into your fist. That's a sure way to break your thumb. Number two, sometimes your fists aren't the best weapon. Fingers in the eyes, an elbow to the throat, stomping on his foot with the heel of your foot—these strikes can hurt much more than a punch to the face."

Kelly practiced on the punching bag while Graham looked on. Donovan needed to come up with a way to help Graham feel more confident without encouraging him to fight at school.

"How would you feel about doing some lifting with me a few times a week? I could set you up with a schedule and we could work on building muscle the right way."

"Yeah? You'd let me use your stuff?"

"As long as I was here to supervise you. Yes."

"That would be awesome."

Donovan loved the sound of that. "Awesome" from a teenager was much better than "lame."

"You know, your dad wanted to become a personal trainer once he got discharged. He was obsessed with working out. That's how he got so big. He worked for it." And worked and worked.

Kelly wasn't very focused on her attacks. "Graham's dad was in the military?"

"He was," Donovan answered. "The only reason he met my sister was because we were really good friends." He had loved Oliver like a brother, so it only made sense that he should become his brother by marriage.

"It's nice that you were close to him as well as your sister," Kelly said.

"Could Daddy jump rope?" Avery asked from the other side.

"He could jump rope really fast." Ollie was larger than life. He had boundless amounts of energy like Avery, but he had a bit of a stubborn streak like Graham, as well. As much as the kids reminded Donovan of his sister daily, they equally made him think of his dear friend.

"He sounds like a cool guy. Kind of like some kids I know," Kelly said. She threw some playful punches at Graham until he smiled.

Jessica would be disappointed in Donovan for letting Kelly be around the kids so much if he had no intention of developing this relationship further, but Ollie would have been ticked off. He would have liked Kelly so much, he would have stopped at nothing to get Donovan to like her, too. Ollie had a thing for matchmaking. He was always setting Donovan up with women he thought were perfect for him.

Watching her make Graham laugh, Donovan wondered if Ollie was enjoying this because there was no shaking these feelings she stirred up inside of him.

## *CHAPTER TWELVE*

"WHERE IS MY favorite bodyguard?" Juliette asked when Kelly arrived at the station Thursday morning. She had picked up her car yesterday afternoon and got to drive herself to work for the first time in forever. Donovan was supposed to meet her here.

"You shouldn't get so attached. I'm starting to think my secret admirer has gone into hiding. I might not need a bodyguard for much longer."

"Oh, I'm so torn! I don't want anyone to stalk you, but I kind of enjoy having the detective around. My husband's stomach likes him, too."

Kelly needed to take her own advice about getting attached because like Juliette and her husband, she also liked having Donovan around a bit too much. It had been over a week since Kelly's stalker had left the apology note on her door. Juliette did not recognize Hunter in the photo Donovan showed her. Donovan wasn't convinced that meant he wasn't still a suspect. He made Kelly order from Johnny's Grill one night this week. When Hunter showed up, Donovan was the one to answer the door and pay for the food. It was a test, but if that was supposed to make Hunter jealous and push him to act out, it didn't work or Hunter wasn't the guy they were looking for.

There had been no stalker activity all week. No gifts, no notes, no phone calls. Nothing. The guy had never gone more than a couple days without making contact. Maybe getting the police involved had scared him off.

The elevator pinged and Donovan stepped out dressed much more casually than the first day they had met. Later this evening, they had to attend a concert at Ryman Auditorium where Kelly was emcee. Dressed in a black button-down and dark denim jeans, Donovan was looking more like a hot date than a bodyguard. He also was holding a tray of coffees.

"Good morning, Detective," Juliette greeted him and was the first to receive a drink.

"Sorry that I'm late. I stopped to get you guys some coffee. Juliette, yours is a latte with sugar-free vanilla."

"It's a good thing my husband loves the recipes you share with me or else he would be very jealous of how much I love you."

He pulled another drink out of the carrier and handed it to Kelly. "Chai latte for Miss Bonner."

He paid attention to things Kelly didn't realize he had noticed about her. Between the way he looked and the kind gesture, her heart skipped a few beats.

"Thank you, Detective Walsh," she said, gratefully accepting the drink. "You didn't have to do that."

"I am celebrating one week without any calls from the high school about Graham. He's gone to all of his classes. Stayed out of trouble. We only have to get him through one more week and some finals and he will successfully finish the year."

Kelly was so proud of Graham. He didn't have an easy time at school with some of the bullying going on. Since they had talked about the issues last week, he had begun to open up more and more about school and his classes. He still hadn't confronted the girl, but he was thinking he might do it the next time she chose not to say anything when her friends picked on him. Thankfully, those guys had backed off a bit.

"Excellent reason to celebrate. I'm glad he's doing well."

"Thanks to someone who is a very good listener." He tipped his cup in her direction.

Kelly couldn't take any of the credit. Graham was choosing to make different and better choices for himself. This was all him.

"Kelly, I'm glad you're here. I need to talk to you." Nancy came out front and snatched her friend away and into Kelly's office.

"What's the matter?"

Nancy shut the door. "I need your help with Lyle."

Kelly's brow furrowed. "What kind of help?" As far as Kelly knew, Lyle had played it cool and kept things professional after Kelly had let him down easy about Nancy not being interested.

"Ever since you mentioned that he likes me, I can't stop thinking I am a giant fool for not at least trying," she said, pacing around the small space. "And the more I regret my choice, the more he seems perfectly content to just be friends. I thought you said he really liked me."

"He does really like you, but I told him you weren't interested, so he's moving on. What did you expect?"

Nancy sat down and crossed her legs. "I don't know. I expected that things might be awkward for a little bit, but he hasn't made it awkward at all. And I caught him chatting it up with Trish the other day. I would definitely characterize it as flirting."

"You're jealous of our twenty-two-year-old intern? She was literally in college two months ago. Come on, Nancy, Lyle is not interested in Trish."

"I think I'm going to ask him to go to dinner this weekend. Do you think that's a good or a bad idea?"

"It doesn't matter what I think. Do you want to go to dinner with him?"

"Yes."

"Then ask him. If he wants to go with you, he'll say yes." She was all for them getting together if that was what both of them wanted. "But I do ask that you think about why you've had this change of heart. If you're doing this because you don't like it that he's giving Trish attention instead of you, please don't ask him out."

Nancy seemed genuinely perplexed. "Why?"

"Because he really likes you. If you're just jealous and not really interested in being in a relationship with him, then please don't ask him out. He deserves better than being that someone who feeds your ego."

Nancy pressed her hand to her chest. "Hurtful. This is not about my ego."

"Then you have my blessing."

"Thank you," Nancy said, getting to her feet. She stopped in the doorway. "I see you and the cute bodyguard are getting along nicely. Anyone else having a change of heart around here?"

"What?" Kelly was shocked by the accusation. What had she seen that made it so obvious that Kelly was torn about what to do? "No," she lied. "Donovan and I have become friends. He's teaching me how to take care of myself and I am helping him figure out how to take care of two kids. There's no romance going on here."

"Says the hopeless romantic who has a knack for knowing two people belong together before they do unless one of those people is her."

It was true. She did have a gift for recognizing when people belonged together. She also was terrible at finding a good man for herself. Did that mean she was missing something going on between her and Donovan?

Kelly turned her back on her friend. "Good luck getting a date. Lyle and Trish are kinda growing on me."

"Super hurtful!" Nancy said on her way out.

A few minutes later there was a knock

on her door. Lyle's lanky frame stood in her doorway. "Oh, good. She's not in here." He came in the office and shut the door behind him. "I need to talk to you."

Kelly set down the pen she was marking her notes with and gave him her full attention. "About?"

"Trish asked me out for drinks after work tomorrow."

Kelly's eyes nearly popped out of head. Had she jinxed Nancy with her jokes? "When did that happen?"

"This morning."

She leaned forward, fearing what this meant for Nancy's change of heart. "And what did you say?"

Lyle grimaced. "I said yes. Why did I say yes? She was in diapers when I started high school."

"Nancy's planning on asking you to dinner this weekend." The words fell out of her mouth on their own. She hadn't planned to spill her friend's secret. In fact, that was the exact opposite of what she'd told herself to do.

He put his hands on his head. "Don't mess with me, Kel."

"You've been doing such a good job of playing it cool, she realized she's more interested in you than she had originally thought she was." Thankfully, Kelly managed to leave out the part about being jealous of Trish.

"Are you kidding me?" he asked. Kelly shook her head. "You're telling me that she realized she likes me as soon as I acted like I didn't like her?"

"Pretty much. What are you going to do?"

Lyle threw his hands up. "I don't know. It's not like Trish and I have decided we want to go steady. I agreed to get drinks."

"The fact that you call exclusively dating someone going steady means you are way too old for her."

"If Nancy doesn't ask me to go to dinner, I will never forgive you for giving me this anxiety," he said, pacing around her office.

"You better hope Trish doesn't tell Nancy that you agreed to go out with her. That's the only thing that might stop her from following through."

Lyle's eyes went wide. "Do you think they would talk to each other about me?"

Kelly couldn't picture Nancy sharing personal information with Trish since she already saw her as a rival. Of course, Trish might say something about going for drinks since she was oblivious to Nancy's feelings for Lyle. "Maybe?"

"Oh, great. Should I tell Trish I can't go?

What if Nancy doesn't ask and I pass up the chance to get to know Trish better? What if they find out I said yes to both of them and they both cancel on me and I die alone?"

Kelly got up and stopped him from pacing. She put a reassuring hand on his arm. "Deep breath. You are not going to die alone. Saying yes to both of them is not a crime. Like you said, you aren't going steady with anyone. I think you can have drinks with Trish tomorrow and go out to dinner with Nancy this weekend."

"It's been a while since I dated one woman and more like forever since I dated two at the same time."

Kelly smiled up at him. "That's because you are a good guy. And because you are such a good guy, you have two wonderful ladies hoping you'll want to spend time with them. There are worse problems to have, my friend."

For example, you could be attracted to a great guy with awesome kids who just so happens to also be a cop working for your uncle, which was a deal-breaker. He could have also said you were amazing but at the same time would never, *ever* be in love with you. Those would be much worse problems to have.

DONOVAN BEGAN TO think this stalker wasn't planning to ever show his face. The gifts had stopped coming to the station ever since Donovan started manning the lobby. He wondered if it was possible for the stalker to know he was there. Was he watching without making himself known?

There was no way for Donovan to know for sure unless he set some kind of trap. Maybe he needed to not be in the lobby for a few days to see if the gifts started up again. He didn't like the thought of leaving Kelly unprotected. He'd have to find a way to be close but less visible.

Kelly came out to the lobby. "Ready to go?"

Her dark hair was pulled up in a sleek ponytail that accentuated her long neck and high cheekbones. Her skin was a little pink from being outside in the late-afternoon sun yesterday. She had come over to the house to do some self-defense training but ended up sitting on the porch with him watching Avery jump on the trampoline for a couple hours instead.

"Ready when you are," he replied. "I'll see you tomorrow, Juliette. Have a good night."

"Bye, you two. Keep her safe, Detective."

They got in the elevator and Kelly pressed the button to get to the parking garage. "I need to be at the auditorium at six. The station is sponsoring the meet-and-greet before the show."

It was four o'clock. Avery would be home by five. He was hoping to feed the kids dinner before he had to leave, but if she needed to be there by six, he'd be cutting things close.

"I can pick you up so you have some extra time at home to get the kids settled," she said as if she had read his mind.

It was a good idea but not possible. "Can't do that because I have to check your apartment at the end of the night. I have to drive. I could meet you at the venue or I can pick you up when you're ready to go."

"I don't want to make you drive all over the city for me. What's easiest for you?"

The elevator opened and they stepped out into the basement garage. "Easiest would be to go straight to my house, make the kids dinner and go to the show, but I'm sure you need to go home first."

Kelly dug through her purse and pulled out her valet ticket. He walked with her to the valet station. "Well, I don't have to." She smiled at the valet, handing him her ticket. "How are you doing tonight, Miller?"

"I'm doing well, Kelly. How are you?"

"It's been a good day, but I have to work tonight."

"No rest for the weary, huh?"

"Not for me," she said.

"Do you have a ticket, sir?" the man asked Donovan. He was one of the valets Donovan had talked to that first day on this case.

"No, I self-parked." Donovan turned his attention back to Kelly. "If you want, you can freshen up at my place and we can leave for the show from there. It would definitely save me some time."

"Let's do that then. I'll follow you to your house. I wanted to hear how Graham did on his chemistry test, so it's all good."

Donovan noticed the valet had found the keys but was still standing there. "Are you going to get her car?"

The man didn't bother to acknowledge Donovan's question. "I'll be right back with your car, Kelly."

She gave him another smile. "Thanks."

"You and the valet are on a first-name basis?" Donovan asked when the young man finally jogged off to retrieve the car.

She shrugged. "He's worked here for a little while. I thought I told you the guys who work here are always pretending to fight over who's going to help me. Miller is always really nice, so I asked his name one time. He acted like no one had ever bothered to ask him that before. We've been buddies ever since."

"Buddies like you and the food delivery guy, huh?"

"It's exactly like that. Miller asks me how my day was, I ask him how his day was. We do a little small talk. It's nothing, but he seems to appreciate being treated like a human being instead of just a car valet."

"You are a very nice person, you know that, right?"

"Because I treat people like people?"

Miller was back with her car quite quickly. Being nice probably helped with the wait time. Kelly folded up a couple dollar bills and handed them to him when he got out of the driver's seat. "Have a good one. I'll see you tomorrow," she said.

"Don't work too hard tonight," he replied, holding the door open for her.

Donovan came up behind him. "I've got it, man. I need to finish talking to her."

The valet gave Donovan a once-over. "Aren't you that guy who was asking a bunch of questions last week?"

"That was me. You have any new info? See anything suspicious down here recently?"

"Are you a cop or are you a friend of Kelly's?" he asked instead of answering.

"He's both, Miller," Kelly said. "If you have seen anything out of the ordinary please let him know."

"I haven't seen anything."

"Well, if you do, I'm here whenever Kelly is," Donovan said, switching places with him. "You can let me know if you see anything. Big or small."

Miller nodded and stepped away.

"Wait for me and you can follow me to my place," he told her.

"Okay." Even though he'd watched her smile at other people all week, when she beamed up at him, she made Donovan feel like he was the only person capable of bringing her that much joy.

He needed to shake off that feeling. If there was no threat, there was no need for a bodyguard. No bodyguard, no reason to spend time with each other anymore. Donovan had to be prepared to go back to his life before Kelly Bonner stepped into it.

Graham was in his room when they got to the house. He came jogging down the stairs minutes later. "Guess who got an A on his chemistry test?"

"You already know your grade?" Kelly asked.

"He didn't grade it yet, but I knew everything. I didn't have to guess on any of them."

"That's awesome, man." Kelly gave him a high-five.

"Good job, Graham," Donovan added, not that his approval mattered a tenth of what Kelly's did.

"I also said something to Mia today." Graham didn't seem as excited about that as he did the test.

Kelly flopped down on the couch like she owned the place. "Oh, my gosh, how did that go? Please tell me it went okay. You don't look devastated, so I feel like it didn't go badly. Did it go badly?"

Donovan loved that when she got so anxious she talked too much instead of giving someone a chance to ease her mind.

Graham sat down next to her. "I told her that she needed to decide. Either she wants to be my friend or she doesn't."

"What did she say?"

"She tried to act like she had no idea what I was talking about. She said she's always been my friend. She didn't understand why I thought she wasn't."

Kelly shifted her body so she was facing him. "Did you tell her?"

"I said she sure doesn't act like it when

certain people are around. When it's just us, she's cool. When we're not alone, she acts like she doesn't even know me. I'm not an idiot. I know she's afraid to tell them we're friends."

"Good for you. What did she say?"

"She just said she had no idea what I was talking about. I said we will see. I told her I'd be sure to point it out when she ignores me next."

"You handled yourself perfectly. You didn't attack her. You stayed cool. You let her know you want to be her friend if she wants to be yours. You left the ball in her court. Hopefully, she comes through for you."

"Who are you guys talking about?" Donovan asked, trying to get back into the loop. They had said a name earlier, but he hadn't been paying attention.

Graham clearly hadn't planned on letting his uncle be part of this conversation. "It doesn't matter."

Kelly shot him a disapproving look. "A name isn't going to kill you. He's not going to do anything. He just wants to know who we're talking about."

"Her name is Mia," he said to Donovan. "I don't know how that helps you understand what is going on. You don't know who she is."

Feeling a bit defensive, he replied, "Neither does Kelly."

"Okay, let's not start this. The good news is the chem test went well. Mia has a chance to step up and be a real friend. And your uncle and I are going to a concert in an hour, so I need to get ready. No one wants to see me looking like this." Kelly waved a hand around her face, which looked just fine to Donovan.

Kelly went to get ready, Graham disappeared back upstairs and Donovan started dinner. At five o'clock Avery came skipping in like she hadn't a care in the world.

"Hi, Uncle Donovan."

"Hello, my favorite little one. How was your day?"

"It was good." She pushed up on her tiptoes to see what he was making. "My teacher said I am a nice friend to my friends. And she laughed at my joke about why the kids crossed the playground."

"Why did the kids cross the playground?"

"To get to the other *slide*!" she said with a giggle. "Get it? Slide. The other slide."

Avery never failed to brighten his day. "Hilarious. High-five for being funny and nice. That makes me very proud."

Her smile lit up her whole face as she

jumped up and high-fived him. "Where's Kelly?"

The fact that she assumed Kelly would be there gave him pause. Donovan had lost sight of all his personal boundaries when it came to Kelly. "She's getting ready in the bathroom. I have to take her to a concert tonight."

"I'm going to say hi," Avery said, scurrying off to find her favorite person in the world.

A few minutes later, Donovan could hear Kelly say, "I don't think pigtails is the right look for tonight, but thank you. You are very sweet for trying to help."

The two of them came into the kitchen, where Donovan almost had dinner ready. "Hey, Avery, why don't you help me by getting four forks and knives out and set on the table?"

Instead of being high on the back of her head, Kelly's ponytail was pulled together at the nape of her neck and her hair was draped over one shoulder. Her makeup had been reapplied with a heavier hand, making those blue eyes even more stunning.

She sat on the stool by the island. "I'm pretty sure that I've eaten more home-cooked meals here in the last week than I have in the last year at my own place."

Donovan set the dinner plates with a clatter. “I wonder how much longer your uncle will want me on this assignment if there’s no more contact by the stalker.”

“He has been quiet since you came on the scene.”

“I’m wondering if my presence has spooked this guy or if you getting the cops involved in general has helped. I’m just not sure that if I backed off, he wouldn’t reappear.”

“Probably should try it and see, don’t you think?” Kelly picked up the napkins on the island and set one next to each plate.

His experience said they should try backing off her security detail, but Donovan’s imagination ran wild with all the possible things that could happen to her if he wasn’t there to keep her safe, making it much harder to walk away.

“I’ll talk to your uncle tomorrow.”

“Or you could talk to me. We could decide.” Kelly’s voice was rife with indignation. “My uncle doesn’t run my life. He’s not the boss of me.”

“Well, he *is* the boss of me. Or did you forget?”

“I didn’t forget. Maybe we should both talk to him in the morning.”

Donovan called Graham down for dinner and the four of them sat and ate, sharing tidbits of their days with one another. Kelly and Graham laughed rather convincingly at Avery's slide joke. After dinner, Donovan followed Kelly to the auditorium.

Working backstage at the show was easy. Everyone there was way more interested in the band than they were Kelly. He led her through crowded hallways and opened doors for her. With the threat level so low, Donovan could relax. Her professional responsibilities were done as soon as she finished announcing the band to the crowd.

"I have two seats to the show… You want to stay with me for a little bit and have a listen?" she asked him when she got offstage.

"You're the boss. If you want to stay, I am obligated to stay with you."

There was a glimmer in her eyes. "Getting to have my own way is pretty irresistible. You sure you're okay with staying?"

He wasn't a huge country music fan, but seeing her have a good time might be entertaining enough. "Whatever you want."

Kelly wanted to stay for a couple of songs. Once they settled into their seats, it almost felt like they were out on a date. Feeling that way may have been more dangerous than any stalker. Dating wasn't part of any of Donovan's plans. Avery and Graham had to be his first priority, but Kelly's smile was bright and she sang adorably off tune. She wasn't making it easy on him.

Kelly sidled up to him and put her mouth close to his ear. "I'm ready to go. Follow me home?"

Donovan nodded as his heart crashed against his ribs. She smelled like the flowers at the farmers market. He was relieved that they had driven separately so she couldn't cloud his judgment any longer.

"I had fun tonight," she said once they made it back to her apartment building.

All he needed to do was get her into her apartment and he'd be able to go home and clear his head. "I'm glad."

She quirked a brow. "Did *you* have any fun?"

He clasped his hands behind his back and avoided her eyes. "It wasn't terrible."

"It wasn't terrible? Jonah Vincent is Grace Note Records' next big thing. Believe you me."

"He's got a great voice. Much better than some people who were singing along..."

Kelly's eyes widened. "Are you calling me a bad singer?"

"Do you hear yourself when you sing at those things?"

Her mouth fell open and she swatted his chest. He could only laugh at her.

The elevator doors opened and Kelly bumped him with her hip to get out first. “You are mean,” she said, turning around to face him as she walked backward toward her apartment.

“Honest. I think the word you’re looking for is honest.”

“Well, not all of us can be great at everything. I am not a great cook. I am not a very good singer. This may be true,” she said. “But I am…”

“Kind,” he finished for her. “Beautiful. Compassionate.”

Her expression serious, she came to a stop in front of her apartment. Her cheeks flushed red. “Thank you.”

“I’m just being honest,” he replied. If he was truly honest, he’d have to admit he cared about her a great deal. She was someone he wanted to be around and not because it meant getting off desk duty.

“You want to open your door?” he asked after she stood staring at him wordlessly for a few seconds.

Kelly snapped out of it and unlocked her door.

The moment he walked into the apartment, the hairs on the back of his neck stood straight up. “Get back in the corridor,” he said to Kelly, who had followed him in. They’d had so many days of nothing to worry about, she had been joining him in the apartment before he completed his walk-through.

Something immediately felt off. Even in the dark, he could tell it wasn’t right. It didn’t even smell the way it should. For the first time while handling Kelly’s protection detail, Donovan wished he had his service weapon. He flicked on the lights and his fears came to life.

“What’s the matter?” Kelly said from the hall.

Donovan didn’t bother going any farther without backup. He pulled out his phone. “I’m guessing you did not leave rose petals on the floor before you left for work this morning.”

The color drained from Kelly’s face. “What? No.”

He was already dialing 9-1-1. “We have a huge problem.”

# *CHAPTER THIRTEEN*

KELLY USUALLY HATED watching the action from the sidelines. This time, however, she was happy to be safely away from the problem.

"The door was locked?" one of the investigating officers asked.

Kelly closed her eyes and visualized putting the key in the lock and turning it. She nodded. It had absolutely been locked.

She looked at Donovan. "How could he have gotten into a locked apartment?"

"Who else has a key to your apartment?" Donovan said instead of answering her question.

"It's a short list," Kelly said. "Me and my uncle Hal are the only two people on it. Unless you want to count Aunt Laura, too. But her key is the same as Uncle Hal's."

What if the man had been in there when she had been? Could he have been hiding while she got ready this morning? She shivered with fear. She couldn't think that way if she was going to hold herself together.

"You can't stay here," Donovan said. "Do you want me to grab you some things?"

She shook her head. "Can I pack my own bag?"

"You okay, Kelly?" Trey Parker from down the hall held his Jack Russell terrier in his arms after what looked like a late-night bathroom break. Trey was always asking to borrow things like a cup of sugar or a couple of dryer sheets. Kelly suspected his requests were always more excuses to talk to her than anything else.

"I'm okay, but someone broke into my apartment tonight."

"Tonight? Oh, my gosh. That's terrible. I always considered this building as being super safe."

She thought so, too. Until tonight.

"Have you been home most of the night?" Donovan asked.

Trey shifted his hold on the dog. "Yeah, I've been home since around five. Took Killer out for a walk right away, so I was gone for about twenty minutes. I didn't hear anything or see anyone, though. I'm so sorry this happened to you, Kelly. If you need anything, don't forget I'm right here." He nodded toward his door. "Don't hesitate to stop by."

"Thanks, Trey."

Donovan placed his arm around her shoulder. "Thanks, Trey."

Did he really think Trey could be a suspect? She thought about the way that he always seemed to show up in the building's gym whenever she did. How he asked about things that she had said on the radio like he listened to her every day all day. Her unease didn't dissipate when Trey went inside his own apartment.

"It would be helpful if she could look around and tell us if anything is missing or was moved around," the other officer said to Donovan.

Kelly sighed, frustrated that they were acting like she wasn't standing right there. She didn't need Donovan's permission and he knew it.

"Come on inside and have a look around and grab a couple days' worth of stuff," he said, his voice controlled and even. Everything she wasn't. Kelly felt anything but in control.

Her heart hammered in her chest as she stepped into her home. Nothing seemed out of place in the living room. There were rose petals all the way across the room and down the hall to the bedroom. Her stomach rolled. Had he planned to wait for her but something happened?

The petals went into her bedroom and ended in a heart on the floor in front of her bed. Again, nothing looked out of place, but she had never felt so violated before. He had been in her room. A person's bedroom was their sanctuary. Their private space. The thought of some stranger being in there without her permission, able to go through her things, made her tremble.

None of her jewelry was missing. She opened her dresser drawers and everything was still folded and seemed in its place. Nothing noticeable was missing from her closet. In her bathroom, she thought it looked like things were in place until she realized her perfume was missing. So was her bottle of shampoo from inside her shower. Bile rose in her throat. She was afraid she was going to be sick.

She reported what was missing and quickly grabbed what she needed. Donovan stayed by her side the whole time. She wished his presence had provided her with more courage than it did.

"Are you sure you've got what you need to last you a couple days?"

Kelly wasn't coming back here in a couple days. The fear she felt right now made her want to move tonight. How could she ever sleep soundly in that bed, in that room, in that whole apartment?

"I've got plenty." What she needed was to get out of there.

"Do you want to call your uncle or should I?" Donovan asked. "We should call him before we show up at his door."

"I'm not going to Uncle Hal's. If this guy can find me here, he can find me there. It wouldn't be hard to figure out he's related to me." If it was Trey, he knew she had an uncle in the area. They had talked about things like her holiday plans before. There was only one place she would feel safe. "Can I go home with you? I know that it's a lot to ask, but no one I suspect knows who you are."

Donovan remained stone-faced as he mulled it over. She knew she was making a big ask. Maybe too big. He had children at his house. Clearly, Kelly didn't want any harm to come to Avery or Graham.

She was about to tell him to forget it, to take her to a hotel when he said, "Let's go."

"Are you sure?"

"I can't think of anywhere else you could go where you'll feel safe and I'll trust you're safe."

"Thank you and I'm sorry." She felt so guilty for putting him out.

Donovan's cool and calm demeanor began to crumble. "Don't apologize. You didn't ask for this." He clenched his fists as they walked to the elevator. "I am going to find this guy. He doesn't get to do this to you. This is not okay."

Kelly's bottom lip began to tremble. She reached for his hand, hoping the contact would calm them both down. He unclenched his fist and let her thread her fingers in between his. She held on to his hand all the way down to the ground level and to his truck.

The gravity of what happened tonight sank in during the drive and the tears began to fall. "I'm scared," she admitted.

His gaze flicked to her and he put his hand on top of hers. "I will *not* let anyone hurt you."

"Sending me stuff was one thing. Going into my apartment, my home? That's a different level of wrong."

"I will find him," Donovan said without any doubt.

Kelly let his words ease some of the anxiety, which was why she wanted to stay with him. If there was one thing she knew about him, it was that he never did anything halfway. Donovan took care of business. If he said he was going to find the stalker, Kelly believed him.

When they got to the house, it was after nine. The hope was Avery was in bed, so they would only have to explain the situation to Graham. Thankfully, the house was dark except for the light on in Graham's room.

"We should call Captain Bonner."

Kelly dreaded this call because it meant she would also have to call her mother, who would most definitely be in the car on her way to Nashville to bring Kelly back to Knoxville thirty seconds after she heard the news.

"Can we tell him in the morning?"

Donovan's thumb hovered over the contact number on his phone. "I won't have a job in the morning if I wait to tell him something this important."

"How about I call my mom and you call my uncle?" She wasn't looking forward to either call, but it was best if her mom heard what was happening from her rather than Uncle Hal. She dialed her mom and waited for her to pick up.

"Kelly Renee, since when do you call your mother two weeks in a row?"

Kelly inhaled slowly to try to keep her voice from cracking. "Hey, Mom."

"What's wrong?"

All her plans to hold it together crumbled with that one simple question. The tears were back and Kelly fell apart as she explained what had happened. All the fear and the anxiety poured out.

"Oh, sweetheart. Are you with Hal and Laura?"

Kelly sniffled. "I'm staying with a friend. It feels safer to stay somewhere no one would think to look for me."

"Your uncle is a police captain. There is nowhere safer than under his roof."

Of course her mother would disagree. Kelly kicked off her shoes and sat down on Donovan's couch. "I feel safe where I am, Mom. My friend is a detective in Uncle Hal's department."

She took a second and then said, "Fine. Do you want me to come to Nashville? I have some days I could take off."

"No, don't waste your vacation days on me. I'll be fine. I just needed to let all of my emotions out. I feel better now."

"I'm going to call Hal and see what he thinks."

Kelly didn't know why she bothered having an opinion. It wasn't as if it mattered.

"He's on the phone with Donovan." Kelly looked over her shoulder at Donovan pacing back and forth in the foyer as he filled Hal in on what happened.

"Donovan? That's the detective?" When Kelly confirmed, she continued, "And his wife is okay with you staying there?"

Not very subtle. "There's no wife, Mom, but he is the legal guardian of his niece and nephew. This is where I feel the safest. You and Uncle Hal are not going to change my mind." She looked back at her host. Hopefully, Uncle Hal wouldn't be able to change Donovan's.

Thankfully, her mom didn't try to sway her again. They said their goodbyes and Kelly promised to call her in the morning. After hanging up, Kelly noticed Donovan was missing. He wasn't in the foyer or the kitchen.

She got off the couch and went looking for him, hoping she could stay there. She found him in the upstairs hall whispering with Graham and holding a pillow and some bedding.

"Hey, are you okay?" Graham asked. "I can't believe what happened."

"I'm totally fine. I'm sorry if you heard me falling apart down there. I didn't mean to let my emotions get the best of me like that."

Graham stepped around Donovan and gave her a hug. "I'm glad you're here. Uncle Donovan won't let anything happen to you."

She loved that he had so much confidence in his uncle. Graham could give Donovan a hard time, but he knew his uncle was a good man.

"I put your bag in my room," Donovan said. "Let me change the sheets and then I'll be out of your way."

"No way," Kelly said, putting her foot down. "I am not taking your room. I'm sleeping on the couch. Don't even try to fight me for it."

"I'm not going to fight you, but I'm also not letting you sleep on the couch."

"And I'm not letting you let me sleep in your bed." Before he could argue, she ran back downstairs and claimed the couch.

THERE WAS STUBBORN and there was Kelly Bonner. She was stubborn on steroids. Donovan followed her downstairs and found her lying on the couch looking at her phone. He placed the pillow and a blanket on the floor in front of her.

"I know you think you're not imposing by doing this, but you're actually making this more difficult for me by refusing to sleep where I planned for you to sleep."

Kelly sat up. "I don't want to sleep in your bed. I know you think that it's the polite thing to do for a guest, but it will make me uncomfortable to be in your room. Especially since I am here because some creep was in my room."

Donovan dropped into the chair across from her. He scrubbed his face with his hand. It had been a long day. He understood it had been a long, hard day for her, as well. "I get that. I just want you to be comfortable."

"I'll be most comfortable right here." Kelly pulled the hair tie out of her hair and shook it out. "I really appreciate that you're letting me stay here. I'm sure my uncle had other ideas. Do I need to call him?"

"He wanted to come get you, but I convinced him that it might be best to stay here tonight and we could talk about things in the morning." He had a few other things to say, but Kelly didn't need to hear it. After hearing her on the phone with her mom, crying about what had happened, he wanted to protect her from anything that would make her upset.

"So I have a reprieve until the morning?"

She bent over and picked up the pillow and blanket. "Is it weird that I feel exhausted and yet totally wired at the same time?"

"It's weird but understandable. Your body is still experiencing some of the flight-or-fight aftereffects." He was suffering from the same thing. Part of the reason he wanted her upstairs was because he knew he couldn't sleep. His mind was whirling and all he wanted to do was find the person who had broken into Kelly's place and made her feel this way.

"Thank you again for taking me in. I truly don't think I would have felt safe anywhere else."

Donovan felt his heart clench. He was glad to be there for her but sorry the situation called for it. He stood up, needing to move. "I'll run up and get your bag. You can sleep down here for tonight. Tomorrow is another story, though."

"My feelings about taking over your space are not going to change overnight," she replied as he headed for the stairs.

"Oh, I'm not talking about my room. If you stay another night, Avery's going to insist on a sleepover in her room, and you know by now, when Avery really wants something, she usually gets it."

Kelly's head dropped in defeat. She had

to know there was no telling Avery thanks but no thanks. Tomorrow, if Captain Bonner thought it was best for her to stay here, Kelly could be rooming with Avery until her stalker was arrested.

THE NEXT MORNING, Donovan awoke to the smell of bacon and the sound of his smoke detector going off. He leaped out of bed and found Graham and Avery rubbing the sleep from their eyes in the hallway. He ran downstairs. Kelly stood under the detector with a dish towel, waving the towel like mad.

"I'm so sorry. I don't know what happened. I thought you'd be so impressed if I made something on my own and, of course, I messed up."

Donovan opened the window above the kitchen sink in an attempt at getting some fresh air in the place. A large pan of bacon and another pan of scrambled eggs sat on the stove. There was a plate of some cooked bacon on the counter, but what was in the pan was "extra crispy."

He grabbed another towel and helped her fan the detector until it stopped beeping. Kelly looked so defeated. She sat down at the kitchen table with tears in her eyes.

"Hey, it happens to the best of us. Bacon is

not easy. It looks like you did great with the first batch," he said, trying to cheer her up.

"Kelly! How did you get here?" Avery said, running over to her and hugging her tight.

"I bet it's going to taste good," Graham said, sitting down next to her.

Kelly took a napkin from the holder on the table and dabbed her eyes. She had the whole table set for breakfast. "I was trying to do something nice for you guys for letting me stay here. I knew I would mess it up."

"You stayed here?" Avery was rightly confused.

"Kelly had to stay at our house last night. She can't stay at her apartment for a few days," Donovan explained.

"You can stay in my room! I have two beds." Avery had a trundle bed, so there was another twin mattress for Kelly to sleep on. Donovan had warned her that Avery would be all over that when she found out she was here.

"That's very sweet of you, Avery." Kelly gave the little girl another squeeze.

Donovan checked on the food one more time. "I think plenty of this is salvageable. Who wants some bacon and eggs?"

Both kids raised their hands and said, "Me!"

"You guys don't have to eat it. It's probably terrible. I should have run out and got doughnuts instead."

"I love doughnuts," Avery said unable to turn off her honesty.

"These eggs are going to be great," Donovan said, bringing the eggs over and spooning some on each plate. "Maybe we'll get doughnuts tomorrow morning. Doughnuts taste best on the weekend."

Graham got up and brought over the bacon that wasn't burnt. "Does anyone want some orange juice?" he asked, being more helpful than Donovan had expected.

"I do!" Avery said, peeling herself off Kelly and taking the seat next to her.

Everyone got settled in and breakfast was served. Donovan quickly made some toast. The kids tried very hard to be complimentary. The eggs were a tad overdone but still palatable. The bacon that wasn't burned was just right. All in all, it was a perfectly acceptable meal.

"Thanks for breakfast, Kelly," Graham said, standing up but swiping one more slice of buttered toast. "I'm gonna get ready for school."

Kelly smiled. It was good to see her relaxed. "You're welcome."

"I can clean up if you want to use my bathroom to get ready," Donovan offered to Kelly.

She pushed her chair back from the table and started to get up. "I should clean up. I made this mess."

"No," he insisted. "Please let me take care of it."

Avery and Kelly went upstairs together, leaving Donovan alone to do something with the mess. He hadn't gotten a lot of sleep last night. He had gone over everything they knew about Kelly's stalker and came up with some questions to ask her about who might have had access to her apartment. The guy needed to be found and needed to be found now.

Graham came back downstairs and dropped his backpack on the kitchen table.

"I haven't wiped that down yet," Donovan warned.

Graham picked it back up and set it at his feet. "Is there any way the guy stalking Kelly could find her here? Would he come here to get her?"

Donovan could hear the worry in Graham's voice. It wasn't only worry for Kelly but for all of them. He tried to be reassuring. "It would be very difficult for someone to find her here unless they followed us, and

I am very aware of who is around us at all times. No one is going to follow me without me knowing about it."

Graham nodded his head. "I hope you find this guy before he finds her. You're going to find him, right?"

His anxiety was palpable and Donovan was hit with a cold bucket of guilt. Graham and Avery were attached to Kelly and now Kelly was at risk. Surely, Graham was thinking worst-case scenario. If something was to happen to her, these kids would be devastated.

"Don't worry. I have complete faith in the police. They are going to find him. It's my job to make sure no one lays a hand on her, and I am very good at my job."

Graham nodded again but didn't seem fully convinced.

"The only thing you need to be thinking about is how to survive these last couple days of school. Finals are coming up. You have to stay focused."

With eyes rolling, Graham let out a sigh. "I won't worry about Kelly if you don't worry about my finals, how about that?"

"I'll worry about everything because I'm the adult in charge. You and your sister are my responsibility and protecting Kelly is my job. Your only job is school."

Graham shoved his earbuds into his ears. “You can’t tell me not to care about what happens to her. I can’t just pretend it doesn’t matter.”

“I’m not telling you not to care. I’m telling you to trust me.”

Slinging his backpack over his shoulder, Graham turned his back on Donovan and headed for the front door. “I trusted the grown-ups to make my mom better and look at how that worked out for me.”

He’d been waiting for the kids to throw that back at him. Nothing had been harder when his sister was sick than trying to balance giving the kids hope with being realistic. Jessica had struggled with it, as well. She wanted to believe she could beat it but did everything she could to prepare Donovan for the possibility she wouldn’t.

After all that planning, Donovan still messed up. He was letting the kids get close to someone in danger. If anything happened to Kelly, not only would he be devastated but so would the kids.

## *CHAPTER FOURTEEN*

"I UNDERSTAND THAT it's not my jurisdiction. All I am asking for is some information." Uncle Hal was fired up. His face was red and his tone sharp. He looked like Kelly felt—tired, frustrated and ready for this to be over. "Yes, she has an off-duty detective from my division providing her with some personal security. You can relay anything to him that you think would be helpful for us to know."

Kelly glanced over at Donovan, who had been quiet since breakfast. He was probably regretting being this deeply involved in someone else's problem. She began to question if she should go to her uncle's instead of bothering Donovan. He had a family to take care of and she, even when trying to be helpful, was just one more problem for him to fix.

Uncle Hal hung up the phone and pinched the bridge of his nose. "I have never been so frustrated with another house. These guys act like I'm trying to take over. All I want is some information. I want to know what they've found out, which by the way, is nothing."

"I'm sure they need to ask Kelly some more questions. At this point, she's the only one who could shed some light," Donovan said.

Defensive, Kelly clasped her hands so they would stop shaking. "Ask me anything you want. I don't know who this guy is. I have no idea how he could have gotten into my apartment."

"Relax, sweetheart," Uncle Hal said. "We don't think you're holding something back. It's possible you know something without realizing it. You could have information that connects some of the dots."

"Was there ever a time when you gave your house key or a spare key to a neighbor or a friend?" Donovan asked. "Anyone other than your uncle? Trey?"

"I don't think so." She racked her brain for an instance where she would have asked someone to go to her apartment for her. "Definitely not Trey."

"Someone at work, another neighbor when you went out of town, a friend who needed to borrow something," Donovan said, trying to jar her memory. "Maybe you needed someone to grab something for you when you couldn't.

Maybe you forgot something at home and you had to be on the air."

Finally, one of his suggestions struck a chord. "There was one time, but it was probably over a year ago. I was flying to Mexico right after my show and I forgot my passport. I asked our intern at the time to go get it for me."

"Do you remember who that was?"

"His name was Lucas. I don't remember his last name. Interns are only at the station for less than a year usually."

"Do you remember Lucas having any interest in you beyond learning about being on the radio? Did he try to spend time with you?"

Kelly tried to remember what Lucas even looked like. She didn't remember him being overly enamored with her. "I don't remember anything like that. I just remember asking him if he could go get my passport and giving him my key fob to get in the building and my key to get in my apartment. He brought me the passport and I made my flight."

Donovan jotted down a few notes. "Anyone else come to mind?"

Under pressure, Kelly couldn't think of anyone else. She shook her head.

"This is a good start. If you think of anything or anyone who would have had access to your keys, let me know."

"Are we sure they had keys?"

"There were no signs of forced entry. Nothing was damaged. I doubt you left your door unlocked," Uncle Hal said.

That was somehow scarier than if someone had simply broken in. If they had a key, they were close enough to her to get it and they could have had access to her apartment for who knew how long. If it was Lucas, he could have had access for over a year.

"Are you sure you're okay staying with Detective Walsh? You know there's a place for you at my house," her uncle asked.

Kelly glanced at Donovan for his reaction. His face was frozen in concentration as he wrote things down in his notebook. "I don't want to be a bother to anyone. Should I get a hotel room?"

"No," Donovan and her uncle replied at the same time.

"At a hotel, you have people coming and going all the time. It would be harder for me to have someone watch over you," Uncle Hal explained.

"It's fine if you stay with me," Donovan said. "Knowing where you are all the time makes things easier on me."

Then it was settled. She would stay at Donovan's until she could have some reassurance that no one could get into her apartment again.

They called the landlord about getting the locks changed. He didn't think they could get it done until Monday. Uncle Hal offered to have someone go in and sweep the whole place for any recording devices the stalker may have left behind. That was something she hadn't even considered until he mentioned it and agreed to let him do it.

Donovan drove her to work and all she could think about was that someone could have put cameras in her apartment. How could she feel safe there? The answer was she couldn't.

"I need to find a new place to live. The landlord can fix the door lock and Hal can tell me there are no bugs or video cameras hidden in my vents, but I am never going to feel completely safe, and isn't that what home should be? Your safe haven from everything else going on in the world."

"We're going to find this guy," Donovan said with confidence. "Eventually, he's going to show himself. He wants to be with you, so he's going to step out of the shadows at some point. I will be there when he does and that will be the end of it."

As much as Kelly liked being independent, having someone looking out for her right now felt better than it ever had. Maybe it was because of who was doing the looking. "I hope you're right. Until then, I guess we have lots of time for you to teach me how to knock this guy out if he ever steps out of the shadows and you aren't around."

Donovan cracked a half smile. "There's the Kelly Bonner I've come to know. You've got this. No one messes with you."

That little vote of confidence did her wonders as they got to the station. They pulled into the parking garage and Donovan parked his truck. "Thank you," she said as they walked to the elevator.

"You don't have to thank me. This is my job, remember?"

"It's not your job to house me and teach me how to protect myself. It really isn't even your job to be my bodyguard. I know my uncle is stretching the rules by having you do this instead of making you sit at your desk all day."

"Well, see? Then I should be thanking you because there is nothing worse than being stuck at a desk all day. It's like caging a lion, cruel and unusual punishment."

He placed his hand on her lower back and ushered her through the doors of the elevator. The physical contact made her stomach do a flip. When he was close like this, she couldn't help but wonder what it would be like to let him wrap his arms around her and hold her tight, the way Avery did this morning or Graham did last night.

He took her by the hand, concern emanating from his eyes. "Are you okay?"

She stared down at their connection, wishing she didn't like it so much. He had just said this was nothing more than a job to him. But these kinds of gestures gave her hope that maybe he was willing to let there be something more to what was happening between them. She was definitely softening to the idea.

"I'm fine. Just thinking about how awesome your kids are. They both made me feel like I wasn't a weird stranger coming into their home. When Graham gave me a hug last night, I thought I might totally lose it. That was so sweet of him."

"He is a really sensitive kid under all that attitude. He's very empathetic. Strongly takes after my sister on that one."

"I think I would have liked your sister."

"You would have." He pressed his lips together and stared up at the ceiling. "I think she would have liked you, too."

Kelly felt like Jessica's blessing would have meant a lot to Donovan. "Maybe we could pick Avery up after school and bring both kids to the farmers market this afternoon. They could help pass out promo stuff for the station. We could grab dinner there—my treat."

Donovan let go of her hand and the elevator doors opened to their floor. She wasn't sure if she had overstepped some boundary or not. He exited and waited for her to follow. "My sister would like you as a person, but she would be concerned about there being any mixed messages about our relationship. It's not good for the kids to think that this is something that will go on after this stalker is gone."

From butterflies in her stomach to a good punch in the gut. Kelly felt like a fool for thinking that maybe there was a possibility of something more. "Right. Of course. I don't want to confuse them. I just thought they might like to see how you're helping me with my job."

Donovan's jaw was still tense, but he nodded. "I see what you're saying. It could be good for them to see this is work, not personal. Let's do it."

Not personal. Kelly needed to remember that.

WHO WAS DONOVAN KIDDING? He was keeping things between him and Kelly about as professional as a carnival worker who let pretty girls on the rides for free. This relationship definitely had one foot in personal and the other in professional.

He needed to refocus his attention on the work side of things. The other detectives would be looking into people like Trey, the neighbor who apparently had some intense interest in Kelly, and Hunter, the delivery guy who might have been amping things up after the jealousy trap Donovan had set early in the week. Donovan was going to check out Lucas. The best place to start to get more information about someone who worked there was his favorite receptionist who never forgot a face.

"Juliette, I need your help this morning," he said, leaning against her desk.

"For you, anything."

"Last year, you guys had an intern named Lucas. What do you remember about him?"

Juliette thought about it for less than a second. "Lucas Kimball. He was from Franklin. His parents are friends with Caroline. Nice kid but didn't think he had to do as much as everyone else would have liked because his family was friends with the boss."

"He was a slacker?" The fact that he wasn't eager to help like the current intern made his supposed willingness to go out of his way to get Kelly's passport suspect.

"Always tried to get out of things. Never wanted to work on the weekends unless he was getting free tickets to some show."

"Do you remember if he seemed more willing to help some people over others? Particularly, do you know if he was interested in Kelly at all?"

Juliette took a little longer to think that one over. "Honestly, I don't remember that. I mean, a lot of people are quickly won over by Kelly. She's beautiful inside and out. Makes it easy to want to be around her."

Wasn't that the truth? Donovan experienced it firsthand. He would probably do anything she wanted him to do because disappointing her seemed wrong.

"Any chance you remember him having to help her get her passport before she went on a trip to Mexico?" he asked, hoping she had a tiny bit more insight.

Juliette shook her head. "I don't know anything about that. Maybe Lyle would remember. Lucas used to irk Lyle the most."

Although not exactly what Donovan wanted to hear, having another lead was better than a dead end. Juliette also gave him a lot of little details that helped. Lucas was quite possibly nearby. Franklin was not too far away. He was familiar with the station, so perhaps that was why he had sent all of the gifts there.

Juliette let Donovan head in to find Lyle. He found him and Kelly's friend Nancy in Kelly's office. There were several bunched-up tissues on Kelly's desk and her eyes were red. There must have been more tears when she told her friends what had happened.

"Everything okay?"

Kelly seemed embarrassed that he caught her crying and wiped her face with her hand. "I'm fine. I think I get myself worked up when I talk about it. What's going on with you?"

"I got some good info about our friend Lucas from Juliette."

"Lucas as in Lucas the intern?" Lyle's displeasure was clear. "Do you think he had something to do with this?"

"What do you remember about him?" Donovan asked.

"He was a whiner who thought he deserved special treatment because Mommy and Daddy were friends with Caroline. He did about one tenth of what Trish does around here."

"I don't remember that. I mean, I remember the part about him being friends with Caroline, but I don't remember him giving me a hard time if I asked him to do something," Kelly said.

"Oh, come on," Nancy said, joining the discussion. "Remember how I asked him to help set up the conference room for a meeting with the executives and he told me that he couldn't because Caroline told him he looked a little tired and he should take a break. His break lasted the rest of the day."

Kelly laughed. "Maybe. I sort of remember something about that. I thought he was helpful to me but maybe that's because what stands out the most was him running to my place to get my passport so I didn't miss Gina's wedding in Cancun."

"He went to your apartment?" Lyle seemed concerned.

"I needed someone to go while I was on air. I had to leave for the airport right after work. I had to run to my terminal and was the last person on the plane as it was."

Lyle shifted in his seat and looked up at Donovan. "So, it could be him. He knows where she lives. He had access to her keys. I never liked that guy."

Being lazy was not exactly a strong trait for a stalker. "What do you two remember about how he acted around Kelly? Did he seem to have a fascination with her? Did he flirt or treat her differently than anyone else around here?"

"I just remember him being such a pain. I don't recall him being flirtatious with anyone," Nancy said.

"He used to come around your office, Kelly, to waste time. I remember finding him in here when he was supposed to be somewhere else," Lyle said in contrast.

Kelly shook her head. "I don't remember that. Was I in here when he was in here? If he's stalking me, maybe he liked to snoop around."

Lyle shook his head. "You were in here. He was talking and acting like Mr. Know-It-All."

"I'm going to pass his name along to the detectives in charge. They can talk to him, get him to account for his whereabouts last night. Is there anyone else around here, past or present, who stands out to either of you as someone who might have an unhealthy fascination with Kelly?"

"Everyone loves Kelly," Nancy said, smiling at her friend.

"Everyone loves you," Kelly said back.

"Yeah, right," Nancy said with a laugh. "Kelly looks like she should be on television, not radio. She has a ton of fans, but no one stands out as being as creepy as this guy."

"If you think of anyone, let me know. I can have the detectives interview anyone we think is suspicious."

"Thanks for looking into things," Kelly said as Donovan moved to leave.

"It's my job, remember?"

Her smile faded and she nodded. "I remember."

Donovan needed to contact the detectives in charge, but he had left his notebook with all of his notes from this morning in his truck. He headed down to the garage, passing the valet station as he went.

"You're that guy who's always with Kelly Bonner, right?" The same guy from yesterday was working. He raked a hand through his hair.

"Miller, right?"

The young man seemed a bit taken back by the fact that Donovan knew his name. "Yeah.

Did something happen to Kelly's car again? I noticed she didn't drive today."

"No, nothing happened to her car. I drove her to work this morning."

Donovan's phone rang. It was one of the detectives in charge of Kelly's case. He apologized and explained to Miller that he needed to take the call.

"Detective Walsh? This is Detective Hermann. How's it going?"

"It's been a wild night and morning," Donovan said.

"We're going to need to interview Ms. Bonner, but I can't get ahold of her."

"She's about to go on-air. She won't be available until three o'clock."

"That's fine. We can stop by then. Did she end up going to her uncle's last night?"

"No, Kelly spent the night at my place. She'll be staying with me indefinitely. She's not feeling real safe at her place."

"Well, I don't blame her for not wanting to stay in that apartment. Does she have any ideas who could have gotten their hands on her key? We have a call in to the landlord and plan to talk to him face-to-face today."

"You might want to check in with a guy named Lucas Kimball. He was an intern at the station last year. Had access to the key and knows where she lives."

Hermann didn't want to look into Kimball until they spoke with Kelly. Donovan didn't understand why they had to waste time and ask the same questions he'd just asked, but this wasn't his case.

"We'll see you at three?" Donovan asked to confirm.

"Around then," Hermann answered. He was annoyingly noncommittal.

"She needs to be at the farmers market at four. If you don't get here by three, you'll have to go there."

"Thanks for the heads-up," Hermann said before letting Donovan go.

These guys were not making this case their priority. They could have a lot going on. He couldn't judge; there could be more pressing cases. Donovan was simply frustrated that he had all the time in the world but couldn't do anything about it.

He sat in his truck and spent the next little while on his phone, searching for Lucas Kimball. He had a Facebook account, Twitter and Instagram. He didn't post regularly and mostly posted memes about sports and dogs.

Scrolling through his Instagram, Donovan saw that he did post a bunch when he was working at the station. There were two pictures of Kelly. The first one was of her at some event and he was more focused on the event in the caption than Kelly. The second picture was more concerning. It was a candid shot of her. He had zoomed in on her face and she didn't seem aware that she was being photographed. His caption for the photo was, "Most beautiful DJ in Nashville" and tagged her. The photo had over five thousand likes.

Donovan took a screenshot of the picture and caption to show to the detectives. It wasn't much, but it was something. He felt this enormous pressure to solve this case. To give Kelly some reprieve from her worry. It would also help rid him of his obligation to her. He could cut ties and go back to the way things were.

Once Kelly had finished her time on the radio, Donovan went inside to be with her when the detectives interviewed her. When he walked into the lobby, Juliette looked relieved to see him.

"Detective! Finally. Where have you been?"

Donovan's stomach dropped. "What happened?"

"The delivery guy—he was here. He had a note for Kelly. I couldn't stall him. He wouldn't stay."

"Give me the note." Anger with himself flashed through his body. If only he had come back inside instead of sitting in his truck.

Juliette handed him the folded piece of paper. "No envelope?" he asked. She shook her head. Donovan read the note.

*I tried to do something nice for you and you ruined it by bringing that man home. I don't know what you're thinking or why you won't give me a chance to prove to you that we belong together. I don't know why you want to hurt me. You've always been so kind. Do you want to hurt me, Kelly? Because if you do, I might hurt you back.*

There was no signature. Just the threat. Donovan had to restrain himself from tearing it to shreds. It was evidence. The guy knew Donovan brought her home last night. He didn't know Donovan came to the radio station or else he wouldn't have risked delivering the note. Given Juliette's description of his mannerisms, it had to be the stalker who gave Juliette this note. That much Donovan knew for sure.

## *CHAPTER FIFTEEN*

KELLY WRUNG HER hands in her lap. The man had been here, according to Donovan. He had walked into the station office and handed Juliette a note. A note that said he was going to hurt her if she hurt him. All Kelly wanted to do was hide out at Donovan's until someone caught this guy.

"Do you have any questions for us?" Detective Hermann asked. He and his partner were waiting for her when she got off-air.

"Not that I can think of," she answered. She had a bunch of questions, only not for them. She needed to talk to Donovan alone.

"Is there anything we should be doing to keep Kelly safe?" Caroline asked. She had joined the discussion with the detectives after hearing about what happened. Her concern was appreciated.

"She's got private security. You could have visitors and delivery people sign in as an extra layer of office security."

"She's supposed to represent the station at

the farmers market tonight. Should she do that?"

Kelly didn't want Caroline to think she couldn't do her job. "It's fine, Caroline. Like they said, I have private security."

"We aren't going to tell Miss Bonner where she can go," the detective answered.

Caroline nodded.

They walked the detectives out and Kelly checked her watch. She was due at the farmers market in a few minutes. Luckily, Trish and Lyle agreed to go and set up. Donovan wore a grim expression.

"Thanks for your concern, Caroline."

Caroline placed a hand on Kelly's shoulder. "No one messes with my employees. Plus, think of the terrible press we'd get if something were to happen to you."

Not surprising, she seemed more concerned about the ramifications for the station than about Kelly's well-being. Compassion didn't come easy for everyone.

Caroline went back to her office and Donovan rubbed the back of his neck. "I'm sorry," he said. "I should have been up here. If I had been, we would have him in custody."

She couldn't blame him. Who would have expected this guy to show up today? At least they knew it wasn't Lucas Kimball or Hunter the delivery guy. Juliette would have recognized them.

"I'm going to remember," Juliette said when they walked out to leave. She was frustrated with herself, as well. She couldn't place where she had seen the man before, but she had seen him somewhere other than in the lobby.

Kelly tried to ease her guilt. "I'm sure it will come to you. Don't beat yourself up. I'm safe. It will be okay."

Juliette came out from behind her desk and gave Kelly a hug. "You are the best. I am sorry you have to deal with all this."

Kelly squeezed her back, knowing she had said all that more to convince herself than Juliette. She let go and walked out with Donovan.

"I get it if you're mad," he said as he pressed the button in the elevator.

"I'm not mad at you. I wish this was all over. Maybe it would have been if you had been there and maybe it wouldn't. Who knows?"

She couldn't dwell on it or she was going to start crying again. Part of her wanted to get on the radio and call this guy out. Tell him to show himself or go away. She was done with these games and threats.

"Are we still going to bring the kids to the market?" she asked, fearing he would cancel their plans because of what happened.

"I'm not sure if we should."

"Are you worried he's coming after me? Hasn't he always been coming after me?"

Donovan nodded. "You're right. Nothing has really changed. He fluctuates between being in love with you and being angry with you for being with someone else. He's consistent with being inconsistent."

They stopped at the house and got Graham, who claimed he was only coming because of the food. After picking him up, they stopped by the after-school program to get Avery, who was thrilled to be going out with Kelly.

"Okay, you two, I need your help," she said to the kids when they got to the K104 booth. "We have to pass out all these fun prizes. We have these flashlight key chains and some can cozies."

"What is this?" Avery asked, holding up a little pouch.

"Those are earbuds. We also have these tiny Bluetooth speakers. Cool, huh?"

"And lame pens? Some people only win a pen?" Graham asked, giving the wheel of prizes a spin of his own.

"They can't all be awesome prizes. It would

take the fun out of it. They could win a chance to be entered in the draw for tickets to see Boone Williams and Piper Starling or they could win a lame pen. There's risk."

"Can I win tickets?" Graham asked.

Donovan shook his head. "You win tickets from me when you make it through the last couple weeks of school without getting in trouble."

"You're going to go see Boone Williams after you almost attacked him at the restaurant?" Lyle asked Donovan.

Graham looked mortified. "You almost attacked Boone Williams?"

"I wasn't going to attack him," Donovan said defensively. "I was asking him what he was doing there."

"That's so embarrassing." Graham covered his face with his hands. "What if he remembers you when Kelly introduces us backstage? Can you not come with us? Can we go with Kelly and you stay somewhere else?"

Kelly tried to hold back a giggle. She felt Graham's pain. "I promise I will not let your uncle embarrass you. Boone will think you are cool, don't worry."

A couple holding hands walked by and Avery encouraged them to come over and spin the wheel. She was quite the little salesperson. The man won a flashlight key chain and the woman won the earbuds.

Trish took Graham under her wing and showed him how the sound system worked so they could broadcast K104 over their speakers. Lyle pulled Kelly aside. "I'm rethinking my decision to go get drinks with Trish after this."

"Why?" As much as Kelly loved Nancy because she was her best friend, it was hard to find anything wrong with Trish.

"I've been standing here, watching her chat it up with Graham, and I realized something very weird—they are closer in age to each other than she and I are."

Kelly's hand covered her open mouth. He was right. There were many more than seven years between Lyle and Trish. "I don't know what to tell you. That is weird. You're not wrong."

"I can't do it. All I've been thinking about for the last twenty-four hours is that I'm going out to dinner with Nancy tomorrow."

He was really looking forward to that and it made Kelly's heart happy. "I think you should do what feels right. If going out with Trish feels weird, don't do it."

Lyle looked relieved. Getting permission to listen to his heart was exactly what he needed. Kelly glanced in Donovan's direction and her heart felt like it was doing double Dutch in her chest. Why did her heart think it needed Donovan? Didn't it get the memo that he wasn't interested? That didn't stop it from reacting to the very sight of him.

He had crouched down to talk to Avery. His sunglasses hid those hazel eyes that were full of so much warmth. Maybe that was a good thing. If she couldn't see them, they couldn't affect her. When he interacted with Avery, though, it didn't matter if she could see his eyes or not. Witnessing the sweetness of the two of them together turned her insides into jelly.

"Graham?" A teenage girl came over to the booth. She had curly, golden-brown hair that was pinned up in the front.

He struggled to play it cool. It was obvious who this girl was. "Hey, Mia."

"Do you work at K104?"

"No, I don't work there. I'm friends with Kelly Bonner," he said, motioning in Kelly's direction.

"Hi. Mia, is it?" she asked, pretending she had no idea who she was.

"I'm Avery, Graham's sister. Want to spin the wheel and win a prize. You would win a chance to win tickets to come to the concert with us. We're going to meet Piper Starling!"

Mia was definitely impressed. "You get to meet Piper Starling?"

"And Boone Williams," Graham added. "Probably Sawyer Stratton, too."

"Shut up." Mia looked like she might pass out. "I am in love with Sawyer Stratton."

"Why don't you spin the wheel and see what happens?" Kelly led her over to the wheel of prizes.

Mia tucked some hair behind her ear and glanced over at Graham. He wished her luck. She spun it and it landed on the pen. Kelly knew Graham wasn't going to be okay with his friend only winning a lame pen.

"You won this incredible K104 pen," Kelly said, waving her hand in front of it like they did on game shows. "But if you choose to give us back the pen, you can have another spin."

Without hesitation, Mia chose to spin again. "Avery, can you help me? I feel like you might have better luck than me."

Avery would have spun the wheel for everyone if they asked. She spun it so hard and fast it took forever for it to slow to a stop. Graham looked at Kelly like she could make it stop. He smiled at Mia, who smiled back even though the whole thing was awkward. Finally, it stopped right on the concert draw.

"You did it, Avery!" Mia said, giving her a high-five. Avery beamed up at the teenager.

Trish handed her a raffle ticket. "Put your contact information right here and you are entered in the draw we're going to have before we leave at six. You don't have to be present to win. We'll call you if you do."

Mia filled it out and shoved her hands in her jean pockets. "Can Graham walk around with me for a little bit?"

Graham glanced at Donovan, who was barely paying attention to what was happening at the booth and more focused on surveying the crowd. "What? Can you go walking around with your friend?"

"May I?" Graham asked, his eyes begging him to say yes.

"Go ahead," Donovan said, making Graham the happiest teenager in all of Nashville. "But be back before six."

"We'll be back for the draw," Mia said.

"Can I go, too?" Avery asked, eager to be like the older kids.

Kelly interrupted to keep her out of Graham's hair. "I need you here to help me. Who is going to pass out prizes if I don't have you?

And don't say that your uncle can do it because he has other jobs to do."

Graham mouthed *"thank you"* when Avery wasn't paying attention. Mia thanked Kelly for the chance to win and off they went. Kelly could only hope that this meant she had considered her options and chosen to be Graham's friend all the time and not only when it was convenient for her.

"WELL, THAT SHOULD be interesting." Donovan came up behind Kelly. He wasn't sure if letting Graham go off on his own was a good idea or not, but Mia came across as a good kid. He just hoped she wouldn't break Graham's heart.

The market seemed busier this week in comparison to last. It was also possible that all that had happened over the last couple of days was making him more on edge. Donovan found himself staring down every man who walked by, waiting for him to announce he was Kelly's stalker. As if that was how it would go down when it happened for real.

"I was really hoping it was Lucas. I would have loved to see you wrestle that guy to the ground and haul him off to jail," Lyle said, coming to stand by him.

"You really disliked that guy, huh?"

"He was a terrible intern. I also don't like people who take advantage of their friendships, and he acted like being friends with Caroline made him something above reproach. People like that deserve to get knocked down a peg. People like Kelly, who are humble and hardworking, they earn my respect."

"You are an excellent judge of character. If I ever have to arrest Lucas Kimball, I will make sure to tackle him to the ground."

Lyle chuckled. "Perfect."

"I feel like I owe you another apology for what happened last week when I thought you were attacking Kelly."

"You don't have to apologize for that," Lyle said. "You were trying to keep her safe and I can't fault you for that."

Donovan nodded and held out his hand. Lyle shook hands and went back to helping Kelly greet people walking by their booth. Avery was having the time of her life helping out. She was such a people person that getting to be a part of this was like putting a sugar addict into a candy store. She would be exhausted when all this was over and ready for bed.

Kelly was also in her element. She had a wonderful way with people. She could engage anyone no matter their age, gender or background. It was impressive to watch her interact with listeners. If her boss needed proof that she was a draw for the station, she only needed to come to one of these events to see it live and in person.

When there was a lull in the activity, Kelly came over to Donovan. "I need to draw a winner for the tickets to the show. Do you think Graham will be mad at me if I don't pick Mia to win?"

"Mad at you?"

"Do you think he's expecting me to pick her name? Rig it in her favor?"

Donovan felt bad that she had put that pressure on herself. "He would never ask you to cheat and please don't feel like you have to do that to make him happy. He'll be happy when he gets to the concert. He'll get over whether his friend comes, too, or not."

"I hope he's having fun. This is the girl."

He smiled, finding it funny that she wasn't sure he had picked up on that. "Yeah, I figured that much out."

"If she wins and then hurts Graham, her tickets will get lost in the mail."

Donovan's eyes went wide. "Wow, you

won't cheat to make him happy, but you'll happily wield your power to get revenge."

Her grin was wide. "What can I say? I am very protective of the people in my circle."

He tried to make sense of how her words made him feel. As much as he appreciated that she had Graham's back, he wasn't sure what that meant for everyone in the long run. Once Donovan found this stalker, what kind of relationship could they even have with Kelly? Maybe she could come over for dinner every once in a while? What would happen when she met someone? How would she explain why she hangs out with some guy and his two kids?

Graham and Mia returned just in time for the draw. Graham was smiling, which was a good sign. Kelly definitely noticed. She announced that they would be picking the winner and called Avery over to be the one to draw the name. Avery pulled out one of the slips and handed it to Kelly.

"The winner of two tickets to the Grace Note Records Concert for the Kids is…Mia Harris!"

Mia immediately turned and hugged Graham. She had won fair and square. Donovan could see that Kelly was a little wary about celebrating this as a win for Graham, too. There was no guarantee this girl wouldn't break his heart down the road. Tickets or no tickets, she was still a teenager and teenagers were fickle.

"Trish and I will take all the stuff back to the station," Lyle said to Kelly. "You have had a rough twenty-four hours. You need to go and have a good weekend. Starting now."

"Are you sure about that? I can help box things up at least. I have six extra hands to help."

"Don't stop putting the kids to work now," Donovan chimed in.

"Um, let's not stop the nice man from letting us go get dinner, especially since some of us are starving," Graham said.

Avery raised her hand. "I'm starving."

"Please don't let the children starve," Lyle said. "Go get some food and I'll see you on Monday."

"Everyone say thank you to Lyle and Trish," Kelly said to the kids.

They were more than happy to do that before begging to go get food. Donovan had adopted two of the hungriest children in the world. They seriously couldn't go more than a few hours without filling their bellies.

"Mia, would you like to come with us to get some dinner?" Kelly offered. She was paying, after all.

"Oh, my parents are here. They own a bakery that sells pies in a booth over on the other side of the market. I told them I would be back after the draw for the tickets."

"Well, congratulations on winning the tickets," Kelly said. "Maybe we'll see you at the show."

"That would be cool. Thanks. You folks have a good night. Bye, Graham."

"See you on Monday," Graham replied.

Donovan had so many questions but knew Graham was unlikely to answer any of them if they came from him. He could only hope Kelly would ask a few while they were all together so he could hear the answers.

They walked to the Market House to get dinner. The kids wanted pasta while Donovan and Kelly opted for wood-fired pizzas. They sat around a table like at home and shared about their days. Kelly was careful not to mention any of the bad stuff. She told the kids that the highlight of her day was being at the farmers market with them.

Avery shared a long story about what she learned during math today. They got to use manipulatives and Todd Gregory shoved one up his nose and had to go to the nurse's office. The nurse couldn't get it out so his mom had to come to school to get him so they could take him to the hospital, where a doctor was probably going to stick giant tweezers up his nose to get the cube out.

As riveting as that story was, Donovan wanted to hear about Graham's adventures with Mia, the pie girl. Thankfully, Kelly came through.

She led with, "Mia seemed nice."

"She was nice today. We weren't around anyone we knew, though," Graham said, sounding more skeptical than Donovan expected.

"But it's a good sign that she wanted to be friends since you gave her the ultimatum." Kelly's optimism was helpful.

Graham shrugged. "I guess. Can we talk about it when we get home and not around…" He glanced around the table.

Donovan pretended he was only talking about Avery. He liked to think Graham would let him hear the rest of the story as long as he stayed quiet and just listened.

"Can we get ice cream?" Avery asked before she even finished her dinner.

"If you eat all of your noodles," Donovan

said. "What do you guys say to Kelly for buying you dinner?"

"Thank you," they both said at the same time.

"You're welcome. You have fed me and given me a place to sleep. I feel like I'm just paying you back."

"You're our family," Avery said. "You don't have to pay us back."

"Yeah, you're our family," Graham said. "Right, Uncle Donovan?"

This was Donovan's chance to set them straight. To reestablish the boundaries and make it clear where Kelly fit in their lives. He wanted to say she was nothing but a friend. Barely a friend. A temporary fixture in their lives.

But he was kidding himself if he thought they would believe that to be true. Kelly had found her way into the hearts of these kids and there was nothing he could do to change that. The only person who needed to think about how he felt was Donovan.

Kelly's phone rang and she answered it. "Whoa, slow down. What happened? Oh, no. Listen, he didn't want you to find out. No, he wasn't trying to play you. I knew about it, but—"

Whoever that was apparently hung up. “What’s going on?”

“Any chance you can drive me to the station? I need to clean up a little mess.”

## *CHAPTER SIXTEEN*

IN ALL THE years they had known each other, Nancy had never hung up on Kelly before. She understood why she was mad, but if Kelly could explain, she would see that she was simply trying to be a good friend to both her and Lyle.

"Why don't you take the kids home and I'll text you if I need you to come get me or maybe I can convince one of them to bring me back to your house," she said when she got out of Donovan's truck.

"I don't know how I feel about that."

"No one is going to be looking for me here at this time of night. Plus, I'm going to be with Nancy and Lyle. It's fine, I promise. Avery needs to get home and in bed."

Donovan couldn't deny the little girl was wiped out. He agreed to take the kids home and come back. It was a compromise.

Kelly ran to the elevator and prayed her friends wouldn't give up on each other before they even gave it a chance. Nancy had somehow found out that Lyle had agreed to get drinks with Trish even though he had decided not to go in the end.

How everything had unraveled was a mystery since Nancy hung up on her and Lyle wasn't responding to any of her texts other than to say she'd better come help him fix this mess.

"What happened?" she asked when she found Lyle in his office.

"I told Trish I couldn't get drinks with her and for some reason she took that as a major brush-off and decided to complain to *Nancy*. Does the woman not have any friends she could talk to about me that aren't the woman I wanted to date in the first place?"

"Where is Nancy now?"

"Last I saw her, she was in the staff lounge. I told you this was what would happen if I said yes to both of them. You have to help me sort this out or I am pretty sure I'm destined to die alone."

The drama was high at K104. "You aren't going to die alone. Once she knows what happened, she'll be fine." At least Kelly hoped so. Nancy had been so jealous of Trish in the beginning. Hearing that Lyle had accepted a date with her before accepting a date with him probably had her all tied up in knots.

Kelly went to check the staff lounge, but no one was in there. The station was much quieter this time of day. The night deejays didn't have as much help producing their shows. Nancy had to be somewhere. She checked her office, but found her coming out of the ladies' room.

"I am not talking to you. You should leave," Nancy said, pointing toward the exit.

"I'm not leaving." Kelly hooked arms with her friend and dragged her toward her office. "Come talk to me."

"Why should I talk to you when you haven't been talking to me?"

Lesson learned. Kelly could not allow herself to be put in the middle of two friends. No matter her good intentions, her words and actions could always be misconstrued. She unlocked her office door and pulled Nancy inside.

"You are my friend, but Lyle is also my friend."

"I am your best friend. That should trump all other friendships," Nancy argued.

"Explain to me why you're mad. Because I didn't tell you that Trish asked him out before you asked him out?"

Nancy held her head in her hands. "How about because you told him that he should go out with her if he wanted to instead of being loyal to me and telling him to remember that he thought he liked me."

Kelly sighed. Leave it to Lyle to rat her out when he was confronted by Nancy. "He does like you. Why do you think he told Trish he didn't want to go out for drinks tonight? He's been so excited about going to dinner with you tomorrow that he couldn't even pretend to be interested in going out with Trish."

"That does make me feel a little bit better. And worse because she was really upset about it. She likes him a lot, or so it seems."

They should all be feeling sorry for Trish. She innocently asked Lyle out, not knowing he had feelings for Nancy, the same day Nancy decided to give Lyle a chance. Lucky for her, she was young and beautiful. She'd be single only as long as she wanted to be.

Kelly picked up the phone and dialed Lyle. When he answered, she told him to come to her office. There was no reason for her to still be playing middle man for these two.

Lyle stubbornly stood in the doorway even though she asked him to sit down.

"You know, all of this could have been avoided if you two were brave enough to tell each other how you feel instead of telling me and asking me to play your messenger. Lyle, you need to tell Nancy how you feel about her. If you think this is a woman you want to have a relationship with, you have to be able to trust that you can tell her how you feel and she's going to be kind and compassionate in return. And, Nancy, you need to be honest with Lyle about how you feel because he can't guess when you change your mind or realize that you've been having feelings all along. If he's someone you want to have a relationship with, shouldn't you be able to trust that he's going to understand?"

The two of them were staring at the ground. Lyle lifted his head and so did Nancy until their gazes met.

"I'm so sorry for agreeing to go on a date with Trish when the only person I want to date is you," Lyle said. "I did it because I was afraid that if I turned her down, I would turn everyone down who isn't you. I thought I didn't have any chance with you."

Nancy cleared her throat. "I'm sorry for freaking out when you did nothing wrong. You have every right to go out with anyone you want to go out with. I think I was mad that I might miss out on a great guy because I was too scared to admit that I had feelings for you when I heard you had feelings for me."

"See? Isn't that better than saying these

things to me?" Kelly stood up and pulled Lyle into the room and out of the doorway. "You two keep talking and I will see you on Monday. I love you both and I can't think of two people more perfect for each other. But what do I know? I've only been right about everyone else I thought that about."

"Oh, my gosh. She's so obnoxious about that, isn't she?" Nancy said to Lyle.

"I know. She loves to take credit for the weirdest things. Does it really make her a matchmaker if she only *thinks* two people would be perfect together and then they actually get together no thanks to her?"

"Right? And I would bet there are people she thought would get along who never got together. She doesn't remember those because nothing ever happened beyond her thinking they would make a cute couple."

"That probably happens all the time," Lyle said, nodding his head like Nancy had made some huge discovery.

"I'm still standing right here. I can hear everything you two are saying about me. You know that, right?"

The two of them burst into laughter. At least they had found common ground about something even if it was to roast Kelly. She could take it as long as they would all be friends in the end.

She left them to discuss where they wanted things to go, moving forward, and texted Donovan that she was ready to be picked up. He texted back that he was already outside. He had dropped her off, run the kids home and come straight back to the station. She was beginning to think this was more than just a job to him. Maybe he cared about her.

Tonight at dinner, the kids told her she was part of the family, but Donovan said nothing. At first, she was hurt, thinking his hesitation meant he did not feel that way at all. Now, she wondered if he had been scared to admit that maybe he felt more connected to her than he wanted to admit.

It was time for Kelly to take her own advice. She needed to be honest with herself in regard to how she felt about Donovan and then she needed to tell him. If he was someone she wanted to have a relationship with, she needed to trust him to listen to what she had to say and be honest back.

Fear crept up her neck and left her a bit unsettled. There was a possibility that if she laid it all on the line, he could say he wasn't interested at all and that would hurt. But even though she might lose, she wouldn't gain anything if she didn't try.

DONOVAN WAITED IMPATIENTLY for Kelly to come out of the building. He didn't like the idea of her being in there unguarded. Not when the stalker had been there earlier today. Relief flooded his body when she stepped outside. He unlocked the door so she could get in.

"Did you solve all the world's problems?" he asked.

"Not the world's, but maybe Lyle's and Nancy's. They needed a little push to actually talk to each other about how they're feeling."

"Talking about feelings is overrated. A lot of time can be wasted worrying about how everyone feels."

Kelly cocked her head. "Are you serious?"

"As a heart attack."

"A lot of time can be wasted when people don't talk about feelings. Misunderstandings abound. People get hurt unnecessarily because they assume things instead of being up front."

"People get their feelings hurt whether they talk about it or not."

"You sound like someone who is afraid of

what they feel or maybe what other people feel."

Donovan was offended. He wasn't afraid. He simply had more important things to worry about than how he felt about this person or that. Or how they felt about him. He had kids to take care of and a stalker to catch.

"I'm not afraid."

"You're important to me. I like being around you. I like being around your family. I'm terrified because I hate that you're a cop because I grew up in a house full of them. I swore to myself that I would never date one, but I care what you think and I sometimes wonder what it would feel like to kiss you," she said, dropping bomb after bomb without any warning.

Donovan was so thrown by what she said he had to slam on the brakes to avoid hitting the car in front of him. Kelly braced herself by putting her hands on the dashboard. His heart raced and all of his senses were heightened.

"Still not afraid?"

He shifted his gaze from the car he almost rammed to her pretty blue eyes. That didn't help his heart slow down. He wasn't afraid of her or how she felt about him. At least he tried to tell himself he wasn't.

"I don't know what you want me to do with all that information."

"I want to know how you feel. Even though you think feelings are stupid, I want to know what yours are."

This was where Donovan always failed. He wasn't good at sharing his feelings. Kelly might have thought he was good at everything, but this was his Achilles' heel.

"I don't know what I feel. I'm not thinking about my feelings. I'm thinking about catching this guy who wants to hurt you. I'm thinking about how Graham needs to do well on his finals so he can pass his classes this semester. I'm thinking about how I have to take Avery to the dentist next week. Worrying about how I feel is a luxury I can't afford right now."

"Ignoring how you feel doesn't make it go away. How you feel about me and how you feel about what I just said impacts everything you do. You can't hide from it. Just tell me."

Donovan didn't know what she wanted to hear him say. He didn't have a laundry list of feelings like she did. Was she important to him? Sure. It was his job to serve and protect. If someone was in danger, it was important to protect them. Did he like being around her? Sure. She was a nice person. Nice people were pleasant to be around. Did he think about kissing her? He didn't try to think about it. Had he ever thought about it? He had and it caused this strange sensation in his chest. It started in the center and emanated outward. It made him uncomfortable. Uncomfortable wasn't how he wanted to feel.

"I want to help you," he offered.

"I know you want to help me, but how do you feel about me?"

She was relentless.

Donovan turned onto his street and pulled into his driveway. There was only one way to prove that these feelings didn't matter. He got out of the truck and walked around to her side. He opened her door and helped her out. He had her somewhat trapped between his body and the truck. He would move if she asked him, but she was silent.

"I'm going to kiss you to prove there's nothing going on," he warned her, waiting for her to protest. She didn't. Her lips slightly parted and she stared deep into his eyes, making it hard to breathe.

He leaned down and pressed his lips to hers. Softly, gently. Convincing himself that this made him feel nothing was hard to do when it made him feel so much. His whole body felt like it was on fire and she was both the flame and the balm that would take away all the pain. His hand cupped her cheek and he tilted her face upward so he could deepen the kiss just a bit. Her arms snaked around his neck and held him in place.

The whole world dropped away and there was nothing but Kelly and this feeling—this feeling he couldn't begin to label. All he knew was he loved it and hated it at the same time. He wanted to push her away and pull her closer. Nothing made sense. Instead of giving him clarity, he felt more confused than ever.

She pulled away first, breathing heavy and staring up at him like he was the most important thing in the world. "Nothing?" she asked. "Because that didn't feel like nothing to me."

He kissed her again because he wasn't ready to talk about it. She didn't seem to mind his avoidance of the subject. The only problem was he couldn't stand out here forever in his driveway, making out instead of admitting he was wrong. She brushed the back of her fingers against his cheek and he decided they could stay a little bit longer. He felt like a cat getting a scratch behind the ear. She made him want to arch his back but simultaneously beg for more. Man, she was confusing him.

When she pulled back a second time, the

smirk on her face left him a tiny bit annoyed. She wouldn't break her stare. It made him want to kiss her again because he knew they'd both close their eyes.

"You like me. Just admit it."

He sighed and broke their gaze. "Fine, I like you. Are you happy now?"

"I know it's messy and we're not even close to being ready to handle this. But it is what it is. I can't pretend I don't feel it."

At least she was being honest about what a disaster this was. He didn't even know where to go with these feelings. Saying it out loud didn't exactly make anything better and the way the kissing made him feel only added to his confusion. Being vulnerable made him want to crawl out of his skin, but kissing felt better than he expected.

"We can't do this in front of the kids," he said. "I don't even know what to call this. I certainly don't want the kids trying to make sense of it. Until I know, we need to protect them from being misled into thinking we're going to live happily-ever-after."

Kelly took a deep breath and nodded her head. "I respect that. I won't let you kiss me when they're around."

"You won't let me? You act like it was all me and you had no say."

She held out her hands, palms up. "I didn't kiss you. You kissed me both times. I was standing here, minding my own business and you attacked me with those lips."

"Attacked you?" He put his hands on her waist and she squirmed, giggling. He pulled her flush against him and he kissed her one more time. Nothing about this made sense.

The kids were going to start to wonder what was taking them so long. Since Graham had heard what happened today at the station, he didn't want him to worry unnecessarily.

He broke the kiss this time. "We need to go inside. Graham will be worried something's happened to you."

She nodded and pressed her lips together, like that would stop him from going after them again. They walked toward the house and she reached for his hand.

"In the interest of transparency, I need you to be aware that I kind of hate you for being such a good kisser. It makes it about a thousand times harder for me not to think about it," she said as they climbed onto the porch. "Thanks for that."

"Yeah, well, that makes two of us," he said, tugging her closer.

"I am completely in love with those kids. I

need you to know that I would never do anything that would bring harm to them."

He believed that more than anything else. They were both very much on the same page about Graham and Avery.

When they got inside, both kids were upstairs. The lights were off in the family room, but someone had lit a bunch of candles. Romantic music was coming from the TV. A bowl of ice cream with two spoons sat on the coffee table. There was a note that said: *Here's some ice cream for you guys since you didn't get any at the market. Enjoy!*

Graham had done some work to put all this together. Donovan was actually shocked that the teen had come up with this on his own. He usually had such a self-centric way of looking at the world.

"I think someone might be trying to set us up," Kelly said, setting down the note.

"Graham!" Donovan shouted from the bottom of the stairs.

He shuffled out to the top of the stairs. "What?" he whisper-yelled.

"Come down here, please."

"Seriously? You really know how to kill a mood." He trudged down. "What?"

"I appreciate what you're trying to accomplish here. I know you like having Kelly around, but I need you to let me do my job and figure out things outside of that on my own."

"Avery and I both approve. We both like her. You don't have to worry about us."

"I'm fully aware of how much you two like her. I understand that I have your full blessing, but can you please let me and Kelly decide how we want to proceed." Donovan wasn't sure how to explain adult relationships. "I need you to understand that there are no guarantees that this ends up with us being one big, happy family. I don't want you getting your or your sister's hopes up."

"Why do you have to make this so complicated?"

Donovan didn't make things complicated. Whenever he was in a relationship, they ended because he tended to keep things too simple. He never let himself get deep enough to let it get complicated.

"You are making it complicated by lighting candles and turning off lights. Let the grown-ups handle the grown-up relationships."

Graham turned on his heel and marched back upstairs. "I told Mia you would probably mess this all up."

Graham had talked to Mia about Donovan and Kelly? What else did Mia know?

"No one is messing anything up," he called up after him. Maybe he was. Donovan had been outside kissing her a minute ago and now was trying to convince his nephew there was nothing going on. With the kids involved, he was deeper than he'd ever been.

Back in the family room, Kelly had her feet up on the coffee table and the bowl of ice cream in her lap. She spooned some ice cream into her mouth and didn't say a word about the conversation she most definitely overheard.

"Whatever this is—I am totally going to mess it up," he said, taking a seat next to her.

She handed him the other spoon and held the bowl of ice cream in between them. "Well, if you don't, I will. So..."

Now they had two things in common. They both would not be able to stop thinking about kissing and they were sure one or both of them would ruin everything.

It would be interesting to see who would wreck it first.

## *CHAPTER SEVENTEEN*

IT HAD BEEN a very long time since Kelly had slept on a twin-size mattress on the floor. Probably not since college. It was as uncomfortable now as it was then. It was highly unlikely that Avery would understand if Kelly went back to the couch, though.

"Are you awake?" Avery whispered in the dark.

Kelly was sure it could not be time to wake up yet. She lay still, hoping Avery would fall back asleep.

"Kelly?" No such luck.

"Avery, it's not time to get up yet."

"Why not? You're awake. I'm awake. We can get up and make pancakes."

Kelly had no intention of trying to cook in this house unsupervised again. One smoke detector fiasco was enough.

"Let's wait until your uncle is awake. I bet his pancakes are way better than mine."

"He's awake. I heard him go downstairs."

Kelly propped herself up on her elbows

and scanned the floor around her bed for her phone. It was just after five in the morning on a Saturday. There was no reason anyone needed to be up this early on a Saturday unless they were a first responder or they delivered babies. No one else was needed.

"Are you sure it was your uncle?"

"I think so."

Kelly rolled out of her bed and onto the floor, army-crawling to the door. Her body resisted as she pulled herself up to her feet. It was way too early for this, but it made her nervous that Donovan was up. Maybe there was news about the stalker.

"Maybe he went to get us doughnuts!" Avery hopped out of bed and bounced all the way over to Kelly like a carefree bunny. "Remember he said he would get doughnuts this weekend?"

Doughnuts was reasonable at this unreasonable time of day. "Let's go check."

The door made a noisy creak when she opened it. Avery would never be able to sneak in and out of this room when she was older. The two of them padded downstairs in search of Donovan. No one was on the first level, either.

"See, he went to get doughnuts," Avery said, gripping the hem of Kelly's sleep shirt.

The sound of metal clacking on metal came from the basement. He was working out? They followed the noise down the second set of stairs.

Donovan was in the basement wearing shorts and a tank top. He had dumbbells in each hand and he lifted them parallel to the floor or until his arms were even with his shoulders. The muscles in his biceps and shoulders bulged under the strain.

Strength and power emanated from him. Donovan didn't just look like he was in the military, he looked like he could take on an army. Watching him made her feel like she had a superhero for a bodyguard.

"Are we getting doughnuts for breakfast?" Avery said, scaring Donovan half to death. He dropped one of the weights as he spun around and clutched his chest.

"How long have you two been standing there?"

"Only for a minute," Kelly said, hoping he didn't think she was a creeper.

"You said we could have doughnuts today, remember?" Avery persisted.

"Let's leave your uncle alone to finish his workout and then we can talk about breakfast." Kelly grabbed Avery by the hand and tugged her gently up the stairs. "Sorry for bothering you."

"I'm really hungry for doughnuts now," Avery complained.

"Let's go back to bed until the sun comes up." She tried to get Avery to follow her back to her room. Kelly stopped halfway up the stairs. "Come on, Avery. It's too early."

"Did someone say they were hungry for doughnuts?" Donovan's voice came out of the darkness.

"Me!" Avery squealed.

"We can go back to bed for a little bit. You can finish your workout."

"Or we can get doughnuts," Avery suggested. "Can I go with you?"

"Why don't we all go? Run upstairs and get dressed."

Avery sprinted past her. Donovan stopped one step below Kelly so their faces were even.

"Sorry," she said again. "She's an extremely early riser and, since she's my roommate, she makes me one, too."

"Did you sleep okay?"

"Yeah," she lied. "Did you?"

"I tossed and turned because I can't turn off my brain," he admitted. "That's why I got up and tried to work out. Thought maybe I needed some physical activity to calm my mind down."

"Why do I feel like I'm responsible for the overthinking?"

He reached up and tucked her hair behind her ear and cupped her cheek. "Probably because you were."

Even in the shadows of the early morning, she could see that warmth in his eyes. She put her hands on his shoulders and gave a little squeeze to reduce some of the tension there.

"If it makes you feel any better, thoughts of you kept me up for a while, as well."

His thumb brushed across her cheek, sending a shiver down her spine. She stared at his lips, remembering how nice it was to kiss him yesterday. She had been imagining it for so many days, she had worried the actual kissing wouldn't live up to the fantasy, but thankfully she had been so very wrong.

"We are really good at torturing each other," he said.

All Kelly wanted to do was kiss him again. She closed her eyes and prepared for takeoff.

"I'm ready! Let's go!" Avery came racing by, causing them to jump apart. "Why aren't you ready? I'm hungry."

Kelly marched up the stairs and slipped into Avery's room. She pressed her back against the door and caught her breath. As much as she wanted to be here, he wasn't wrong about the torture.

She changed into some shorts and a T-shirt and brushed her hair into a ponytail. Nothing fancy needed for an early-morning doughnut run. She opened the door to find Donovan in the hall.

She held up her toothbrush. "I'm going to brush my teeth and use the bathroom. Are you going to wake up Graham to see if he wants to come with us?"

"Are you serious? Have you ever tried to wake a teenager before dawn on a weekend? Not only do you risk your life by doing that, if you do survive, it makes them extremely irritable the rest of the day."

"I vote we let him sleep. We can bring him back a couple of his favorites for later."

"Much better idea," he said with a wink.

Kelly finished her morning routine quickly, knowing Avery's patience was running thin.

She found the two of them waiting for her by the front door. "Come on, Kelly. I've starving."

"How can such a little girl eat so much?" Kelly asked, giving Avery's side a tickle.

She giggled. "I don't know. My belly just growls."

Donovan opened the door and held it open for the ladies. "Your carriage awaits, princess."

They took off for the doughnut shop. Donovan swore the best doughnuts could only be found at Three Sisters Donuts. It was owned by three actual sisters who loved different flavor combinations and unusual toppings.

It was an adorable little shop with a country farmhouse theme. The menu was written in pastel-colored chalk on chalkboards hanging on the wall behind the counter. At least two dozen varieties of doughnuts filled the display cases.

"I want the one with the Froot Loops!" Avery said, her face practically pressed against the glass.

"If you like chocolate, those white chocolate brownie doughnuts are pretty amazing." Donovan came up behind her and reached around her to point at some delicious-looking goodies.

"I think we need to get all of them and do a taste test to determine the best."

"All of them?"

Kelly turned around to face him. "You're not going to make me choose, are you?"

"How does someone so small eat so much?" he asked with a smirk.

"My belly just growls. I need all the doughnuts. Except the jelly-filled. I am not a jelly fan."

"What? Strawberry jelly doughnuts are delicious."

"If you're an old man."

"Wrong. Old men eat plain doughnuts dunked in black coffee."

Kelly made a face. "That's so gross."

"The things you learn about a person when you go doughnut shopping," Donovan said, shaking his head.

As unwilling as he had been about sharing their feelings with one another, once they did, he seemed to lighten a little. She already liked him on a regular day, but silly, doughnut-buying Donovan was almost irresistible.

"We will take one of each except for any jelly-filled or plain doughnuts. My friend here is not a fan," Donovan told the woman behind the counter.

"MY FAVORITE IS the bacon one," Avery said, picking the last piece of bacon off what was left of the maple bacon doughnut they had cut into four pieces.

Donovan figured Graham would either be amused or a bit disturbed to find a quarter each of eighteen different doughnuts when he finally dragged himself out of bed. They had massacred them all so they could each get a taste.

"I am going to have to vote for the s'mores one. I love marshmallow," Kelly said, leaning back and giving her belly a rub. It wasn't growling because it was empty anymore. Now, it probably moaned from being so full.

Donovan hadn't been able to really tell the difference between them after about doughnut number five. They all started to taste sweet and capable of putting him in a sugar-induced coma if he ate one more bite.

"I'm voting for the old-fashioned. Those are the kind I remember eating when I was a kid."

"Back in the olden days?" Kelly teased.

Donovan didn't know how old Kelly was exactly, but he figured she was still in her twenties. At thirty-six, he was probably close to ten years older than she was.

"You know what doughnut your dad would have liked, Avery?"

"Which one?"

Avery had only been three years old when Ollie died, and the majority of those three years, he had been in Afghanistan. She never really knew her father and that made Donovan sad for both of them.

"He would have liked the milk and cookies one because he was obsessed with cookies. Our squad used to call him a cookie monster because he would trade everyone for their cookies at dinner."

"He did?"

"He did. Sometimes he'd eat a whole plate of them for dinner."

Avery laughed like it was the funniest thing she'd ever heard. "I bet Mommy didn't let him do that. She says no dessert until you eat your dinner."

Jess was a stickler about healthy eating habits. She and Ollie were so different, but somehow it worked. They complemented each other because where one was weak, the other was strong.

Avery and Graham were a lot like that. They both had different traits of their mom and dad in them. Avery had her dad's laugh and his love of sugar. Not only did she look like her mom, but she had her compassion and love of family. Graham had his dad's temper and technical skills. From Jess, Graham got his artistic ability and her seriousness.

"Your dad was my kind of man," Kelly said to Avery. "I could have handled making him dinner every night. Open up some Chips Ahoy one night, Oreos the next. Super easy."

"Can we have cookies for dinner tonight?" Avery asked.

"No way, kiddo. You just ate a million grams of sugar for breakfast. I need to make sure your mom doesn't strike me down with some lightning."

"Mommy can make lightning?"

Donovan and Kelly exchanged a look. He knew he had to watch what he said around Avery, but things still slipped out that she took literally.

"No, it's just a saying. Some say that when people do things that make someone in heaven mad, the person in heaven throws some lightning at them."

Avery seemed satisfied with that answer and asked if she could watch some cartoons. Donovan agreed but asked her to keep the volume low so they didn't disturb Graham.

He scooted his chair closer to Kelly's and reached for her hand. "What do you want to do today? I was thinking we could do a little self-defense training."

"I need to find a new place to live." She held his hand in both of hers.

"You're serious about that?"

"I can't go back there. My lease is almost up. I was thinking about actually buying a place once I signed my new contract at work.

When you're in radio, you run the risk of having to move from town to town. A new contract at K104 means I can put down some roots finally."

"Roots are good." He intertwined his fingers with hers and lifted her hand to his lips. "We can fire up my laptop later and search the web for the best house in Nashville to put down roots."

Her smile was crooked and perfect. "You think we'll find the right house if that's what we put in our Google search?"

"Why not?"

She leaned in close and he wanted to kiss her just like he had wanted to kiss her on the stairs earlier that morning.

"Why are you guys up so early?" Graham's voice startled them both.

Donovan pushed away from Kelly. "Your sister wanted doughnuts. We brought some home for you."

"Well, we have some parts of doughnuts for you," Kelly said, flipping open the lids to the boxes. "This one was my favorite, this one is your sister's favorite and your uncle is an eighty-year-old trapped in a thirtysomething's body and this was his favorite."

"I don't know what you're talking about," Donovan said. "I am very young at heart."

Graham narrowed his eyes as he checked out the decimated doughnuts. "Did you guys eat part of every doughnut? How are you not sick from eating all that?"

"We're going to go downstairs and do some self-defense training. One of the moves we're going to learn is how to barf on the guy so he runs away from you," Kelly said.

"Wow. If I'm an eighty-year-old, you're a twelve-year-old in a twentysomething's body."

"Twenty-year-olds think barf is funny," she argued.

"No one thinks barf is funny," Graham countered.

"What?" Kelly dared to look shocked. "Avery, do you think barf is funny?"

"Barfing is gross!" Avery yelled from the couch.

"Not even the seven-year-old thinks it's funny," Donovan said with a laugh.

"You guys need to get a sense of humor."

"Uncle Donovan?" Avery said, running into the kitchen.

"Avery?"

Her little face scrunched up in pain. "I don't feel good. I think I ate too many doughnuts." Before Donovan could respond, she threw up all over him and it was the least funny thing he'd ever experienced.

"I AM SO SORRY. I feel like I jinxed you," Kelly said as they threw some clothes into the washing machine.

"I don't think it was all the talking about barf as much as it was the eighteen pieces of doughnuts she ate. I'm pretty sure the barf was my sister's version of lightning."

"The good news is Avery seems to be feeling better."

Donovan started the wash. "This is what I get for being the fun uncle. From now on, it's fruit and cereal for breakfast only."

"Poor Avery will never forgive herself."

Donovan's laundry room was barely big enough to house the washer and the dryer. They were in very tight quarters and finally alone. He put his hands on her hips and finally got that kiss he had been waiting for. Kelly's hands slid up his arms and rested on his shoulders.

"Why does it feel like we've known each other forever?" he asked when she pulled away.

"It does, doesn't it?"

Less than two weeks and he was attached. Donovan Walsh didn't get attached. He was too logical for that. Yet, here he was in his tiny laundry room, thinking about how he wanted to ask her to forget about buying a house and move in with him and the kids instead.

That thought was actually running through his head. He had lost his mind. Somehow, in just under two weeks, this woman had managed to get him to completely reconsider how he saw the whole world.

"What?" She lightly scratched the back of his neck. "That scares you, doesn't it?"

"It doesn't scare you?"

"I promised myself I would never, ever let myself fall for a police officer. My parents were cops and I was not going to spend the rest of my life living in a house that was run like a police station. You walk into my life with your matter-of-fact attitude about everything and I hate you at first. Then I find out being a cop is one sliver of who you are and that there are all these beautiful facets. You have totally changed the way I think about everything."

"So, yes. You are as terrified as I am?"

"Completely," she said with a laugh.

"I need to find your stalker so we have one less thing to worry about." Donovan kissed her forehead and let her go. "I think we should do something to lure him out into the open. There are a couple things that make me believe you know him. He said you've always been kind. How would he know that if he hadn't met you?"

"I'm nice on the radio."

"Yeah, but being nice on the radio and being kind seem like two different things to me." This is how Donovan had spent his night. Trying to make sense of the little bits of evidence that they had. "I also think he sees you sometimes but not all the time. He knew I was with you at the apartment the other night, but he asked you on the radio if you were wearing the earrings he gave you."

"Do you think he was in the apartment when we showed up and got out before the other cops got there?"

He knew she wasn't going to like his answer. "I don't think he was inside when we got there. I think he watched us go in, though. Maybe it's Trey or maybe it's someone else who lives in your building. You have this tendency to be nice to *everyone*."

"You say that like it's a terrible thing. I need your laptop so I can get a new place and get my niceness away from you," she said, turning to leave.

He pulled her back against him. "I think your niceness is one of your best traits. I also don't know for sure that he lives in your building because if he did, it makes more sense that he would have sent the first few gifts to your apartment. Everything was focused on the radio station to begin with. That makes me think it isn't someone who lives by you. I feel like this guy knows you through the radio."

"Well, I don't live by anyone I work with. At least, I don't know of anyone. Some guy in accounting used to live in my building, but he moved out after he got married. I doubt it was him."

Donovan's head hurt from trying to make sense of clues that added up to practically nothing. He only saw one solution to their problem.

"I think we need to set a trap. I'll have to coordinate with the other detectives, but I think we have you say something on the radio and you invite him somewhere to make amends. If he thinks you want to apologize, he could come into it without any thoughts of doing harm."

Kelly cringed. "I don't like that idea. Lying to trap this guy? I feel like that could backfire. What if he finds out I'm lying?"

Donovan rested his forehead against hers. "I won't let anything happen to you."

Kelly wrapped her arms around his neck and buried her face in the crook of it. He held her tight, hoping she knew how serious he was. No one would lay a finger on her as long as he was around.

"Can I go to Davey's? Whoa, sorry. I didn't know—" Graham was in the doorway one second and gone the next. So much for shielding him from this relationship. Kelly and Donovan untangled themselves and Donovan went after Graham.

"Hey," he said, trying to get his attention as he walked away. "You weren't interrupting. We were talking about the stalker and she got upset and I was trying to console her."

"You call it whatever you want." Graham held his hands up like he was under arrest. "I am not judging. I already told you that Avery and I give you a big thumbs-up when it comes to Kelly."

Donovan was no good at making things less confusing for these kids. He decided there was no point in trying to deny anything else. "You want to hang out with Davey? Was that what you were coming to ask?"

"Yeah, is it okay if I go over there?"

"It's okay. Thanks for asking." The last

couple of months, Graham would walk out, announcing where he was going, not asking.

"Cool. You can go back and hug it out with Kelly, who is *not* your girlfriend." Graham flashed him a big, old grin.

Donovan shook his head. Smart aleck.

## *CHAPTER EIGHTEEN*

"ARE YOU SURE you know what you're supposed to say?" Detective Hermann asked for the third time. If there was one thing Kelly was good at, it was reading a script over the radio. That part wasn't going to be difficult at all. The hard part was going to be mustering up the courage to follow through with things later on.

"I've got it." She held up the paper with her lines all written out. They had spent three days coming up with this plan. She was as ready as she was ever going to be.

"Just stick to the script. We have everything in place to trace a call if he calls in."

Stick to the script. The plan was to repeat the same message throughout her show. They had no idea if he listened every day or not. They had no idea if he would call in so they could get to him first or if they would have to go through with the actual trap and lure him in with Kelly as the bait. That was the part she wasn't feeling too good about.

"It's going to be okay," Donovan reassured her. "There are lots of people working on this. Lots of cops will be in the area if we have to smoke him out. No one is going to touch you."

She wasn't sure if he was saying that for her sake or for his own. She had listened in on his conversations with the other detectives and he was very vocal about what he would allow her to do and what he wouldn't allow her to do, much to Detective Hermann's dismay. If anyone was as anxious as she was about this, it was Donovan.

It was like being in the middle of her worst nightmare. She felt like a prisoner. Police monitored her every move. They told her what to say and do, who she could interact with and when. She had lost all sense of independence, and she wasn't happy about it.

Lyle gave her the cue that the song playing was coming to an end and she was going on air in three…two…one…

"Good morning, Nashville. This is Kelly Bonner, excited to be spending this fine Wednesday with you. We are halfway through the workweek and I don't know about you guys, but I am so ready for the weekend. My favorite part of the weekend is kicking it off at the Nashville Farmers Market located right downtown. I will be there this Friday from four until six giving away some prizes, chatting it up with listeners and hopefully signing some of you up to be K104 Insiders. But what I'm really looking forward to is hopefully mending some fences, which leads me to my question of the day. How do you tell that special person in your life you're sorry? I recently hurt the feelings of someone who has been nothing but nice to me. He bought me presents, he writes me the sweetest notes, he puts up with my carelessness. You guys have to help me out. How do I say I am sorry?" Kelly rattled off the station's phone number and begged Nashville to call before playing the next song on the playlist.

Kelly didn't really want all of Nashville to call. She only wanted the person who thought she needed to say it to call in. She wanted him to call in, give up his location and get arrested. Once this guy was off the streets, she could be free.

"Great job. That was perfect," Donovan said, entering the studio and taking a seat next to her.

"Are you going to be my cohost? Juliette is going to be missing you today."

"I think Juliette will understand. I want to

be here with you if he calls. I'll help you with what to say."

"I thought that was Detective Hermann's job." She knew it originally was, but clearly, Donovan had weaseled his way into that role.

He grabbed her hand. "You're shaking."

She was way more nervous than she had been letting on. Her stomach ached and her shoulders were so tense they hurt.

"I hope I don't mess anything up or make him madder than he already is. Plus, I feel like I'm thirteen again and all I want to do is go to the movies, but I'm not allowed because it wouldn't be safe to go unsupervised."

Donovan pressed his lips against her knuckles and she felt some of the tension leave her body. Maybe it was better that he was here instead of Detective Hermann.

"I get it. You feel trapped. It could be worse, though, right? At least you're trapped with me and I'm not so bad."

He was cute. "I guess you're not *that* bad."

He laughed and nodded. "Oh, really? Great."

"I like being in control of my life, but I can't be. And I'm worried I'm not going to live up to everyone's expectations. I'm going to mess it up and we won't catch him."

"You aren't going to mess anything up. This is a great plan. If he's listening, his curiosity is piqued. He is going to want to know what you're willing to do to prove you're sorry. He's either going to tell you what it is by calling in or he's going to show up at the farmers market."

That was the plan. She was supposed to repeatedly mention her appearance at the farmers market and keep the apology theme going throughout her show. The hope was that if he chose to listen at any point in the show, he'd get both messages and either call or show up at the market on Friday.

"Calls are coming in," Lyle said through the headphones. "Operation Catch the Stalker has begun."

Kelly spent the next five minutes fielding calls from listeners. One lady told her that a simple *I'm sorry* should be all it takes if the man really loves her. Another caller said she should cook him his favorite dinner and dessert because the way to a man's heart was through his stomach. That was great advice for people who could cook.

The first batch of calls didn't get them their stalker. Not even one male caller. Kelly reminded herself that she might have to do this all week long. They had no idea if he was even listening.

At the top of the next hour, Kelly made

a second attempt at reeling in her stalker. "That was Boone Williams's song 'Too Late for Sorry,' which goes along with our theme today. I took a bunch of calls last hour from our lady listeners who had good ideas on how to say sorry. I have someone out there I need to apologize to and I'm hoping I don't end up like Boone, feeling like it's too late. So, I need you gentlemen out there to call in and let me know what the best way is for the lady in your life to show you they are sorry."

Round two of calls didn't lead them to the stalker, either. Kelly did get a few men to call in with some good answers and a couple with answers she couldn't put on-air.

"I'm frustrated and we aren't even halfway through the show," she said to Donovan, who sat there with incredible patience.

"Don't get frustrated. This could take all day. It could take the rest of the week. We might completely strike out. We have to be prepared that he might not be listening."

The anxiety of not knowing made Kelly want to crawl out of her skin. She propped her head up on her hand and blew out a long breath. It wasn't going to be easy and she needed to prepare for the long haul.

Hour three and four didn't get them what they wanted, either. Going into her last hour on-air, she wasn't confident that they were going to catch any bad guys today.

"So, what does this thing do?" Donovan pointed to the VoxPro controller.

"This is what I use to cut down the calls that come in. When somebody calls, we answer it and record it through this. You would be surprised how much of a call actually gets cut when we talk to people. I can take out long pauses, I can take out parts of the conversation that ramble and I can erase parts that aren't appropriate."

"Interesting. I thought you used a time delay to catch people swearing or whatever, but I didn't realize you sometimes shortened the conversation altogether."

"Radio is all about time management. We need to play music, get our advertisements out there and squeeze in our original content. It's harder than you'd think."

"What does Lyle do in there?"

"Lyle is my content producer and my board operator. He helps me come up with content for the show, he handles music choices, makes the playlists. He helps me when we have a special guest. He also operates all the technical stuff like volume control. He can screen calls for me in there. He does a lot actually."

"If someone calls in and requests a song,

can you play it or do you have to do what the computer tells you to do?"

"We could play something that was requested, but we don't usually take requests. Lyle has to go into a program and search for the song and mess with the playlist, which could screw up the flow of the show. Like I said, it's all about timing. We can't have any dead air and we have to make sure we fit in all of our advertising."

"Do you feel better now?" Donovan asked, a pleased expression on his face.

"What?"

"I was trying to get your mind off your worries. Did it work?"

She actually did feel better. She'd totally forgotten that she was in the midst of a sting operation.

"Nice work, Detective Walsh." Kelly smiled and ran her fingers through her ponytail. He was good at distracting her. "Can you keep that up for another hour?"

"I'll do my best."

"This is Kelly Bonner, coming to you from the K104 studio. I'm getting ready to pass things off to Jax, who's going to get you through your commute home this evening. No apologies for that, but we have been talking about what it means to say you're sorry and we heard from a lot of you loyal listeners who shared your ideas of the best way to apologize. My last question to you all is this—what do you do when your apology is not accepted? I need to apologize to someone special, who has been so kind and generous to me over the last few weeks, and I'm a little worried he's not going to accept my apology. What do I do then, people? Help a girl out." Kelly gave the number for the station one last time, hoping the stalker had finally tuned in.

"Fingers crossed. You did everything we asked you to do," Donovan said. "Let's pray it works."

The phone calls slowly trickled in. The two o'clock hour wasn't very interactive on a good day. Caller number one was a young woman who wanted to request a song for her boyfriend. Caller two wanted to know when Kelly was giving away tickets to the Grace Note concert. She started to worry they weren't even going to get any calls answering her question.

"K104, this is Kelly," she said, hitting Record as she answered the next call.

"Did you mean it?" His voice was like a shot of adrenaline. She motioned to Donovan that this was it. Detective Hermann and his partner jumped into action in the control room with Lyle. Donovan put on headphones so he could listen in.

"Did I mean what?"

"Did you mean it when you said you were sorry for how you treated the person who has been nothing but nice to you?"

"I did. I do. I mean it. I feel really bad because my intention was never to hurt anyone."

"You hurt me. You hurt me more than once by treating me like I am some kind of bad guy."

Kelly's heart was racing. "I don't think you're a bad guy."

"Then why did you call the police?"

"You damaged my car. I had to file a police report so the insurance company would fix it." She was so nervous. This wasn't one of the questions she had been prepared to answer. Donovan gave her a thumbs-up.

"Don't lie. You have a cop with you at all times. He's either looking for me or he's your boyfriend. Which one is it?"

Kelly looked to Donovan for help with that one. Neither answer was going to make this guy happy. Donovan wrote a note on a piece of paper and held it up.

*Blame your uncle.*

"That's because my uncle is a police officer. He had his guys follow me around because he doesn't understand what's going on between us."

Donovan jotted down some more notes. Kelly wondered how long it took for them to trace this call.

"What do you think is going on with us?" the caller asked.

*Apologize. Say you're confused. You don't understand what he wants from you.*

"I don't know. Everything that's happened lately has been confusing me. I don't know what you want me to do. I don't even know who you are, but you keep getting angry with me because I'm scared." Kelly's hands were shaking and he had to hear how nervous she was.

"I didn't mean to scare you."

"Who are you? Can you tell me that? Knowing who you are will make me a lot less scared of you."

There was a muffled noise in the background. "Get out of here," he said to someone. He must have covered the phone or put it down. He began talking to someone, but Kelly couldn't make out what he said and then there was nothing. He had hung up.

Donovan took off his headphones. "We got all that, right? It's recorded?"

"Yeah. It's all here."

Detective Hermann came in the studio room. “That was great, Kelly. Really great. You did a good job of keeping him on the line.”

“Were you able to get a location?” Donovan asked.

“We have a general vicinity to work off of. A minute more and we could have pinpointed his exact location, but that’s okay. The recording can help.”

Kelly didn’t understand what they thought was so valuable about the recording. He didn’t say anything that made her feel like she knew any more than she knew before she talked to him.

“You look stressed.” Donovan moved closer. “This was good.”

“How was it good? He didn’t tell me his name. I don’t know what he wants. Where’s the good?”

“Don’t worry about it. Let the police handle it. All you need to do is sit tight.”

“I hate this, by the way. I hate everything about this plan.”

“You have to let us do our job, and our job is to keep you safe.”

“Kelly, I need you on-air in one minute,” Lyle said over the intercom.

If they thought they could use what he gave

them so far, she wasn't going to argue about it. She hoped there was something useful on there. She also hoped he'd call back.

Detective Hermann went back to the control room and Donovan needed to go with him. Before he left, he placed a hand on her shoulder. "Are you sure you're okay?"

She had to read an advertisement and give the time and weather conditions. "I'll be fine."

Donovan took her at her word and left her alone. The stalker never called back. Let down, Kelly felt like she had been so close to getting more information out of him. If they hadn't been interrupted, maybe he would have said his name.

Minutes before his show, Jax showed up and strolled into the studio without a care in the world. What Kelly wouldn't do to feel like that again. She waited for him to ask who all the extra people were, but he refrained. She could only imagine the amount of gossip going around the office.

Lyle cued her that she was on. Kelly signed off and turned things over to Jax like it was any other day. Only it was far from it.

Before she took off her headphones, Lyle cut in. "Hey, there's a call for you. Not him but someone else. Line three."

Kelly picked up the line. “Hello, this is Kelly Bonner.”

“Hi, ma’am. This is Officer Holmes with the Nashville Police Department. I have a young man here who says he belongs to you.”

There was only one young man who would get in trouble and call her. “Graham? Is he okay? Did something happen?”

“He’s fine, ma’am. He said you are his guardian, that his parents are deceased. Is that true ma’am?”

“Is he under arrest?” She held her breath, waiting for the answer.

“No, ma’am, but he was in a fight and we need you to come get him.”

“Where are you?”

Officer Holmes gave her the details, leaving her to figure out how to get to King’s Ice Cream without telling Donovan. She slipped into the control room.

“Do you think you can do me a favor?” she asked Lyle.

“Anything.”

“Can you get me the keys to the station’s van?”

“Why would you need that?”

“I need to get out of here for a minute. *Alone*,” she said, hoping he wouldn’t ask any more questions.

Lyle frowned. “I’m not sure that’s a good idea. You were just on the phone with your stalker. You have a gaggle of cops huddled together in the conference room, trying to figure out how to catch him.”

“Perfect timing if you ask me. They have work to do and I will be back before they miss me. If anyone is looking for me, tell them I’m in a meeting.”

Lyle wasn’t convinced. “You’re going to get me arrested.”

“They can’t arrest you. Helping me isn’t against the law. Having a bodyguard is…” An independence stealer, messing with her head, more than she asked for—Kelly could think of quite a few ways to finish that sentence. “A perk of having a police officer uncle,” she finished. “Don’t worry.”

As much as she was falling for her bodyguard, she was still the same person she’d always been. She was willing to help out a friend when they needed her. She appreciated Donovan’s protection but wished she could see him every day because she chose to spend time with him rather than being forced.

“Fine, but if you get busted, I had nothing to do with this.”

Kelly used her finger to cross her heart. She wouldn’t get busted. She could grab Graham, take him home and be back before Donovan even noticed. She knew why Graham had called her and not his uncle. She wished she had had someone to call when she was a teenager who could have saved her from the wrath of her overprotective and overreacting parents. Donovan wouldn't give Graham the benefit of the doubt. Even if he had a perfectly good reason for getting into a fight, Donovan would come down hard on him. Graham knew that and so did Kelly.

# *CHAPTER NINETEEN*

DONOVAN FELT BETTER about the way things were going in this case. They didn't get a name or a location, which would have put an end to all of this, but he was confident this guy would be in touch soon. When he did try to contact Kelly again, he would let something slip. They were going to catch him and put him away for breaking and entering as well as stalking.

"If he doesn't reach out again by phone, we need to be ready for him to make an appearance at the farmers market. He was listening, so he'll go there if he wants to show himself to her," Hermann said. He looked at Donovan. "That means you can't be there."

"What? I'm not sitting this one out."

"You are if we want him to approach her. This guy knows you. He's seen you with her. If you're there, he's not going to make contact."

"Isn't it going to be suspicious that she suddenly doesn't have a bodyguard?" Donovan argued.

"Not if they just talked about how she didn't want one. How it was because of her uncle. Maybe she dropped you because he pointed out that it made him feel like a bad guy. It could be her way of telling him she wants to meet him."

It made sense logically. Donovan was having a hard time thinking logically when it came to Kelly, though. He was too close and Hermann knew it.

"I want to be there. I don't have to be with her, but I want to be on location. Undercover."

Hermann shook his head. "If he spots you anywhere at that market, it's over. You can't be there. You have to trust that we've got this."

"I can be in a van." He needed to be close enough to get to her when she needed him.

"Listen, I get it. You and her, you've got a thing going. But I need you to be a cop here, not her boyfriend."

"I'm not her boyfriend," Donovan fired back. This blurring of the boundaries was not good.

Hermann dared to smirk. "Whatever you want to call it or not call it, the point is you can't be there on Friday. You will put her in more danger. I don't need to call your captain about there being a problem, do I?"

The last thing Donovan needed was for

Hermann to call Captain and tell him that he was interfering in the case because of his feelings for Kelly. Donovan's partner had been clear about how Captain felt about anyone even thinking about his niece that way. Why had he let himself get into this mess?

"Of course not. This is your show."

"Great." Hermann clapped his hands together and got to his feet. "I think we've got it from here. We will come back tomorrow and Friday, see if he calls back during her show. If need be, we'll put things into place to catch him on Friday at the market."

"Great." Donovan stood, as well. It was clear he was no longer needed. The only thing left for him to do was get Kelly home safely. Not home. Not her home. Why had he obliterated the boundaries so immensely? She had somehow managed to get him to completely forget there needed to be boundaries. He couldn't do his job right if they didn't have them. Hermann had pointed that out quite clearly.

Donovan's feelings for Kelly were affecting his judgment. Hence why he hated talking about feelings, thinking about feelings, having anything to do with stupid feelings. Had he been in charge of things, he probably would have ruined everything by placing himself at the farmers market and scaring off the suspect. Why? Because every cell in his body wanted to protect her. It had to be him. No one else could do the job correctly because they didn't care about her the way he did. That kind of muddled, overly emotional thinking would have been his downfall.

Donovan walked the other detectives out before searching for Kelly. He checked her office, but she wasn't there. She wasn't in the break room or in Nancy's office. He looked for her in Lyle's office, but she wasn't there, either.

"Any idea where Kelly is?" he asked Lyle, who usually seemed to know what was going on around the station.

The man looked as if he had seen a ghost. His face paled and he swallowed hard. "Kelly?"

"Yeah, Kelly."

Lyle stood up and rubbed his hands on his thighs. "Kelly. Hmm...that's a tough one. I'm not sure. Maybe in a meeting."

"Maybe in a meeting? With who?"

"I don't know. Maybe Caroline," he said with a shrug, his voice rough.

Something was going on. "Was she supposed to have a meeting with Caroline?"

"I don't know. I honestly don't know."

Donovan stared at him for a minute, waiting to see if he would crack and tell him what was going on. Lyle just stood there frozen. He was no help.

If she was meeting with Caroline, there was no way he could interrupt. He decided to wait in the lobby with Juliette.

"Well, if it isn't my favorite detective."

"Are you sure about that? I've had some competition today."

Juliette pursed her red lips. "I thought about it and you're still my favorite."

She made him smile. "Good to know. Any chance you know Caroline's schedule for today?"

"I know a lot of things," she replied. "That might be one of them."

"What time is her meeting with Kelly supposed to end?"

Juliette's brow furrowed. "Meeting with Kelly?"

"Isn't she in a meeting with Kelly right now?"

"Kelly ducked out of here about..." She glanced at the time. "Oh, my, twenty minutes ago. Said she was stepping outside for some fresh air. I thought you gave her the okay."

Donovan felt his blood pressure rise. "Twenty minutes ago? She's been gone twenty minutes?"

Juliette nodded. "You don't think…?"

Donovan didn't want her to finish that question, nor did he want to answer it because he surely thought it was possible that the stalker had come here to talk to her and found her outside unguarded.

He skipped waiting for the elevator and took off down the stairs. He made it down to the ground level and didn't find her anywhere in or outside the building. He called her cell phone but got her voice mail. Not a good sign. He went back to the stairs and went down to the parking garage level. He didn't find her by his truck and she wasn't hanging out around the valet stand.

"Have you seen Kelly Bonner?" he asked an unfamiliar-looking valet.

"Who's Kelly Bonner?" the man asked.

"She works in the building. Dark hair, blue eyes. About five eight." Donovan held his hand up to show him how tall that was.

"This is my first day, man. I have no idea."

"Where's Miller? Or the other guy? Dark hair, lanky." They both knew who Kelly was and would be able to tell him if she had been down there.

"Carl? He's parking a car. I don't know who Miller is. Like I said, this is my first day."

Carl, thankfully, came jogging back to the valet station.

"Have you seen Kelly Bonner down here recently?" Donovan asked as soon as he was close enough.

"Kelly? I saw her a little while ago. Took off in the station van. Why?"

Donovan's heart stopped. "What? Took off, like drove away?"

Carl had a puzzled expression. "Yep. Drove away all by herself."

"No one was with her? No one seemed to be making her go anywhere?" He had to be sure she wasn't taken before he blew his lid.

"She was by herself as far as I could tell. Said hello when she walked out here."

Donovan didn't even bother to thank him for the information. He grabbed his phone out of his pocket and called her. How dare she take off like this. Where in the world did she need to be and why would she risk going alone?

It rang four times before she picked up. "Don't be mad," she said.

"Don't be mad? That's how you're going to start this conversation?"

"I'll be back in a few minutes. I had to run an errand for the station and you were busy with the other detectives. I didn't want to bother you."

"You didn't want to bother me?" He let out a humorless laugh. "That's rich. You are my responsibility, Kelly. If you need to leave the premises, you need to bother me so I can do my job."

"Listen, I can't talk right now. I'll be happy to hear about how mad you are when I get back."

"Tell me where you are," he demanded.

Instead of answering, she hung up. When he tried to call her back, it went to voice mail. *Mad* was an understatement.

If something happened to her, how was he going to explain this to his captain? Telling him that she was missing would be worse than telling him that they were in a relationship. He waited in the parking garage for her to return. This was where feelings had got him. Nowhere good.

"You all right, man?" Carl asked.

Donovan rolled his shoulders. "I'm fine. Just waiting for Kelly to come back."

"You're a cop, right?"

"Yeah."

"I thought so," Carl said with a nod. "Miller thought you were like her boyfriend or something."

Boyfriend. There it was again. "I'm not her boyfriend. I am her bodyguard, though."

"You're her bodyguard? How's that working out for you?" Carl snickered.

"Not as well as I'd like." Donovan checked his phone. She had ten more minutes and he would call her again.

"Too bad Miller quit the other day. I'm sure he'd be relieved to hear Kelly is still single."

After weeks of working out this puzzle of a case, it was like Carl had handed him the missing piece that had been giving him the most trouble. "Why would Miller care if Kelly was single?"

Carl rolled his eyes. "Dude had the biggest crush on her. Always talking about how they were going to be together someday. I was like, 'Bro, you're a car valet and she's on billboards. You don't have any chance.' But he acted like because she was nice to him that meant he had one. Poor guy didn't realize she was nice to everyone."

"Why didn't you tell me or the other detectives about this?"

Carl stepped back and held his hands up defensively. "You asked me about seeing anyone out of the ordinary or guys showing up with deliveries. You never asked me if I knew anyone who had a crush on her."

He wasn't wrong. All this time, the guy they were looking for had been right under their noses. He had access to her car. He had access to her keys. He could have found her address on the car registration. He saw her often but not every day.

"What's his last name? Miller what?"

Carl had to think about it for a second. "Miller Green, I think."

Donovan bolted upstairs to find Juliette. If she could confirm one thing, he'd be able to hand Hermann his suspect. Once in the lobby, he had to wait for Juliette to get off the phone. Seconds felt like hours. As soon as she hung up, he pounced.

"The delivery guy. The one you said looked familiar, but you couldn't place him. Any chance he was one of the valets down in the parking garage?"

Juliette snapped her fingers. "That's it! Oh, my gosh. He's one of the valets! How did you figure it out?"

Donovan didn't have time to discuss anything more with Juliette. He needed to get this information to Detective Hermann. They had their man. All Hermann and his partner had to do was go pick him up.

He called it in and was left with nothing else to do but wait for Kelly to get back. It would have been easier if he didn't have tons of adrenaline flowing through his body. He could run ten miles without breaking a sweat right now.

Antsy, Donovan went back down to the parking garage to wait for her. As soon as he got there, the station van pulled in. His emotions were all over the place. Anger, relief, frustration, hope that this would all be over tonight.

"I know you're mad. But I'm fine. Here I am, totally fine," she said as she got out of the van.

"Miller. Miller the valet. He's the guy."

Confusion fell over her face. "Miller?" She shook her head. "No way. Miller?"

"He's had a crush on you for a while, apparently. He had access to everything. Juliette identified him as the man who delivered some of the gifts."

She clearly was trying to make sense of it all. Looking over his shoulder in the direction of the valet station, she asked, "Did they arrest him?"

"He quit a couple days ago. Hermann is looking for him now. I'm sure we'll hear something soon."

Kelly leaned back against the van and placed a hand on her forehead. "Miller." She closed her eyes. "It was his voice. It was him. I can't believe I didn't realize it."

"You've been under a lot of stress. It's understandable that you didn't recognize his voice when he called."

Before he could stop her, Kelly threw her arms around his neck and hugged him tightly. "It's over. It's really going to be over."

As much as he wanted to hug her back, he couldn't forget that she had run off without him. The fear he had felt, the anger. These were feelings he wanted nothing to do with. They were inevitable when he let someone get close, though.

"Where were you?" he asked. She pulled back and bit down on her lip. "Don't tell me station business because no one in the station knew you were gone."

"I can't tell you."

He could add frustration to the list of the ways he hated to feel. "Why?"

"You're not my keeper, Donovan. I am sorry I didn't tell you I had to leave, but I have the right to go where I want when I want with or without you."

She was right, but something about her attitude rubbed him the wrong way. "You know what? I'm not your keeper. Maybe you should stay with your uncle until you find a new place. Now that we know who we're looking for, there's no reason for you to be in hiding."

"You don't want me to stay with you anymore?"

"I think you should return your keys so we can get out of here. The sooner I get you to your uncle, the better."

Kelly opened her mouth but shut it. Without a word, she stepped around him and into the building. He was being a jerk. He knew it, she knew it. Being a jerk was another thing he was good at. It was the only way he knew how to deal with all of these negative feelings.

They walked to the truck in silence. The air between them was thick with all the things they wanted to say but wouldn't. It was better this way, Donovan kept telling himself.

"I know you're mad. Will you just talk to me?"

"I'm not mad. I have nothing to say."

"Don't do that."

"Do what?" He glanced at her, which was a mistake. She was beautiful even when she was sad.

"Shut me out. I'd rather listen to your mad voice than have you sit there and seethe in silence."

He did not have a mad voice. Why did she and Avery keep saying that? "I'm not mad."

"Just because I needed to be alone doesn't mean my feelings for you have changed. I care about you and what you think and feel."

If he told her how he felt, he would be handing her the weapons she needed to rip out his heart. His feelings had done nothing but cloud his judgment. She couldn't hurt him if he didn't feel anything.

They pulled in the driveway at the same time as Mrs. Finnegan, who was dropping off Avery from after-school club.

Donovan cringed at the thought of how difficult it was going to be to explain to the kids why Kelly was leaving tonight. He waved to Mrs. Finnegan as Avery jumped out of her minivan.

"Kelly! Guess what happened at school today." Avery had Kelly by the hand before Donovan shut his door.

"Tell me all about it, sweetheart," Kelly said as they made their way to the front door.

Avery went on and on about a science experiment the teacher did for the class. The house was otherwise quiet. Graham must have been in his room. It was a little strange that he wasn't in front of the TV, playing video games like usual.

"Avery, Kelly needs to go upstairs and get her stuff packed. She's going to stay with her uncle just like you stay with yours." Donovan hoped that making it seem like something they had in common would lessen the blow.

"What? No! I don't want Kelly to leave."

"I know, but this is good news," Donovan said. "It means that Kelly is safe to go."

Avery wrapped her little arms around Kelly's waist. "No."

Kelly stroked Avery's head. "I know it's sad. No more sleepovers. But it's time for me to go."

"No!" Avery didn't let go.

"What's happening?" Graham came flying down the stairs. "Why is Avery shouting?"

"Uncle Donovan is making Kelly leave," Avery said.

"I'm not making her leave." Maybe he was. He was trying to rip the bandage off instead of prolonging his misery.

"Why are you making her leave?" Graham looked panicked. "Is it because of me?"

Kelly's eyes went wide. "No," she said firmly. "Absolutely not because of you."

"Why would it be because of you?" Donovan's gaze shifted from Kelly to Graham and back again.

"Is it because you left work?" Graham asked Kelly, who was shaking her head.

Donovan's jaw ticked. "How do you know she left work?"

"Blame me," Graham said. "Not her. Don't kick her out because I asked her for a favor."

"Graham—" Kelly started to say, but Donovan cut her off.

That familiar heat crept up his neck. He couldn't hold back this anger if he tried. "You left the station because of Graham? Start talking and don't even think about lying to me."

"I gave him a ride home. It's not a big deal."

"Gave him a ride home from where?" he asked. Kelly and Graham exchanged another look. That's when Donovan noticed the cut by Graham's right eye. "What happened to your eye?"

Graham came over to stand next to Kelly while Avery still clung to her like a wet blanket. It was a standoff. The three of them against Donovan.

"I went to hang out with Mia after school today and we ran into the guys from math class who hate me. They thought it would be really funny to humiliate me in front of her. Only, they didn't know I could fight back. They got one hit in and I took the three of them out thanks to everything you taught me."

"You got in a fight? I didn't teach you to fight. I taught you how to get away."

"I didn't want to fight, but it was three against one. I had to."

Donovan shook his head. "And why did Kelly have to pick you up?"

There was another exchange of looks, which meant whatever it was, it was not going to make Donovan any less angry.

Graham sighed. "We were at King's Ice Cream. Someone there called the cops."

"You got arrested?" Donovan could only see red.

"No," Graham and Kelly answered at the same time.

"He didn't get arrested, but they had to release him to his…guardian," Kelly said with a grimace.

"Which is me. Not you." He threw his hands up. His mind was blown. "But you chose to go anyway. You put yourself at risk, lied to the police about being his guardian and then plotted to keep all this from me?" She wanted to know how he felt? She cared about what he thought? She was a liar.

Kelly pried Avery off her and wrung her hands. "I know what it's like to be a cop's kid. He wasn't in trouble. The officers on the scene were actually pretty cool about everything. They understood Graham didn't have many options. I planned to talk to Graham tonight about telling you. We weren't going to keep it a secret forever."

Donovan couldn't talk about this anymore. The fact that she thought it was okay for her to have any secrets with his nephew made him furious. He had opened himself up to this woman. He had let her into his home, around his kids, and she stabbed him in the back. Conspired with his nephew. Agreed to lie. The sooner he got Kelly out of this house, out of their lives, the better.

"Please go pack your stuff. I need to take you to your uncle's. Now," he added when she didn't move.

"No!" Avery cried. "I don't want her to go. We love her."

"You don't love her, Avery. You barely know her. Graham, go to your room. You're grounded indefinitely. Avery, go in the kitchen and take out your coloring books. You can color until I get back."

Avery resumed her clinging to Kelly, who crouched down and gave the little girl a hug back. "I love you, too, sweet girl. I have had the best time being your roommate, but it's time for me to go. Your uncle found the bad guy who was trying to hurt me, so I'm safe now."

"I still don't want you to go," Avery cried.

Kelly had tears running down her cheeks. Donovan had to look away. "I know. I'm going to miss you like crazy. I need you to be a big girl and go do what your uncle said, okay?"

Avery sniffled all the way to the kitchen table. Graham wrapped Kelly up in a hug. "I'm sorry. This is all my fault."

"No, it's not. I'm the grown-up. It was my call. You're an amazing kid, Graham. Don't forget that."

"I wanted to show you my drawing. I get it back on Friday after my last final."

"You have my cell number now. If it's okay with your uncle, you can send me a text. I'd love to see it." Kelly glanced in Donovan's direction. He nodded. That was the one and only concession he would make.

Kelly and Graham walked solemnly upstairs. Donovan waited at the bottom, his head spinning with all that had happened. He held his head in his hand and gave his temples a rub. His head wasn't the only thing hurting, though. The pain in his chest was a million times worse. Between the tears and the obvious bonds that had been formed between Kelly and the kids, he could hardly stand it. There was also this resentment. Why was he always the bad guy? Why did they ask for his trust but refuse to give him theirs?

He drove Kelly to her uncle's and had nothing to say when she got out of the truck. That didn't stop her from saying her piece.

"I know you don't want to talk to me, but I hope you talk with Graham. He cares about what you think more than you know. He only called me because he was afraid of how you would react and I went because I thought I could help him."

"Don't. Don't act like you lied and put yourself and Graham at risk because I might not have reacted the way a fifteen-year-old wants me to."

That left her speechless. She closed the door and walked away. When he got back home, Avery was at the kitchen table like he had asked her. Donovan went upstairs to talk to Graham. Not because Kelly told him to, or at least that was what he was going to tell himself.

He knocked on the door and got no response, so Donovan pushed it open. Graham was on his bed, sitting in the dark. Donovan flipped on the light.

"We need to talk."

"What's there to talk about? You hate me.

You hate Kelly. You wish you never had to take either of us in," Graham said.

Donovan sat on the end of his bed. "Why do you always assume the worst? Why am I always the bad guy?"

"You're the bad guy? I'm the bad guy! I'm the one always getting in trouble. I'm the one who does nothing but disappoint you. Why would you want me to live here?"

Kids were more confusing to Donovan than women. He thought Graham hated him, but it appeared the boy hated himself more.

"Is that what you really think? Graham..." He wasn't sure what to say. He tried to put himself in the kid's shoes. To see it from his perspective. "You are my nephew. You will always be welcome here. This is your home. I...I love you, buddy. No matter what you do, no matter what you say. We're family. Family is the most important thing in this world."

Graham shook his head. "I make you mad. I bet you wish you could kick me out like you kicked Kelly out."

"I didn't kick Kelly out. And this isn't about Kelly. This is about trust. We have got to find a way to trust each other. I need to be able to count on you and I need you to believe you can count on me. I know I'm not as easygoing as your dad was or as patient and understanding as your mom was, but I am trying so hard to do right by you and Avery."

"I know you didn't want the burden of two kids."

"Hey," Donovan said, waiting for Graham to look at him. "Your mom was my favorite person in the entire world. The fact that she asked me to take care of her kids when she passed away means everything to me. It's a privilege to get to raise you two for her. Not a burden. Never a burden."

"Never?" Graham's eyes were wet.

"Never," he replied, patting his nephew on the leg. "If you had called me today from the police station, I'm sure I would have used my mad voice, but I would not have grounded you for life or whatever you thought was going to happen. If you had given me a chance and talked to me, I would have understood. Maybe not right away like Kelly probably did, but eventually, I would have understood."

"That's what Kelly said."

"Oh, yeah?"

"She said you have more layers than I think."

"Layers? Like a cake? Because if Kelly was talking in food metaphors, that could be dangerous."

The right side of Graham's lip curled up

into a half smile. "She said you're more than just a big, bad cop. More than a mad voice. She also said I should talk to you about what happened. I was going to, but then everything happened..."

Kelly had not conspired to keep the truth from him. He felt some relief in that. Donovan had been so afraid of what his feelings for her meant, he had lashed out without giving her a chance to explain.

"I'm really sorry, Uncle Donovan. Please don't hate Kelly because of me."

Donovan gave Graham a hug. "I don't hate anyone." Hating her was impossible, but was he capable of loving her? Or would fear stand in his way?

## *CHAPTER TWENTY*

"HE'S NOWHERE." UNCLE HAL threw his phone on the couch Friday morning. "He's not at his apartment, his mother's house or with anyone his mother identified as a friend."

The hunt for Miller Green was not going as expected. What was supposed to be an easy arrest had become more like finding a needle in a haystack. It meant that Kelly's lockdown continued. Only not with Donovan.

"Maybe I should call Walsh to meet you at the station. Without him, they can't seem to get this done," he said.

"No!" Kelly said a bit too roughly. Uncle Hal's brow quirked up. "No reason to make him come to the station when the other detectives are there."

"I guess you're right." Uncle Hal sat down next to her at his large oak kitchen table. "I'm sorry, Kell Bell. I thought this would be over by now."

"Don't be sorry. At least we know who

we're looking for. It'll be over soon. I'm not worried."

She was much more worried she might not get the chance to make amends with Donovan. Kelly had managed to ruin everything with one decision.

Uncle Hal placed his hand over hers. "Walsh really went above and beyond. Not only did he watch over you like I asked him, but he solved the case."

Kelly's heart ached. Donovan had done everything to keep her safe and she only made it harder for him. On top of that, she let her personal baggage destroy any chance they had at having a relationship. "You really know how to pick 'em."

"Maybe once all this is over, we'll have him over for dinner to show our appreciation," Uncle Hal said, unaware of all the reasons that was a terrible idea.

"Sounds good," Kelly replied with a tiny smile.

"Are you nervous about this Miller guy showing up at the farmers market today?"

"I'm more worried about him not showing up. If he does, this is over. If he doesn't, who knows how long it could take."

He patted her hands. "I'll say a little prayer.

Your father is up there, making sure we get our man. I'm not worried."

Kelly gave Uncle Hal a hug. Hopefully, her dad was watching out for her, even though he was probably disappointed in the way she'd handled everything up until now.

At the station, nothing happened to get them any closer to finding Miller. The detectives were more concerned with setting a trap at the farmers market. They had a female detective working undercover as Kelly's intern and a few others who would mill around, waiting to pounce.

All of this was supposed to make Kelly feel safe, but the truth was she missed having Donovan there to watch her back. He had a way of calming her when she had that flutter of anxiety in her chest.

"If you see him, you make Detective Roman aware. We want him to get close enough for you to positively identify him, but far enough away that he can't touch you," Detective Hermann explained.

Kelly nodded. She understood the plan and hoped it would work. There were all these conflicting emotions. As much as she wanted Miller to show up, it was terrifying to think he could get close. She had to trust the police would make sure that wouldn't happen.

They set up their booth and Kelly organized all the promotional giveaways. Lyle was there, as well. He was in charge of the spinning wheel. His nerves were evident.

"You going to be all right?" Kelly asked him.

Lyle readjusted his K104 hat on his head. "Am I going to be all right? I'm not the one with a target on my back. You are. Are you all right?"

"As good as I'm going to be."

"I wish Detective Walsh was here," Lyle whispered so Detective Roman couldn't overhear. "That guy took his job seriously. I have no doubt he'd take this stalker down in a heartbeat."

Kelly's chest tightened. She wished he could be there, too. She wished she could take back some of the things she had said and done so he didn't hate her like he probably did. "Me, too. Let's hope the rest of the MNPD is as good at their jobs as he is."

There seemed to be twice as many people at the market today compared to every other Friday they had been there this summer. Kelly found herself distracted by searching the faces of everyone in their immediate area. It made being interactive with listeners a bit challenging. There was a man with a mustache. A boy around ten years old just out of his mom's reach. A pregnant woman and her husband. A lanky young man and his friend in cowboy hats. None of them was Miller.

"Kelly!"

She looked up at the sound of her name being called. Graham and Mia were holding hands and coming her way.

"What are you doing here?" she asked.

Graham gave her a hug and she hugged him back, grateful for the opportunity but fearful that Donovan had not exactly given his permission for Graham to be there.

"I wanted to show you my final art project, which I got an A plus on, by the way." The pride in his voice almost brought Kelly to tears.

"An A plus! I didn't expect anything less."

Graham took off his backpack and unzipped it to remove a tube. He popped the lid off the tube and carefully slid out the paper rolled up inside. "Mr. Reed said he thinks I should enter it in the city's art competition."

Kelly watched him unfurl it and hand it to her. It was a gorgeous drawing in colored pencil. Kelly had seen pictures of Jessica around the house, and this looked exactly like her. It was just her profile and her head was tipped down. She wore a smile that made the corner of her eyes crinkle. Kelly imagined it was how she would have grinned down at Graham when he was little.

"This is absolutely beautiful," she said. "I definitely think you should enter it in the competition. You should enter it in every competition. You would win them all."

"He's so talented," Mia said, giving him a light punch to the arm. Graham's cheeks turned pink. They were cute together, but most likely in a lot of trouble.

"Please tell me your uncle knows you're here."

Graham grimaced. "Not really."

"Graham," she said with a sigh. "As happy as I am to see you and grateful you wanted to show me this in person, I don't think you should be here. You should head home." Kelly rolled up the drawing and handed it back to him.

"I was going to go home right after we saw you. I need to be home when Avery gets there. Don't worry—I think you were right. Uncle Donovan has more layers than I thought."

Kelly wasn't sure what that meant. The man didn't have enough layers to be okay with Graham sneaking around to meet with the enemy. Hopefully, Donovan didn't truly believe she was the enemy. She pulled Graham in for one more hug.

"Get going. And let me know how the art competition goes. I see a blue ribbon in your future."

The teenagers took off, leaving Kelly to nurse her broken heart once again. As she faked a smile and greeted another listener there to spin the prize wheel, she couldn't shake the feeling that Miller was near. She scanned the crowd but didn't see him.

"What's wrong?" Lyle asked. Detective Roman stepped closer.

"Nothing. I'm paranoid. I imagine him popping up every time I turn around, but he's nowhere. I don't think he's coming."

"There's still plenty of time," Detective Roman reminded her.

The anxiety made Kelly's skin tingle like she was being shocked. She wanted him to show up. She needed him to show up. That was the only way this would be over.

Time seemed to be in slow motion. The two hours felt like ten. About fifteen minutes before their time was up, Kelly's phone rang. It was Graham. He was either calling to tell her he got away with sneaking out or totally busted.

"What happened? Please tell me your uncle is not even more mad at us," she said.

"Kelly." Not Graham. Not Graham at all. Miller. Definitely Miller. "Don't say anything. I know you brought the police with you. I've been watching them while they've been clueless about me."

"Where are you?" she asked, trying to maintain her composure. He had to have Graham if he had his phone. She couldn't put him at risk. She tried to control her tone as she pretended to be talking to someone else. "I need to get you home safely, Graham."

"Come meet us in the parking lot. Alone."

Heart beating out of control, Kelly tried to swallow her fear. "I can't do that."

"You have to try. For us. You said you were sorry. Now, prove it. Call me when you are alone."

Before she could argue that it was impossible, Miller hung up. The police told her they would have eyes everywhere. Detective Roman would never let her go off on her own. She couldn't tell them he had Graham. He always seemed one step ahead.

"I need to use the bathroom," Kelly said.

"Okay," Lyle said. "We can draw for the tickets when you get back."

Detective Roman adjusted her sunglasses.

"Can you not hold it for a few more minutes? We are almost done here."

There was no time to waste. The thought of Graham being with Miller made her stomach turn. "I can't. I need to go now."

"Fine," she said in a huff. "Let's go."

"I don't think I need an escort to the bathroom," Kelly tried.

"You need an escort wherever you go." Detective Roman was wearing an earpiece and a mic. "On the move," she said to whoever was listening.

Kelly knew she wouldn't get to go on her own. What she didn't know was how many would be following her. How many she'd have to get away from. She led the way to the Market House, where there were multiple restaurants and a bathroom.

"If you really want to look like an intern instead of a bodyguard, maybe you could grab me a sweet tea while I'm in there," Kelly said, holding out a five-dollar bill. She hoped the officer didn't notice how badly she was shaking.

"Seriously?" she scoffed.

"Please? It will make you look a lot less suspicious if he's watching us."

Detective Roman snatched the five out of her hand. "I'm getting myself one, too."

"Of course." Kelly marched toward the bathroom as Detective Roman got in line for a drink. She scanned the room, looking for a familiar face. She knew the officers who had come with them. She didn't see any in the Market House.

Instead of going to the restroom, Kelly made for the exit as soon as Detective Roman looked away. She prayed no one else was waiting right outside. She tried to hide herself amongst a group of college-aged kids. As soon as she could, she took off, sprinting toward the parking lot. She had to save Graham even if it meant putting herself in danger.

DONOVAN DECIDED HE needed to do something spontaneous and fun. He was going to start showing off some of these layers to Graham and Avery. Since he also desperately needed a distraction so he didn't obsess about what was happening at the farmers market, today seemed like a good day to start. Only Graham wasn't answering his phone, which could only mean one thing—he was clearly not sitting at home waiting for his sister to come home like he should have been since he was grounded for lying.

Donovan swung by the elementary school to pick up Avery and Macy Finnegan from after-school club a little early. After dropping Macy off, he and Avery headed home.

"I can't wait to go to summer camp on Monday. I bet I make a hundred new friends," Avery said. Donovan loved her sense of optimism.

"I bet you make at least that."

They got out of the truck and headed inside the house. Donovan was shocked to find Graham sitting on the couch, playing video games.

"Why haven't you been answering your phone?"

Graham pushed his headphones off his ear. "What?"

"Why haven't you been answering your phone?" he repeated, surprised that his instincts had been off.

Graham stuck his hand in his pocket and then the other. He stood up and pulled up the couch cushion, searching for his phone.

"Shoot." He got down on his hands and knees and looked under the couch. "Is it on the island?"

Donovan strolled into the kitchen. There was nothing on the island. No phone on the table or counters, either. "Please tell me you didn't lose your phone."

"I had it." He patted himself down before

running upstairs to presumably look in his room. "Can you call it again?"

Donovan leaned against the kitchen island and took out his own phone. He clicked on Graham's name and didn't bother to hold it to his ear so he could listen for Graham's ringing in the house instead.

The call was picked up. The phone must have been in Graham's room. He was just about to hang up when Graham jogged down the stairs.

"Did you call it?"

Donovan put the phone to his ear. "Hello?"

"She wants to be with me. Did you notice how quickly she got rid of you when I asked her to?"

Donovan's blood ran cold. "Miller?"

"She's coming to me. We're going to be together and all you cops can go back to catching the real criminals."

"That's interesting. Did she tell you that?" He couldn't get out the door fast enough.

"She agreed to meet me."

He jumped in his truck and prayed he could keep this guy on the line until he made it to the farmers market. "Maybe she just wants to tell you to your face that she's not interested."

"That's not true!"

"You thought I was her boyfriend. What if I am?"

"You're not anymore. She wants to be with me."

Donovan didn't bother to stop at any of the stop signs in his neighborhood. He prayed for all green lights, as well.

"I think I need to hear that from her. I think we should all sit down and she can tell both of us to our faces what she wants. If she chooses you, I'll walk away. Will you do the same?"

There was no answer. Donovan worried Miller had hung up. He checked to see if the call was still connected. It was.

"Where are you guys?" he asked. "I will meet you wherever you want."

"We don't need your interference. You need to stay away," Miller said.

It was minutes before six. Kelly should have been working at the farmers market. She should have cops watching her every move. There was no reason to believe Miller wasn't about to be arrested. He was falling right into the detectives' trap.

"How did you get my nephew's phone?" he asked, slowing down a bit. There was no reason to panic. Kelly was safe. She had police with her.

"He was here visiting my girl. I guessed

he had her number and I was right. It was the perfect way to get her to agree to lose the cops."

Donovan hit the gas. Kelly thought that Miller had Graham. She didn't know Graham was home safe. If Kelly thought Graham was in danger, he had no doubt that she would do whatever she could to get away from her security to save him.

"She's calling now. I have to go. No hard feelings. The better man won," Miller said before hanging up.

Donovan dialed Kelly, hoping she'd click over but knowing that if she thought Graham was in trouble, she wouldn't. He decided to leave a message, hoping she'd listen to it before she met with her stalker.

"Kelly, Graham is home. He's fine. He's safe. Miller only has his phone. Go back to your security. Do not try to engage him on your own."

He kept calling her until he pulled into the parking lot across the street from the farmers market. He had to find her. He couldn't let anything happen to her. Not when she thought he hated her. He didn't hate her. Couldn't hate her. He was falling in love with her even though he had done everything in his power not to.

KELLY WAS BREATHING so hard, someone might think she had run a mile to get here. Her heart pounded against her ribs. Donovan kept calling and texting her. She didn't answer nor did she even open the texts. He had to know Graham was missing. She didn't know what to say to him. She couldn't bring herself to tell him that it was all her fault. She had to save him and then everything would be okay. Donovan would forgive them if Graham came out of this safe.

Miller had told her where his car was parked. She needed to find him and convince him to let Graham go. As she made it to the marker where he told her to go, she saw him standing beside a red pickup. Every muscle in her body tensed. Once Graham was safe, she would do what she had to do to get away, but now, she needed to hand herself over to the enemy.

"Hey," she said as she approached him.

He seemed extremely nervous. It was like his head was on a swivel; he kept surveilling the area to make sure he wasn't about to get arrested.

"No one followed you?"

Kelly shook her head. "I don't think so." She stepped closer and scanned the cars around them. She didn't see Graham sitting inside any of them. "Where's Graham?"

"Don't worry about him. Let's get out of here," Miller said, unlocking the doors of the pickup. "Come on."

"I need to see Graham. I need to know he's okay."

"I'll show you when you get in the truck. Come on," he said with a little more urgency.

Kelly stopped moving. "I need you to let him go before I come with you."

Miller let out a growl and barreled toward her. "We have to go, now!"

He grabbed her by the wrist and pulled her toward the truck. Graham wasn't there. He wasn't in the truck. She felt a rush of adrenaline. Her flight-or-fight instincts kicked in and she was ready to do both.

Just like Donovan had taught her, she broke his hold. She screamed for help. Miller wrapped his arms around her and tried to cover her mouth. Unfortunately for him, Donovan had taught her what to do when that happened, as well. She bit his finger and broke his hold again.

Escape, escape, escape.

She ran and yelled for help. Miller wasn't going to be deterred. He chased her and knocked her to the ground. Donovan had emphasized staying on her feet. She couldn't fight if he had her pinned to the ground. She let him lift her up. If she couldn't get away, she had to take him down.

Everything Donovan taught her helped her do just that. She elbowed him in the ribs, turned and popped him in the nose. When he doubled over, she pushed him off balance until he fell forward.

The whole time she screamed for help and people finally came to her rescue. She tried to catch her breath as a couple of guys held Miller down while a woman called 9-1-1.

"Kelly!"

She turned to the sound of her name. Donovan ran full speed at her. In the blink of an eye, she was wrapped up in his embrace. It was the only place she wanted to be.

"You're okay," he said over and over.

She realized that they weren't all okay yet. "I don't know where Graham is. I think he has Graham."

Donovan let her go. "He's home. Miller only had his phone. That's what I was trying to tell you when I called."

The relief was instantaneous. Graham was safe. They were all safe now. Detectives Hermann and Roman showed up and placed

Miller under arrest. Detective Roman was not pleased and Kelly didn't blame her.

"I can't believe you took him out all by yourself," Donovan marveled as the witnesses recounted what happened.

"I had an excellent self-defense teacher."

"You shouldn't have needed to use self-defense. You had a team of police officers here to help you," Detective Roman said, a peeved expression on her face.

Donovan put an arm around Kelly. "Can we save the lecture for later? I need to get her home. She can answer all your questions tomorrow. We'll come to you."

Detective Roman didn't argue and Donovan led her to his truck. Kelly figured he planned a lecture of his own.

"Okay, let me have it," she said once they got inside. "I was stupid. I was reckless. I was easily fooled. You hate me and my refusal to do as I am told."

Donovan turned his body toward her and placed his hands on her face. "You were scared. You were trying to protect my nephew. You were extremely brave. I love you and your willingness to do whatever you can to take care of the people in your circle, as you call them."

She appreciated everything he had to say,

but there were three words that stood out the most. “You love me?”

“You make me use my mad voice more than I like, but I’m going to work on that. Yes, I love you.”

Kelly didn’t know what to say. This was the exact opposite of what she expected from him. She had done everything he would have told her not to do.

“I thought you liked it when we talked about our feelings. Are you going to tell me how you feel about all of this?” Donovan asked.

Instead of using her words, she leaned forward and placed her lips on his. There was no better way to tell him how she felt than to show him.

When they broke apart, both of them were breathing a bit unevenly.

“Let’s go home, huh?” he asked. “The kids will be excited to see you.”

There wasn’t anywhere else she wanted to be.

## *CHAPTER TWENTY-ONE*

"WHAT IF PIPER STARLING wants to be best friends? Can I say yes?" Avery asked as Donovan handed the tickets over to the man at the gate.

"You might hurt Macy's feelings if she finds out that Piper is your best friend instead of her," Graham said. "But if she wants to divorce that husband of hers and marry me, I will definitely say yes."

"Wow, I guess I'll have to pick up the pieces of Sawyer Stratton's broken heart since it seems I will be very much single," Mia said, pushing past Graham.

"I was kidding!" Graham caught up to her and held her hand.

"What if Piper wants to marry Uncle Donovan?" Avery asked.

"Ha!" Graham looked over his shoulder. "Piper Starling isn't going to want to marry some old guy like Uncle Donovan."

Donovan cocked his head. "Old guy?"

"I think she would want to marry you. You're not *that* old," Avery said, smiling up at him.

"Well, thank you." They made their way to the special VIP entrance. Kelly had promised to meet them here. "But I'll have you all know that if this Piper Starling person wanted to marry me, I would tell her no thank you. I already have a girlfriend."

Avery giggled into her hand and Graham rolled his eyes. Mia placed a hand over her heart.

"That's so sweet," she said. "Why can't my boyfriend be that sweet?"

"I can be sweet," Graham argued. "I was kidding. If Piper asked me to marry her, I would point to you and say, 'Sorry, Piper, I'm taken.'"

Donovan didn't realize those two had made things official. Kelly probably knew. Graham had a tendency to tell her everything. He wondered if the kids noticed that was the first time he called Kelly his girlfriend. They had told her uncle they were together last weekend when they moved her into her new place. Getting a new contract at work meant Kelly had a reason to put down those roots. Captain Bonner didn't threaten to take Donovan's badge away again, so it was official for them, too.

"Who's ready to meet some famous people?" Kelly was a sight for sore eyes. They had all had dinner together last night, but she had been busy with station responsibilities all day today.

The kids were more than ready to meet some famous people. Kelly gave Donovan a peck on the cheek.

"What about you? Are you ready?"

"Oh, I can't wait. I sure hope Boone What's-His-Name will sign my hat."

"Please don't call him that when we go backstage," Graham said with a groan.

Kelly shook her head. "He knows his name. Your uncle simply enjoys being difficult. I promise I won't let him embarrass you."

Donovan grinned. He did like to be a little bit difficult. It was only fair. The rest of them were difficult on a regular basis.

"I promise not to say anything that will purposely embarrass you." Donovan held up his right hand like he was making a pledge.

"Are you sure we can't leave him out here?" Graham asked.

Kelly hooked arms with Donovan. "We can't trust him out here by himself. It's better to keep him close. Come on, you guys. Let's go backstage."

KELLY WAS EXCITED to introduce her family to everyone backstage. That was what she considered them—her family. They both almost messed it up, but somehow they rose above. Kelly promised there would be no more conspiring with Graham. Donovan promised to be more open about his feelings.

"When we get in the meet-and-greet room, you need to wait until someone tells us it's our turn to go. We'll get a few minutes with each singer. Okay?" Kelly wanted to make sure the kids understood the rules because she could picture Avery making a beeline for Piper Starling the moment she stepped in the room. They were getting advanced access, but that didn't mean they had free rein.

Avery's eyes were huge when they walked in. She jumped up and down, unable to contain her excitement but following the rules and not racing over to Piper, who was on the other side of the room. She would be one of the last people they would meet.

Graham had his sketchbook with him. He was going to have everyone sign a picture of themselves that he had drawn. Like Kelly, he was most excited to meet Boone, who looked to be the first person they were going to meet.

"Kelly Bonner, how are you?" Boone asked when it was their turn.

He remembered her name. She nearly melted.

"I'm doing quite well, Boone. But I know

I'll be doing better when I'm watching you onstage tonight."

"Well, aren't you sweet?" He tipped his cowboy hat. Dressed in a plaid button-down and jeans that looked like they were made for him, he held his arms open for a hug.

Donovan cleared his throat. Kelly hesitated.

"I'm kidding. Go give the man a hug. I can take it."

After her hug, she introduced Boone to everyone in her group. Avery was her bubbly self. Graham got a little emotional when he explained how Boone was his parents' favorite singer.

They took their pictures and got their signatures and moved on to the next band and then the next. When they finally got to Piper Starling and Sawyer Stratton, Avery was about to burst.

"I love you, but we can't be best friends because it will hurt Macy's feelings, but you are the best singer in the whole world and someday I want to be a singer or I want to be a dog trainer. I can't decide. My brother would marry you if you want, but this is his girlfriend, Mia. She's really nice, so maybe I don't want you to marry him. Can I have a picture?"

Graham almost died of embarrassment. Kelly wondered if they should encourage her to be a singer because she clearly had amazing lung capacity to get out all of those words without taking more than a couple of breaths. Piper was extraordinarily kind and made Avery feel like the most important person in the room.

"I'm glad you're very nice, Mia, so Piper doesn't try to marry Avery's brother," Sawyer Stratton said. The two of them had been married for a couple of years and had the most adorable two-year-old. Kelly had seen him running around backstage earlier.

Mia looked weak in the knees. "I love you," she said, starstruck.

Kelly made eye contact with Donovan, who couldn't hold back his laughter. Everyone got their pictures and signatures before Piper invited them all to go fill a bag at the candy bar she had set up along the back wall.

Avery didn't hesitate. If there was one thing she loved more than Piper Starling, it was candy.

They made their goody bags and went to find their seats in the stadium. They had seats next to Lyle and Nancy, who were on their tenth date. Romance was in the air. Kelly wrapped her arms around Donovan's waist.

"Did you have fun back there?"

"I had fun watching everyone else have fun. Even when you got all gaga over that Boone What's-His-Name."

"I am only gaga for one guy and he's not a singer. He's a cop."

"You date a cop? I hear that's hard."

It was almost comical that she had once thought it would never be something she'd ever do. "Challenging for sure. But he's worth it."

Donovan kissed the top of her head. "Good to know because I'm crazy about this deejay. She looks unassuming, but if she wanted to, she could drop me in seconds."

Kelly laughed. He teased her about her takedown, but she hoped he knew how much it meant to her that he had empowered her to protect herself. Because of him, she knew she could count on someone to be there for her but also rely on herself when she needed to. It was exactly what she needed from a partner in this life.

Kelly knew she had been given more gifts than she deserved. She had faith in herself, she had the love of a good man and she had two incredible kids she'd someday truly be able to call hers.

"Okay, I have to go backstage. I'll be back

after I announce the start of the show. I love you, guys," she said.

"We love you, too, Kelly!" Avery shouted. "Right, Uncle Donovan?"

"Without a doubt, Avery."

* * * * *

COMING NEXT MONTH FROM

HARLEQUIN®

# HEARTWARMING™

Available September 3, 2019

## #295 AFTER THE RODEO

*Heroes of Shelter Creek* • by Claire McEwen

Former bull rider Jace Hendricks needs biologist Vivian Reed off his ranch, fast—or he risks losing custody of his nieces and nephew. So why is Vivian's optimism winning over the kids...and Jace?

## #296 THE RANCHER'S FAMILY

*The Hitching Post Hotel* • by Barbara White Daille

Wes Daniels is fine on his own. He has his ranch and his children—he doesn't need anything else. But the local matchmaker has other plans! Now Wes is suspicious about why Cara Leonetti keeps calling on him...

## #297 SAFE IN HIS ARMS

*Butterfly Harbor Stories* • by Anna J. Stewart

Army vet Kendall Davidson has found the peace she's been searching for until loud newcomers Hunter MacBride and his niece arrive with love and laughter to share, making her question what kind of life she's truly looking for.

## #298 THEIR FOREVER HOME

by Syndi Powell

Can a popular home reno contest allow Cassie Lowman and John Robison their chance to shine and fall for each other with so much—personally and professionally—on the line?